# THE
# LAST
# REPRISAL

Where Memory and Betrayal Collide

RICHARD E. OLSON

QUANTUM SHIFT
PUBLISHING
PORT SAINT LUCIE, FLORIDA

ISBN: 978-1-955533 (print)
ISBN: 978-1-955533-41-6 (eBook)
Available on Audiobook
Library of Congress Control Number: 2025918929

Printed in United States

To my grandparents—
my "country" grandparents, who nurtured my love of nature among the flowerbeds of a Wisconsin dairy farm,
and my "city" grandparents, who opened my eyes to the wider world through tunnel crossings and holiday visits in Detroit—
I posthumously dedicate this book.

Though your lives were different, you taught me many of the same lessons: the value of curiosity, the beauty of tradition, and the quiet strength of love. Thank you.

# FOREWORD

They say you should write what you know. While not everything in this book comes from my own experience, many of the places and events are drawn from my life. Some of the characters, too, are inspired by people I've known—or personalities I've crossed paths with over the years.

Writing this book has taken me on a journey through time. Some pages have stirred old memories; others have led me into unfamiliar territory, leaving me surprised at where the story went. Though this is a work of fiction, I often wonder how much of what we call memory is fiction, too.

This story has been unfolding, in one form or another, since I retired from teaching Spanish fifteen years ago. It's evolved so much over time that I barely recognize the original plot, characters, or even the tone I began with.

I hope, as you read, you'll catch glimpses of yourself—or someone you know—somewhere among these pages. And above all, I hope you enjoy the journey.

First, I would like to posthumously acknowledge Dr. Robert Kirsner, who, while I studied for a master's degree in Guadalajara, Mexico, not only taught me how to read literature but also *why*.

I would also like to acknowledge freelance writer and marketing manager Carrie Gerner, who guided me through the original version of this book.

Also, I would like to acknowledge Keren Kilgore of Quantum Shift Media, whose tough but fair guidance brought this book to fruition.

And finally, to my partner of 36 years, Ray Kraemer, who picked up the slack as I sequestered myself for hours to write.

# CONTENTS

# THE DIARY

*June 17, 2021*

*I haven't been as diligent as I once was in writing in my diary. Of course, years ago, with my boys at home, I had much more to write about. People say it's more difficult to raise girls, but I'm not so sure. At least my four boys stayed out of major trouble and are now married, notice I didn't write 'happily married'. Nobody understands that better than I do.*

*Now, I have some things I must admit.*

*I must admit, I wasn't the kind of wife Karl deserved. I was never a farm wife who spent her time cooking, baking, canning, and volunteering at the church.*

*My parents were both university professors, and I grew up in an urban academic setting. At least some of that rubbed off on Connor. He was rarely seen on the farm without a book in his hands.*

*And now, I sit alone in this wretched farmhouse, as much a prisoner now as I was from the start. At first, I was so in love with Karl, if, in fact, one could be in love at first. When he talked about his farm, it sounded so idyllic. I fancied myself another Willa Cather, writing books about the challenges and rewards of a bucolic rural life. But none of that ever happened, and now, in retrospect, I realize that I unfairly blamed Karl for the bitterness that thwarted my literary ambition.*

*I must admit that Connor, my baby, was the joy of my life. Not that I loved him more than I did his brothers; we just had so much more in common, like reading, watching the clouds and stars, writing poems and short stories, and working in my garden. He never connected with his brothers nor with Karl. He was a lonely boy who never had the chance to learn how to lose.*

*And the last thing I must admit is that Karl was right all along about the money. But none of that matters now. The million dollars will soon be in Connor's hands, I hope. I left him one last treasure hunt for him to find.*

*I remember how much he loved those treasure hunts as a child. I had him running all over this farm as he followed my clues. He especially liked it when I wrote the clues in silly poems. When he was little, the treasures started out as toys or candy, then moved to comic books, and later, a library card and a blank diary. But this, this final treasure hunt, will be one he'll never forget.*

*Connor, I know you know about the money and that it's in the safe. You watched me put it there at least once. You also know I've kept this diary over the years and that I hide it in an old trunk in the basement.*

*When they read my will, they'll find no mention of the money in that safe; the four boys will only inherit the farm and any other holdings I have. But I know Connor, he will put two and two together and try to get the money out before the place is sold. So, have fun, Connor, and spend the money wisely.*

*P.S. This is the final entry in my diary.*
*Roberta Larson,  1945-*

# CHAPTER 1

# THIS OLD HOUSE

## From Generation to Generation

Karl Larson passed away years ago, and his wife, Roberta, lived alone in the decaying farmhouse until her recent death. Built on a county road one mile from the junction of a state highway, the house sat on a 200-acre farm and was home to three generations.

The last of the Larsons' four brothers had put the farm up for sale. It was a buyer's market, as more dairy farms in Wisconsin were going out of business.

Typical of farmhouses of the time, it was built with white oak in the late 1800s. There were two stairways at either end of the house, leading to the second floor, which had four bedrooms, one for each of the boys. Karl and Roberta occupied the bedroom on the main level. At one time, it was a large bedroom, but when Karl's parents, who first occupied the house, put in an indoor bathroom on the main level, they carved out space from the bedroom.

Initially, someone painted the exterior white, and then, a generation later, someone repainted it white again. But much of that paint had either chipped off or faded into a cloud-colored gray. It would likely need two coats of paint if anyone ever intended to paint it again.

Originally, the house had an attached summer kitchen, but Karl's parents tore it down in the 1950s. They replaced the original cast-iron, wood-burning stove with a gas stove that had a wood-burning compartment built into it. The old kitchen wood box showed years of use, and even though no one had used it recently, it still held a few small logs and some kindling.

The lower parts of the kitchen walls were paneled with wainscoting and painted white. The rest of the walls were soft blue. On warm and breezy summer nights, the white sheer curtains in the kitchen fluttered, ghosts of the past coming to life. Handles were missing from some cabinets and drawers. The patterned linoleum installed in the 1960s showed obvious signs of the many footsteps that had worn it down. Although someone had added modern plumbing at some point, the old hand pump still functioned, though people rarely used it.

For the first generation of the Larsons that inhabited the house, Karl's parents, Lars and Hedda, and his many siblings, the kitchen was abuzz with activity. But that wasn't the case in recent years. No longer were the counters cluttered with freshly baked bread, half-eaten cakes, kitchen utensils, and recipe ingredients all vying for space.

On Sundays, Hedda would either have a pot roast or a freshly butchered chicken in the oven that would fill the room with a hunger-inducing aroma. Potatoes would be boiling on the stove, waiting to be mashed, buttered, and smothered in gravy. A jar of carrots, brought up from the basement that morning, might sit on the counter, waiting to be heated on the stove and then served with a large pat of butter on top. There would be pies, depending on the season: strawberry-rhubarb, blueberry, cherry, or apple. The whipped cream would have been made by hand. The coffee would brew during the meal and be ready in time for the pie.

On his darker days, Karl carried those memories of his youth with nagging nostalgia. He remembered being in the house's cellar only a few times to help his mother bring empty jars up to the kitchen or carry full jars back down to the cellar. Karl's mother rarely served anything from a tin can. Her soups were homemade. Her pickle recipe was handed down to her from her mother. The shelves in the cellar reached their capacity in late fall. The shelves on the north side of the basement bore the weight of some three dozen jars of applesauce, apple butter, pears, peaches, jellies, and jams. On the opposite wall were the vegetables: corn, beets, carrots, beans, and peas.

The "odds and ends shelf," as his mother called it, stood against the east wall. His mother reserved it for the more uncommon items, and it included tomato juice, relishes of several kinds, pickles, both sweet and dill, and sometimes chicken and beef stock.

Potatoes, onions, and squash had no dedicated space and thrived in any cool, dry spot.

Very little went to waste when Karl was growing up. If a plastic bag existed in that kitchen, which was rare, his mother rinsed it out and hung it above the sink with a clothespin to dry and reuse it again and again. If there was a hard-to-reach spot of tillable land, Karl's father wiggled his way in and brought it to life.

As Karl's parents grew older and most of their children moved away, family and neighbors encouraged them to sell the farm. Karl, their youngest, was twenty when his parents decided it was time to move off the farm and into town, finally admitting that their bodies were feeling the effects of a lifetime of labor.

Since Karl was the only son interested in maintaining the farm, they leased the property to him with the option to buy it in the future. Karl was the youngest boy, and his older brothers and sisters felt slighted by this arrangement, despite their lack of interest in farming.

## Norwegian Bachelor Farmer

Karl lived alone in the house and tirelessly worked the farm. The new barn his father had built stood next to the old one. Even though the weather destroyed most of the old barn over time, parts of it remained. The new barn was in good shape, although it could have used a new coat of red paint. He had all the machinery he needed, all the cows he could milk, and all the land he could work. At certain times of the year, he even had hired help.

But what he didn't have was a wife.

Having worked on the farm most of his life, Karl knew what hard work meant. His svelte physique, his cheerful manner, and generosity with his time and money made him "the catch of the decade," according to his sister, Edna.

Karl knew he was a prime target for lonely, unmarried women in the area. He had lost track of how many times an anxious mother had introduced him to her available daughter.

In town, he ducked around corners, went into shops he had no intention of entering, or sat in his car with the visor down to avoid pesky encounters. Not that Karl didn't want a wife; he just didn't want to be drawn into the stifling relationships that some of his older siblings had been trapped in. There were already two divorces in the family, and Karl did not want to be the third; he saw how expensive and brutal they could be. But some were wondering why he was still a bachelor farmer at the prime age of 21.

Mothers in the area, who knew what was best for Karl, encouraged their unmarried daughters to save him. "He would be a good catch. He's a Lutheran. He has a farm. He needs a sturdy woman like you," one anxious mother concluded.

"You're not getting any younger. Someone's going to grab him soon. Take over an apple pie. You don't have to tell him I made it," another suggested.

"Maybe if you fixed your hair a different way. I don't know, a bit more eye-catching? Your beautiful hair, which you got from me, is your best feature. A bit of makeup would do you no harm. But don't overdo it. Karl's not the type who would be attracted to a painted lady," another overwrought mother cautioned.

Karl grew weary of the tedious game and just wanted to go at his own pace. With an increasing number of men being drafted to fight in Vietnam, there was an ever-growing number of single women, or young widows, in the area. It was a buyer's market, so to speak, and Karl was no spendthrift.

By late summer of 1966, Karl began harvesting the corn he had planted in the spring. He was pleased with the size of the harvest and could also sell some hay to other farmers. It was this confidence that led him to offer to host Christmas at his house in December. After all, it was much larger than the place his parents bought in town. The only thing he asked was that he wouldn't have to cook.

On Christmas Eve, the house came alive with family: Karl's parents, his brother Bobby and his wife and three kids, his oldest brother Hans with his second wife, and his sister Ida with her husband and six kids. Edna and Lester arrived at the farm as the sun set in the wintry sky. Edna filtered through the house with her tray of traditional Norwegian delicacies as Lester stayed close to the bottle of brandy in the wood box with Bobby and Hans.

By Christmas night, the house was littered with crumbled-up wrapping paper, empty boxes, glitter, tinsel, and assorted ribbons and bows. Ida and Bobby's wife herded the children up the stairs in a noisy scramble. Ida's six tumbled into two bedrooms, Bobby's three boys spilled into another, and Bobby and his wife settled across the hall. Hans and his wife took the last room, closing the door on the chaos.

Feeling overwhelmed by the commotion of the day, Karl found his father's oak rocking chair and slumped into it with an audible sigh that was heard across the room.

"I'll second that," his father replied as he lowered himself onto the couch.

Directing his tired voice toward the kitchen and hoping he could summon the volume needed so he wouldn't have to get up from his chair, Karl waited until the chatter waned and called out, "Someone, grab that bottle of brandy hidden in the wood box and some glasses. Time to unwind."

"Got it," Edna yelled back from the kitchen.

With the house finally quiet and the brandy mollifying frazzled celebrants, it was time for the adults to talk.

"Karl, we've been talking," his sister Edna said. "We are worried about you."

"That's right, Karl," his father agreed. You do nothing but work all day and sit here alone at night."

His mother, who shared the sofa with his father and brother Bobby, nodded in agreement as she removed a hair from the shoulder of her husband's flannel shirt.

"Well, you know me, not the social type. I may spend a lot of time alone, but that doesn't mean I'm lonely. Please don't feel sorry for me," Karl softly replied as he slipped off his shoes.

His oldest brother, Hans, chimed in, "First of all, we don't feel sorry for you. It's your life."

"Honey, we just want you to be happy," Karl's mother said faintly.

"I saw Sam Peterson in town this morning," Edna said. "He's still studying at UW-Madison. And he said he has someone you should meet. Apparently, she's, as he put it, quite the looker." Edna winked at Karl. "He said her name was Rebecca, or maybe it was Roberta. But, anyway, that doesn't matter. I suggested that he whisk you away for a long weekend when he returns for the spring semester. Who knows, maybe—"

"Why don't you give him a call tomorrow?" Bobby cut off Edna. "If you need to get away from the farm for a couple of days, just let us know and we can work something out."

"Maybe I will give Sammy a call," Karl pursed his lips and nodded his head. "But don't worry about the farm, the Jensen twins will step in."

"My, those boys have grown!" Lars observed. "The way they toss those bales of hay around like they were mere shredded wheat."

"Good analogy, pops," Ida opined.

Soon, it was lights out at the Larson farm. By late the next morning, everyone had left, and Karl could enjoy his quiet house again.

# CHAPTER 2

# ROBERTA, MEET KARL

With the Jensen twins tending to the farm, and Sammy Peterson at the wheel of his Mercury Comet rattletrap, Karl was on his way to his long weekend in Madison.

Sam shared an apartment with three other students, four blocks from the campus. Sam provided a personal tour, which impressed Karl. He had never been on a college campus before. Despite the winter weather, he found the small pockets of protesters holding posters and chanting unsettling. Although he was aware of the unrest in the nation, seeing it live and in person, and close to his homestead, the mood suddenly seemed palpable.

"What's all the fuss about?" he asked Sam.

"The unjust war in Vietnam, civil rights, the draft, dumping chemicals on innocent children, aggressive law enforcement, you name it." Sam's mordant response evidenced what Karl deemed to be unpatriotic gibberish.

Parties were going on nearly everywhere. Karl had a brandy or a beer once in a while, but what he saw at a kegger—a new word for Karl—bewildered him.

At his first party, he stood on the sidelines, critically studying the mating ritual as an anthropologist might do. He noticed a woman standing alone with a red plastic glass in her hand. *Why would such an attractive woman be standing there alone?* he asked himself.

Her long, straight brown hair fell casually over her shoulders. Her bell-bottom jeans hung low on her hips and were frayed at the bottom. Karl thought her black sweater might have been cashmere or angora, but what did he know? *And was that a beret on her head?* He wondered as his lips turned into a slight smile.

"There you are," Sam said as he approached the woman. "There's someone I want you to meet." As Sam and the woman came closer, Karl's palms began to sweat. He could see she had very little makeup on and that her eyes were hazel. *Edna was right, she is a looker,* he concluded.

"Roberta, this is my best friend, Karl Larson. Karl, this is Roberta." Sam stuck around for a few minutes as they talked, but soon cut away, leaving the two alone.

"I've never seen you around, Karl. Are you a new student?" Roberta asked.

"No, I'm just visiting Sam for a couple of days," Karl replied.

"So, you must have a job, or something?"

"In a sense. I own a farm near Gailsprings. I raise cattle."

They chatted the evening away, and Karl asked if he might walk her home. On the street in front of her parents' home, Karl asked if she would see him again.

The following night, they met at a coffeehouse on State Street. Karl was curious about the protests on the campus and wanted to know more. Roberta impressed him with her knowledge and insights into the issues, but wondered if he would be suitable for her. He walked her home and kissed her goodnight.

"Mom, he's such a dreamboat. He's handsome, modest, polite, and he owns a farm. He has money! And I think he likes me," Roberta gushed as her mother listened.

"Will you see him tomorrow?" her mother asked.

"Yes."

"Well, we would like to meet him."

The next evening, after Karl and Roberta said goodnight to her parents, Roberta made an observation as they walked away. "I think they liked you. They're always afraid I'll fall for some radical hippie type who doesn't believe in working." Roberta's dreamy eyes met Karl's. "You are quite the opposite, you know."

Karl was over the moon.

It was Karl's last night in Madison; the next day, he would take a bus back to Gailsprings. The party at Sam's apartment was thumping, the beer was flowing, joints were passing from one hand to another, and couples were openly bordering on foreplay.

Roberta ran her finger up Karl's stomach and chest, stopping at his lower lip. Taken in by the moment, Karl responded by doing the same. Their lips met as they fell into each other. Karl breathed in the earthy patchouli oil scent of Roberta's silky hair and was immediately aroused.

They guzzled the rest of their beer, then set their cups down on a table. He led her up the stairs into Sam's dark room and into the garden of earthly delights.

# CHAPTER 3

# OH, WHAT A LONELY BOY!

## Family Ties

Since Connor was seven years younger than the third Larson boy, many considered him to be the unexpected late-in-life child that sometimes happens. But only three people knew it didn't involve Karl.

When Karl first suspected that Connor was not his biological son, he wanted to tell the world. But Karl wouldn't do that; that's not who he was. He didn't want others to know his wife had cheated on him. And he surely didn't want to stigmatize Connor. But the shroud of repressive acrimony that had hung over Karl and Roberta's marriage for years bore down on the household like a cold spell. If their sons heard any conversations between the two of any consequence, it was in the form of muffled bickering from their bedroom, with the words "money" and "Connor" occasionally shouted.

Karl knew Roberta had inherited a sizable amount of money after her parents were killed in a car crash. The ensuing lawsuit against the drunk driver dragged on for years. At least, that's what Roberta told Karl. Karl reasoned that, since Roberta acquired a share of a prosperous farm when they married, she should share her inheritance with him.

He had discussed a divorce with his sister, Edna, who told him if they did divorce, he wouldn't likely get any of the inheritance, but she would likely get some of the farm.

So, Roberta and Karl tacitly agreed to tolerate one another as they became comfortable in their own misery, a misery that neither wanted to disturb.

At any rate, the farm was doing well, and it provided adequate living for the six members of the Larson family.

Connor was eight years younger than his next-oldest brother, Ernest, and fourteen years younger than Matt, the oldest of the Connor boys. Ruben fit in neatly between Matt and Ernest.

Growing up, Connor had seen their father playing catch with the older boys, wrestling with them on the living room rug, and teaching them to tie a fly for trout fishing. He had pet names for them. Matt, he called "Slugger." Ernest, he called "Popeye," because he failed to catch a line drive, and the ball hit him just above his eye. And Ruben, he called Marshall, because that was his middle name. But Connor was always just Connor as far as his father was concerned.

As for his brothers, he was Connie, their mother's little girl.

It started as lighthearted teasing; the kind boys grow into and sometimes never grow out of. Unlike Connor, his brothers were expected to work with their father on the farm, growing stronger and taller. Their interest in girls puzzled the younger Connor, who wondered why his brothers acted so stupidly around girls. But Connor had no one to ask.

At home, Connor learned to sequester himself with a book. He mastered the art of self-imposed exile, ignoring his brother's taunts, ignoring them as they ignored him, and sometimes reading the same page over and over while doing so.

Both Karl and Roberta were aware of Connor's tendency to withdraw into a world of his own. Karl tried to engage Connor in several activities, but Karl no longer had the energy he once had. As the older boys left the farm, his workload increased. By the end of the day, Karl had little energy left.

It was Roberta who would bring Connor out of his shell. She organized treasure hunts for him, first around the house and then around the farm. There was always a reward of some kind. But Roberta saw this as a chance to guide Connor toward a college degree, the one she never got. The prizes were books, a telescope, a calculator, and other things.

## The Diaries

The year after Connor was born, Roberta began keeping a diary. She enjoyed writing about her daily life, her thoughts, and current events.

With the summer winding down and Connor about to start fifth grade, Roberta organized one last treasure hunt for the summer. Roberta wrote some of the clues backward or upside down. One of the clues was in the form of a limerick. The clues led Connor to wear a blindfold into the house and sit at the table where she had placed a book just out of reach.

"OK, Connor, you can take the blindfold off now," Roberta said. She waited for him to pick up the book. He paged through it.

"It's a book with no words," he declared.

"It's a diary. A journal. It's something you write in. I've been keeping one since you were born." Roberta explained, affectionately tousling his hair.

"Write what?" Connor asked, his face blank.

"What you do is this. First, you write today's date, including the year." Roberta opened her diary and showed Connor her first entry. "You don't have to write in it every day, just when you feel like it, when something's bothering you, when you're happy about something."

Roberta handed Connor a pencil. "Let's start right now. First, write the date."

Connor looked at the John Deere calendar on the wall in front of him and wrote the date.

"Now write about what you did today. Then close the diary and hide it where nobody, not even me, can find it. It is your secret diary. Yours alone." Roberta left the room.

At school, Connor blossomed. From early on, he won over his teachers and classmates. *He* organized the games at recess. *He* was the class clown. *He* won the spelling bees. When he was in high school, he served as the editor of the school newspaper for three consecutive years. In his junior year, he scored in the upper 10% on the PSAT exam. But his most significant achievement, as far as he was concerned, was the many debate awards and trophies he had earned.

## Sorry for Your Loss

Connor was eighteen and only two weeks into his first semester at the University of Minnesota when his brother Matt called with shocking news: their father had died suddenly of a cardiac infarction. The coroner performed no autopsy, a surprise to those who had recently seen the man looking well. After notifying his professors, Connor drove his graduation gift—a used car from his parents—to Galesprings for a brief visit. His brothers and their families arrived soon after, choosing to stay at a hotel with an outdoor pool rather than at the farmhouse.

The Halverson Funeral Parlor held the evening visitation for Karl. Roberta sat on a stool at the beginning of the line and cordially accepted the superficial condolences she'd hoped for. As Connor was the youngest son, his position in the line was next to the open casket, and he couldn't help glancing at it throughout the evening.

When Edna arrived at the casket, she hugged Connor and whispered in his ear, "My baby brother. Gone. Senslessly." She stood at the open casket and touched Karl's folded hands. A lone tear ran down her cheek as she walked away.

At the memorial service, the extended Larson family occupied several pews, a black cluster of Karl's brothers and sisters, and Karl and Roberts's children and grandchildren. Edna sat on the third pew next to Lester.

Holding the memorial card in front of her mouth, she whispered into Lester's ear, "Of course, Roberta is putting on a show of grief for the audience. She's glad he's dead. She ain't fooling me."

Lester didn't respond.

The rest of the church was filled with church members, area farmers, and some local business owners with whom Karl interacted.

"I think," the minister took off his glasses as he looked down upon the congregation, "that I can confidently say that almost all of us in this sanctuary knew Karl as a respected, honorable, trustworthy, and caring man. He was always among the first to lend a hand to his neighbors in need. True, he was a quiet man, but, as they say, 'still waters run deep,' and I think that was the case with Karl. Karl Marshall Larson will be missed." He put his glasses back on. "Please join me as we sing hymn number eighty-four."

The cemetery was next to the church, and most of the attendees surrounded the plot. The sexton stood by with his shovel leaning against an oak tree as the minister offered some final words.

Even though the casket was now closed, Connor could still see his father's body in it. He looked at his brothers, wondering if they were seeing the same thing: a distant father Connor barely knew, a stoic man who had withdrawn from a family when Connor was still young, a man who lived and died despite himself. But, no, of course, that's not what they saw. They saw a man who taught them how to throw a pitch, a man who wrestled with them on the living room floor, a man who showed them how to plow a straight row. Connor stood alone at the cemetery plot, the minister's words muted by the pesky voices in his head, some calling him to remember, others to forget.

What was it about seeing his emaciated father lying in the coffin that made him consider their relationship now?

Connor knew there was something buried deep in his memories, something that needed to surface before he could move on. He rewound his thoughts and played them through again—the burning barn, his mother's secrets, his distant relationship with his brothers, his parents' distressed marriage.

And there it was, shaken loose by the image of his father's closed coffin being lowered into the ground; those comments about not looking like his father, comments about not looking or acting like his brothers, his mother's favoritism. Was Karl not his biological father?

After the luncheon, Connor approached his mother. "Mom, I have to go back this afternoon. The semester's just started, and I can't miss any more classes than necessary."

"That's fine, honey. You move on, move on with your life. We failed you as a family, but you, you, are not a failure. I know I wasn't a good wife to Karl. But you and I had, have, a special bond. Remember all those clues I gave you for those treasure hunts? I still have all of them. There is an envelope in the safe. There's also something else in the safe, just for you and you alone. Start with my diary."

"Mom, the Schmidts are about to leave, and they want to see you first," Matt interrupted. "I'll be right there," Roberta promised.

"Connor, come home when you can, but don't feel guilty if you can't. I taught you to explore as a child, but don't stop now. Too many people do, you know, stop exploring when they're adults. I love you, Connor." Roberta kissed Connor on the forehead.

"I love you too, Mom," he mumbled.

Back at school, Connor made minor adjustments to the big city and dorm life. Away from Gailsprings, he found himself to be more gregarious, more willing to explore his surroundings, and more interested in women.

Her name was Leticia and she was a visiting student from Argentina. Her swarthy complexion, her wavy black hair, and her fiery personality captivated Connor. On their first date, they went out for tacos and then saw a foreign film on campus. He walked her to her dorm, where he stammered as he awkwardly stood, not knowing what to do with his hands.

On their second date, Leticia showed him what to do with those hands. That was the night Connor lost his virginity.

Connor had a few more sexual relationships over his six years at college, but things went no further.

He graduated with an MA degree in business management and quickly found a job at 3M. He shared an ordinary office on the second floor of the building with a view of a parking lot.

Often, when Connor entered the building in St. Paul, he would look up at the top floor with longing. Sometimes he would even stop and stare at the window of a corner office. He imagined himself in that office, wearing a power suit and sitting on a leather executive chair behind a mahogany desk. He could smell the coffee as his administrative assistant set his 3M coffee mug on his desk and said, "Here's your coffee, Mr. Larson."

# CHAPTER 4

# BECOMING LANA PAULSON

## Taken for Granted

Early on, Lana's parents were concerned about Lana's willingness to let others determine her actions. She wasn't exactly bullied, but she tended to allow others to take the lead and rarely stood up for herself.

"Lana, sometimes it's best to walk away, or just go along, but sometimes you have to stand up for yourself," her father counseled.

"Lana, if you continue to let others take you for granted or walk all over you, life is going to be tough," her mother advised.

In the cafeteria at school, "Lana, that's where I wanted to sit," someone said. And Lana moved.

On the playground, "Lana, Lucy, and I want to swing next to each other," the girl said. Lana found somewhere else to play.

In her sophomore year in high school, when she chose Ellie to be her partner while dissecting a frog, "No, Lana, I want to be Ellie's partner," that pushy cheerleader butted in. Lana worked alone.

Lana hated group projects because she was always the weakest member.

Her parents met with her teachers and counselors, but the advice they received did little to address their concerns.

"Maybe college will solve the problem," her middle school science teacher said.

"I think she'll be a late bloomer," her sophomore algebra teacher predicted.

"She should join some clubs, like the Spanish Club," Señora Prieta suggested.

Lana excelled at mathematics, completing courses in algebra, geometry, advanced algebra, and AP calculus. She understood numbers, symbols, and equations; they didn't push her around; she pushed them around.

When she became valedictorian of her graduating class, few of her fellow seniors even knew who she was. True, her transcript of academic classes listed a plethora of academics, but there were no activities listed under her photo in the yearbook.

## Macalester College

At the beginning of her senior year in high school, Lana's parents began suggesting that she go to college.

"Your grades are good, and you got a 31 on your ACT score, which is very impressive," her father said. "You're sure to be accepted at many universities."

Lana's mother nodded in agreement.

Lana talked to a school counselor, who also encouraged her to apply for scholarships. She applied to a handful of universities and was accepted by all. But she chose Macalester in Saint Paul, not only because of the generous scholarships she was offered but also because she thought she would be more comfortable at a smaller university.

"I wished I had gone to Macalester," Lana's mother said when Lana told her parents about her decision. "That's where your grandpa Paulson taught economics. I was about to graduate from high school when I met your father; he was staffing a table of Macalester merchandise at the Minneapolis Convention Center. He was so handsome."

"Hey, what do you mean, *was*?" Peter asked with feigned indignation.

"Well, Peter, honey, you had hair then," Ella playfully commented. "Anyway, I went up to the table to see what he was selling."

"Ha!" Peter threw his head back laughing. "I knew from the start that it wasn't the merchandise that brought you over to my table," he added as he stuck his nose up with a self-satisfied smirk.

"He said he was about to take a break, so he invited me to get some ice cream with him. I said yes, and about a year later, I said, 'I do.' We went to Niagara Falls for our honeymoon."

"I remember the drive back, too," Peter picked up the next part of the story. "We were stuck for five hours in a multi-car crash on the highway, but we made the most of it. We think that's when you were conceived, Lana." He glanced at Lana as she rolled her eyes.

"How many times do I have to hear that story?" Lana groaned.

Lana mostly kept to herself during her college years. Her apartment was within walking distance of the campus, a walk she enjoyed until the cold and snowy Minnesota winters blew in. She distinguished herself in her studies, and many of her professors encouraged her to pursue graduate studies. Heeding their advice, Lana applied to the master's program in business administration at Macalester.

But accounting is one thing, and being directly involved in the business world is another. More than one of Lana's professors suggested she take a hybrid course on leadership or assertive training if she intended to pursue an MBA.

In her senior year of her MBA degree, Lana received some good news; she could finish her undergraduate degree and immediately begin her master's program. Since Lana had started her graduate studies as soon as she did, she finished the coursework early in her final semester.

## A Mulberry-Blue Necktie

In mid-February, Lana landed her first job at Benedict's, a well-known supper club near Stillwater. The thirty-minute drive each way—longer in heavy traffic—meant careful planning around her MBA classes.

She worked weekend nights and occasionally filled in during the week when her coursework allowed.

The staff all called the manager Mr. Armand. Assuming the name was French, Lana greeted him in her basic French—only to learn his native language was Greek. When she later discovered his first name was Nelson, she gave up guessing people's origins by their names. *Shouldn't his name be something like Dimitri, Konstantinos, or Aristotle?* she wondered.

Lana quickly warmed up to Carmen, who had been a server at Benedict's Supper Club for sixteen years. She and Lana would sometimes sit at the bar and have a drink at the end of the evening. Carmen always had the most recent pictures of her three grandchildren, and Lana enjoyed looking at them. Seeing the pictures sometimes gave Lana pause to think about her life. Would she have grandchildren someday? Would she even be a mother?

It was a Tuesday evening, a day when Lana would typically not be working, but 3M had reserved the entire supper club for a gathering of leading business entrepreneurs. As the evening drew to a close, Mr. Armand called Lana over to a table where he and five others were having coffee and an after-dinner cordial. Mr. Armand pointed to an empty chair beside an elegantly dressed woman and motioned for Lana to sit. He made the introductions and asked what Lana would like to drink. Lana ordered a gin and tonic.

While she waited for her drink, Mr. Armand told the others that Lana, who had been working at Benedict's for only two weeks, would soon complete an MBA degree from Macalester College.

The younger man at the table chimed in. "Congratulations. I have an MBA from the University of Minnesota and now work for 3M. Maybe our paths will cross at some point."

Noting that none of the others commented, Lana felt irrelevant. She took a dainty sip of her gin and tonic, refraining from knocking it back.

The woman beside Lana shimmered in a powder-blue satin blouse, the fabric catching the light with every movement. A black wool pencil skirt and silver jewelry completed the look—elegant, effortless, expensive. Her silky black hair with dashes of silver glimmered in the ambient light. Across the table, the other woman wore a zebra-print silk blouse, her silver accessories just as polished. Her steel grey hair with wisps of lavender was combed back, highlighting her fine facial features. Their air of sophistication, the kind that came from years of knowing exactly where to shop, made Lana certain they found their wardrobes in Paris or Milan.

They offered her a few polite questions; the kind spoken out of courtesy rather than interest, before turning toward each other, their conversation closing like a door.

Next to Mr. Armand sat three men. Two of them, the women's husbands, were mirror images in Armani suits—dark eyes, silver curls, and the same deliberate gestures. *Brothers*, Lana guessed. The third man, younger by a decade or more, wore a tailored charcoal suit and a mulberry-blue silk tie anchored by a diamond pin that glinted when he moved.

Lana straightened her server uniform, wishing she could disappear under the linen tablecloth. Surrounded by fine fabric, polished silver, and people who belonged in this world, she felt like a misplaced puzzle piece—one that didn't quite fit.

When she overheard Mr. Armand mention her MBA studies to the men, heat crept into her cheeks, and she scanned the room for an escape.

Carmen, aware of Lana's discomfort, approached the table. "Excuse me, I am so sorry to interrupt, but Lana, there is an issue that needs your attention before you leave for the evening."

"Thank you, Carmen," Lana said as she excused herself.

"Drinks are on me, Carmen," Lana told her friend as they walked to the kitchen. "You saved me back there."

Lana had just finished bidding good night to some regular customers who were walking out the door when she felt a presence to her left. She turned to find the man with the diamond tiepin waiting.

"Hi, Lana. I didn't mean to approach like this, but I was afraid you'd leave before I had a chance to talk to you."

Connor's deep yet mellifluous voice left Lana speechless.

"In case you don't remember, my name is Connor, Connor Larson. We met earlier."

"Yes, of course, I remember." While Lana mostly spoke to the two women, she noted how Connor effortlessly socialized with the men. She tried not to stare at his handsome features, but couldn't resist a fleeting glance, or two. She imagined he would be just as dashing as the other two men when wisps of silver streaked his hair. The images of Carmen's grandchildren flashed before her eyes, leading her to wonder what her babies would look like if she and Connor ever got that far.

"I was wondering if we might have dinner together some night, when it works for you, of course. I hear you are completing an MBA at Macalester. I have one from the University of Minnesota."

That voice, that suit and tie, that physique; it all hit Lana at once. She hadn't noticed at the table whether Connor was wearing a wedding band. It would be too obvious to look now.

Untrue to her character, Lana responded, "I'd love to. Nothing too fancy, though. I am afraid I could never match the finery of your lady friends this evening."

Lana wrote her number down and handed it to Connor, their fingers meeting for the briefest moment. He tucked the slip of paper into his pocket, his eyes holding hers as he said he'd call soon.

At first, Lana doubted herself, thinking that she had been too hasty in accepting Connor's offer. *I am not the Lana I once was*, she thought. After six years at Macalester and having completed a summer course in leadership skills, Lana finally knew who she was. She didn't just go along with Connor because she couldn't say no, unlike on the playground, in the cafeteria, or in biology class. She agreed to go out with him because that is what *she* wanted to do.

Lana also wondered what Connor's connection was to the two couples at the table. Did Connor encourage Mr. Armand to invite Lana to join them? What was Connor looking for? *Am I over-analyzing all of this?* she thought. She'd wait and see.

## The Date

Several days passed, and Lana wondered if Connor would call. She had little experience with the dating scene and didn't know what to make of the delay. But Connor's call came in on a Sunday evening when Lana was watching *Call the Midwife*. Lana let her phone buzz a few times, so as not to seem too eager. On the seventh buzz, she answered.

"Hello," Lana answered nonchalantly, even though her caller ID showed who was calling.

"Hi, Lana. It's Connor, you know, from Benedict's. Last Saturday night."

"Oh, yes, sure, I remember."

Connor asked about Lana's day, and she did likewise. He told a funny story about losing his car keys at the gym. Lana confessed she lost her car keys all the time. When Connor finally got around to setting up the date, he suggested a weeknight.

"I would imagine you work most weekends and enjoy your Sundays off," Connor concluded, waiting for Lana to agree.

Lana could feel her heart beating fast, but didn't want to sound too eager. "Yes, that is really the only time I could."

Connor was caught off guard by the comment, but would wait until their date to find out more. "How about Tuesday night?" Connor asked.

"Sure, sounds good," Lana said and gave Connor her address.

As he entered it into his phone, he said, "Yes, I know the area. There's a fabulous Italian place nearby. How does that sound?" Connor asked.

"Great. I hope it's not too dressy; Italian places usually aren't," Lana replied.

"Not at all. I would describe it as urban casual with a touch of class. Does seven work?" He asked.

"Perfect. I'll see you then." They ended the call. *Urban casual with a touch of class? Can I do that?* she asked herself.

In high school, Lana wasn't much into following the latest fashion trends like most of her peers. She wore nice clothes, but nothing was too flashy or revealing. Her wavy blond hair, which cascaded slightly over her shoulders, was manageable without product or much effort and easily blended with whatever colors she wore. She had a bookish charm that often captured a double-take by the boys, especially when she glanced at them with her mysterious dark brown eyes through her Kensie Girl glasses.

Hours before Connor arrived on Tuesday night, Lana went to her closet in search of the only two dresses she had brought with her to college. They stood out easily among the customary casual apparel of university life. One had made its sole appearance at a banquet honoring students accepted into Beta Gamma Sigma, the international honor society for business majors.

Pulling both dresses from the closet, she laid them side by side on her bed. Deciding between them proved impossible. Lana paced in and out of her bedroom, glancing at the two garments as if waiting for one to suddenly declare itself the winner.

The third time, it did.

She returned the black sleeveless dress to the closet, opting instead for the low-cut short-sleeved midi with a matching cloth belt. The subtle burgundy floral print added a springlike breeziness to the dress.

Lana allowed the string of pearls her grandmother had given her to slide through her fingers before putting them on. She got out her lavender flats, dusted them off, and set them next to the front door. She checked her hair and makeup one last time. Then, with her right hand, she flipped back her hair, striking a sassy pose, a Shirley Maclaine kind of sassy. *I'll show them urban casual with a touch of class!* she thought.

A modest gold brooch in the shape of a rose caught her eye, and she pinned it to her dress. The violet shawl from Target came next, casually draped over her shoulders before another glance in the mirror. Earrings—of course. Her fingers brushed her earlobes, and she settled on the silver hoops from J.C. Penney.

Her purse yielded a fresh roll of breath mints. As the wrapper crinkled open, a quick look at the clock told her it was almost time. The mint lasted right up to the moment the doorbell rang at seven o'clock sharp. One final glance in the mirror, and Lana opened the door.

"Lana, you look every bit as fine as those ladies when we met," Connor said, remembering her previous comments about clothing.

Lana graciously accepted the compliment, and they strolled to the restaurant.

The Italian restaurant was just two blocks from Lana's apartment, and the unseasonably warm April evening invited a walk. With each step, Lana felt the tension of getting ready fade.

Connor wore a burgundy ribbed crew neck pullover and a black sports coat. His slate gray slacks and his black Oxfords rounded out what Lana assumed to be his idea of urban casual.

They entered the trendy restaurant, where the maître d' stood at the door, ready to welcome the evening crowd. Lana's ears perked up when he greeted Connor by name. He promptly led them to a table.

"Here you go, your favorite table, Connor. And who might this lovely lady be?" the maître'd coyly asked.

"This is Lana. Lana, this is Giovanni. His family owns this place," Connor explained.

Lana and Giovanni shook hands.

Connor then helped Lana into her chair. "Lana and I met a few days ago at Benedict's, a supper club where she works part-time. She is a student at Macalester College," Connor explained.

"I see. Would you like to see the wine list, sir?" Giovanni asked.

"You must come here often, Giovanni seems to know you well," Lana said. *Is this where he brings all his dates? Am I just one of many?* she thought.

"I don't know if it's often, but I know Giovanni's family. In fact, you met his grandparents the night you sat with us at Benedicts," he reminded her.

"Oh, yes, I remember. But neither of the couples sounded Italian to me. Their accent was more Eastern European," Lana replied.

"You're right about the accent. It's not Italian; it's Greek. They got their start with Greek restaurants in New York and Boston and have branched out into other restaurants." Connor glanced at the wine list Giovanni placed on the table as he passed by. "I'm not sure Giovanni's grandparents even know how many or what businesses they own. The other couple was his grandmother's sister and her husband. All four of them were born in Greece but came here with their parents when they immigrated to the US."

Connor held the wine list with his left hand, giving Lana a chance to notice his unadorned ring finger.

"If I remember correctly, you were sipping a glass of white wine that night at Benedict's. How does a bottle of Pinot Grigio sound?" Connor suggested.

Lana agreed. They concentrated on the menu, distracted only when the wine was set on the table.

"So, tell me about Macalester," Connor said as he poured the wine, her glass first.

"I'm just about to finish an MBA at Macalester and am conducting a seminar for undergraduates going into business," Lana said as she took a sip of the wine.

"I believe I told you I have an MBA, as well," Connor reminded her.

"Yes, you did. But I hope this doesn't mean we have to talk about Robert House's Path-Goal Theory or Accrual-Basis Accounting tonight."

"Absolutely not," Connor emphasized. "That's something better saved for a second date." They both laughed, and from that point on, things could not have gone better.

They lingered outside Lana's apartment building door, Connor with his ankles crossed, the toe of his right shoe touching the ground. He leaned on the door frame with his right forearm, placing his left hand on his hip, poised to fall into the building with a whispered invitation. Lana leaned against one column holding up the awning over the entryway, her hands crossed behind her back. The bright light above attracted an array of flitting moths.

"Lana, I hope I can see you again. This was a delightful evening for me. And we still have the House Path-Goal Theory to discuss."

Lana looked down at the sidewalk with a sigh. She slowly raised her head and, with a determined look, shook her head. "Not going to happen," she flatly said.

Connor put both his feet on the ground and stood erect. The puzzled look on his face made it difficult for Lana to suppress a chuckle.

"I meant the Goal Theory thing—not a second date." Her eyes teased him as they both laughed, his laughter fuller now, ego restored. Connor caught her hands in his, holding them just long enough for her to feel the warmth in his touch.

"Ha, you got me, Lana. I'll give you that," Connor said, his grin lingering as he drew her in and brushed his lips against hers—soft, unhurried. When she turned to unlock the door, her fingers fumbled with the keys, aware of his nearness and the quiet heat in the space between them.

"I'm glad we did this. See you soon," Lana said as she opened the door.

Once Lana was safely inside, she turned and watched Connor as he walked away in a spirited gait and got into a black Ferrari. Since they had walked to the restaurant, Lana hadn't noticed the car. How Connor could afford such a car after his brief time at 3M left her wondering about the connection between Connor and the people he sat with at Benedict's.

The following Wednesday, Connor called late in the afternoon. "Lana. Hi, it's Connor. I know this is short notice, but I was wondering if you'd like to join me for pizza tonight?"

"Hi, Connor. I'd love to, but tonight won't work. I'm facilitating a seminar for potential MBA students, and we usually go out for a drink afterwards. Maybe another night?"

"Yes, sure, of course. Another night it is."

"How about tomorrow night?" Lana suggested.

"That won't work. Duty calls, you know," Connor replied. "I'll get back to you soon." They ended the call. *What did he mean by duty calls,* Lana wondered.

The following Monday, Connor called Lana mid-morning.

"Can you have lunch with me today?" he asked.

Lana hesitated. "Well, I don't know. That's kind of short notice, isn't it? But yes, we can have lunch."

"Great! Meet me at the Asian fusion restaurant on Summit Avenue."

"Well, this was a good choice," Lana commented when they finished their meal. "And for once, I don't have leftovers."

"Lana, my next meeting isn't until four this afternoon." Lana easily decoded the provocative inflection in Connor's hint.

"I see. How would you like to come over for some Ethiopian coffee?" It wasn't the first time Lana had Ethiopian coffee, but it was the first time she'd ever had sex in the afternoon.

Over the next few days, Lana balanced her thoughts. On one hand, realizing she was getting ahead of the game, she could see herself moving into a relationship, whether it was with Connor. Yet she realized she wasn't willing to compromise her professional aspirations. Sure, a woman could do both, but she wasn't sure she wanted to.

As their relationship continued, both Lana and Connor became increasingly confused, not only as to their own intentions, but to each other's as well. He wanted to keep love out of it, and that was clear to

Lana. But even though the sex was great, Lana wanted, no, needed to know where things stood.

"Connor, there's something I've been meaning to ask?" Lana broached the subject delicately. "Have you ever been married? I've noticed you don't wear a wedding ring."

Connor finished his sip of coffee and gently placed the mug on the table.

"I guess I'm the kind of guy who, as they say, is married to his career," he replied. "What about you?"

"I suppose I might say the same about myself since getting my MBA has been my focus until now."

Lana's response was a warning flare in Connor's mind. *Did she say, 'until now'?*

They continued their meal in silence, both reluctant to say anymore, each hoping the other would change the subject.

*Has someone hurt him?* Lana wondered. *Or am I moving too fast? And moving toward what? Why did I bring up marriage?*

*Is she looking for a husband? Is she falling in love with me?* Connor asked himself. *Do I need to end this now?*

As they were about to leave the restaurant, Connor realized he had left his antique green monogrammed L.L.Bean anorak jacket hanging on the back of his chair. Lana waited by the door as he retrieved it.

With the arrival of spring, Lana wanted to do things in public: go on a picnic, walk around the many parks in the Twin Cities area, attend farmers' markets, and flea markets. But Connor wouldn't have it. It had to be a quiet lunch or dinner and always at a place of his choice. And his choices were always the best.

Their dating, if it could be called that, was erratic and centered on Connor's schedule. On the rare occasion that Lana had a weekend night off, Connor was always out of town, entertaining an out-of-town client, or attending a conference. After a while, Lana became accustomed to the spontaneity that defined their relationship. In fact, she found impulsiveness erotic, especially when he would just show up out of the blue and entice her from the mundane to the sublime. She never expected the relationship to go any further than brief dinners with casual sex for dessert.

Lana convinced herself that she was satisfied with the situation. It was clear that Connor was solely interested in companionship and sex. And if a man can do that, then so could she—no attachments, she told herself.

## Chi Town

In keeping with the capriciousness of a Minnesota spring, the mid-May day was rainy one minute and sunny the next. Lana was holed up in her apartment, finalizing her thesis. It was Thursday, mid-afternoon, when Connor called from his office.

"Hi, Lana. Some weather we're having, but this *is* springtime in the Midwest, you know."

Lana still hadn't gotten used to all the comments about the weather Midwesterners made daily.

"Yes, I know," she groaned.

"Listen, Lana, this afternoon isn't going to work out. I need to go to Chicago for the weekend on business and need to get a presentation ready and pack," Connor explained.

"Chicago? How exciting! I've never been there other than one suburb."

Connor's frozen silence spoke loud enough for Lana to hear his message.

"Oh, Connor, sorry. I just thought—" she let it fall flat.

How could he get out of it now? Multiple scenarios of having her along flashed through his mind. "No, no, that's, that's fine. I was going to, um, invite you anyway," he stammered.

"Are you sure, Connor? It sounds to me like you don't want me along," Lana sensed.

"It's not that I don't want you to come with me; it's just that I'll be in meetings all day Saturday and maybe even Sunday morning." He waited for her to decline the invitation.

"No worries. I can entertain myself while you're at the meetings. Then maybe we can go dancing, out for dinner, maybe to a jazz club."

"Okay, I'll pick you up tomorrow at 8 am. Pack a sexy party dress."

Lana waited in the car while Connor checked into the hotel, then they took the glass elevator to their suite on the seventh floor. "Look at this view, Connor. It's stunning. The water seems to glitter," Lana said, gazing at the lake.

Connor joined her at the window. "Maybe we'll have a chance to stick our toes in Lake Michigan while we're here. It's usually on the cool side, though," Connor said as he removed his suit from his garment bag. "But, for now, let's get ready and find something to eat."

The dark gray dress slacks that Connor already had on were perfect for a night out in Chicago, as were his black Salvatore Ferragamo calf-skin Oxfords. He removed a freshly ironed white shirt, a burgundy silk tie, and a black blazer from his garment bag.

In the meantime, Lana slipped out of her black sandals, blue jeans, and white short-sleeved tunic and changed into the black floral faux-wrap dress she had bought the night before at Target. She accessorized with pink tourmaline earrings that accented the pink and white floral pattern of the dress, a three-piece brass beaded bracelet, also from Target, and an ivory shawl that once was her grandmother's.

On the elevator ride down, Connor told Lana that he had already made a reservation at Gibson's Bar and Steakhouse on Rush Street. He had also arranged for transportation, as it was too far to walk.

When they entered the restaurant, Lana smiled, glad to see it wasn't as fancy as she expected. The leather seats at the booth the maître'd led them to were supple and free of tears, unlike some booths she sat at in Saint Paul. The warm lighting and soft music reminded her of a movie she once saw. *Was it 'Pretty Woman'?* she wondered. The voices were muffled, and the usual clanging sound of servers and bussers clearing dishes was absent from the scene.

Their server was a young man in his late twenties. His jet black hair was pulled tightly into a man bun, and he wore a white shirt and black slacks. Connor commented on his narrow retro necktie.

"Thank you. I found it at a vintage clothing shop in London. I—," the server stopped himself from telling them about the shop and the other items he bought, realizing he needed to move things along in the busy locale. "Can I get you anything from the bar?" he asked as he filled their water glasses. "I've served a lot of mojitos tonight, if that's your choice."

"I'll have a Tanqueray martini, straight up and dry, with two olives," Lana breezily ordered her cocktail, feeling like a movie star.

"Nice," Connor approved. "A gin martini for me. Beefeater."

They opened their menus. Lana's eyes widened when she saw the prices.

"Connor, these prices are astronomical," Lana said, her eyes never straying from the menu. "Don't worry, Lana," Connor reassured her. "Order whatever you like. I have an expense account, a generous one."

"I just can't decide," Lana admitted as her eyes bounced from one item to another. "But, I think I'll have the miso marinated Chilean Sea Bass."

"I'm having steak," Connor stated definitively as he snapped his menu shut and placed it on the table.

The martinis arrived at just the right time. "Are you ready to order?" the server asked.

"Yes, for the lady, the Chilean sea bass, and for me, the ribeye, medium rare." Lana quietly watched Connor as she saw what might have been a Hollywood star out with a leading lady. Except Lana wasn't impressed.

"Any starters, a salad, shrimp cocktail, maybe?" The server spoke only to Connor.

"Yes. One shrimp cocktail for each of us. Then, two Caesar salads. And for the sides, one creamed spinach and one grilled asparagus."

"Excellent, sir," the server remarked as he gathered the two menus.

"Would you like wine with your dinner, sir?"

"Yes, a Pinot Grigio for the lady and a Merlot for me."

Lana sat quietly, bobbing her olives in her gin as Connor rambled on about the history of the restaurant. But Lana heard very little.

Finally, after noticing the disconcerted grimace on Lana's face, Connor changed the subject.

"Lana, is something wrong? Is it your martini?"

The tender look in Connor's blue eyes was nearly enough to deflect what Lana wanted to say. And that errant curl of hair above his eye, the curl that invited any woman to twirl it in her fingers, came even closer to sending Lana's reply into oblivion. But she wouldn't back down. She looked up from her martini, sat back, and crossed her arms, ready to answer Connor's misguided question.

"Oh, no, the martini's fine. But you ordered for me. That's never happened to me before. I don't know if I should be insulted or honored, but right now I'm leaning toward being insulted."

"I'm sorry, Lana, I guess I'm just used to doing that with my —"

Just then, the shrimp cocktails arrived. Connor quickly changed the subject. "So, how's it going with your thesis?"

They both raved about their entrees, though Lana thought the creamed spinach was too salty. For dessert, they split a slice of key lime pie.

After paying the check, Connor opened his Uber app and arranged for transportation to the Navy Pier. They rode the Ferris wheel and marveled at the Chicago skyline as they leisurely strolled around the pier. Sensing that Lana was tired, Connor arranged for transportation back to the hotel. But Lana was anything but tired.

The door to their room was barely shut when Lana tossed her purse on the bed and turned to face Connor, who was taking his blazer off. He knew that look, the way she dropped her left shoulder, biting her lower lip in an impish smile. He tossed his blazer on the bed with a free and easy flair.

Lana slowly eased her way over to Connor, one provocative slink at a time. She looked down at Connor's belt buckle and gently tugged at it. But she wouldn't start there. As she raised her head, she casually brushed her hair back with her fingertips, her smoldering eyes locked on Connor's eager face.

They faced each other, two wanton grins sharing an identical frequency, transmitting the same signal. Lana stood in front of Connor, his masculine scent overpowering her subtle feminine essence. He brushed the backs of his fingertips down her bare arm. Lana closed her eyes as she melted, a chocolate kiss in Connor's torrid hand.

She walked her fingers up each arm of Connor's crisp white shirt, closing in with each step until their bodies merged.

"Oh, baby, you're killing me," Connor moaned, his husky voice low and sultry.

Lana skillfully undid Connor's necktie. *Schwoosh!*

She flung it over her shoulders; the first obstacle now removed. It was a Burberry from Neiman Marcus, but that didn't matter to Connor at the moment.

Connor carefully removed Lana's glasses, folded them together, and set them on a suitcase next to the door. He then gradually pulled down the right shoulder strap of her dress and let it hang. He gently kissed her shoulder. Using his other hand this time, he lowered the strap on her left shoulder. He brushed the back of his fingers across her perky breasts as he brought his arm down. He put both hands on Lana's hips and pulled her in. Their lips met softly, a softness that would soon be forgotten.

Still standing just inside the door, they took their time stripping off a variety of fabrics, randomly discarding them on the floor. The scent of their bodies fused, an overture to a building crescendo.

Recalling a scene from a movie, Lana bent over and picked up the necktie. She threw it around Connor's neck and, walking backward, with measured steps, pulled him toward the bed, watching his crooked smile broaden with each step. They kissed again, deeper, harder, as Connor fondled Lana's breast.

She ripped open the carefully made bed, sending the purse and blazer into the unknown. They tumbled in. Sensually teasing each other's flesh with their lips, tongues, and fingertips, their sounds of impending ecstasy intensified.

Connor bounced out of bed, went into the bathroom, and slipped on a condom. He returned to find Lana waiting, vulnerable, his for the taking. Their gentle foreplay aside, Connor entered Lana. Deeper and deeper, he penetrated Lana's core. Increasing, surging, cresting with every thrust of Connor's brawn, Lana's paeans of rapture reverberated, harmonizing with Connor's into a symphonic rhapsody of climax.

Connor's virile body lay collapsed over Lana, pinning her to the mattress. She couldn't move. She didn't want to move.

As their breathing slowly returned to normal, neither said a word. Nothing. Lana was ready to say, "I love you," but doubted Connor was ready to hear it, so she held it in.

## You're Not Invited

The next morning, Connor rose early and quietly left the room so as not to awaken Lana. An hour later, Lana awoke and was soon on her way downstairs to breakfast. She couldn't believe she was so hungry after all she had eaten the night before.

After a hearty breakfast of poached eggs on burned toast with a side of sausage and an order of hash browns, Lana was ready for Chicago. She talked to the concierge about her options and left the hotel with an itinerary of sightseeing, museums, and shopping. She had just paid for purchases at Neiman Marcus on Michigan Avenue when a call came in from Connor.

"Hi, Lana. I hope you've been having a good day."

"I'm having a great day!" Lana ardently proclaimed.

"Lana, I have something to tell you. I need to go to a business dinner tonight."

"Great, I can wear the new dress and shoes I just bought at Neiman Marcus."

"It's a business dinner, Lana. I told them it would just be me. You'd be terribly bored."

A lag in Lana's response prompted Connor to revisit his concern that Lana thought their relationship was anything more than a physical attraction. But that wasn't what Lana was wondering. *Why would Connor think that I, someone who is about to earn an MBA, would be bored at a business dinner?* She would ask him that later, or tomorrow.

"I see. But I know you're here on business, and I will miss not having another dinner with you and maybe a repeat of last night. In the meantime, I'll grab a bite to eat somewhere and read until you get back to the hotel. No worries!"

Connor felt bad enough about leaving Lana alone in Chicago on a Saturday night. *But did she have to be so agreeable? Shouldn't she at least be a bit disappointed?* he asked himself.

"I'll be back as soon as I can. I promise. And wouldn't it be a nice surprise to see you in your new dress and shoes, so that I can peel them off you."

"We'll seeee," Lana teased before she hung up and hailed a taxi to their hotel.

After freshening up in their room, Lana returned to the lobby for an early dinner in the hotel's restaurant. The white and powder-blue floral sleeveless dress, paired with the white pumps she bought at Neiman Marcus, went well beyond the smart casual dress code of the steakhouse. She wore her hair in a high ponytail. As she walked past a crowded bar, her ponytail swaying in sync with her step, it wasn't her diamond earrings, her pearl necklace, or her tanzanite bracelet that more than one man noticed; it was the lack of a ring on her left hand.

"Table for one, ma'am?" the smartly dressed maître d' asked.

"My husband will be joining me later, so please bring two menus." Lana wanted to signal that she was not alone to deter unwanted attention.

She ordered a Sapphire Gin martini and looked over the menu. When the server returned, she ordered the grilled salmon with a snow pea salad. Once her meal arrived, Lana left those memories behind as she thought about her future and what she might do when she's finished her MBA.

Lana finished her meal but declined dessert. She wrote their room number on the check and signed Connor's name. After buying a coffee, she returned to their room. She stood by the window, sipping her coffee while looking down at a vibrant Chicago, alive with the nightlife she might otherwise have been a part of. But that was no loss; she had had enough of Chicago for one day. She would curl up in the easy chair and continue reading *The Midnight Library* by Matt Haig.

## The Jacket

When Connor entered the room, Lana closed her book using her index finger as a bookmark.

Without making eye contact with Lana, Connor's shoulders sank as he spoke. "I'm really sorry about tonight, Lana, but I thought I was doing the right thing."

"It's fine, Connor. I'm not angry or hurt. I did want to show off my new dress, though," Lana admitted.

"It's lovely." Connor's wispy voice sounded deflated. She could see from his tight face that he was either tired or distressed.

"At any rate, I'm glad to be back," he mumbled as he shuffled across the carpet on his way to the bathroom. Lana returned to her reading but struggled to concentrate on the words in her book. She knew Connor could be moody, especially when things went awry. *Had he not attained the success in Chicago that he was used to?* She doubted it.

Connor was very successful in his career. Even before he received his MBA, he'd been hired by 3M. What started as an entry-level position quickly turned into a string of promotions. Often, when walking into the office, he saw the same corner office on the top floor. Someday, that would be his. He would be called Mr. Larson, have a company credit card, and preside over meetings at the head of the table.

Lana attributed some of his success to his commanding demeanor. He was six feet, three inches tall and weighed 160 pounds. His mid-length curly black hair had a way of diverting a single curl slightly over his left eye. His penetrating blue eyes often left others wondering what he was really thinking.

No, Connor's mood was surely due to something else.

Lana closed her book completely when Connor came out of the bathroom. She watched as he mechanically hung his clothes in the closet. After he slid into bed, Lana went to the bathroom to prepare for what she now doubted would be anything like the night before.

When she came out, Connor was sound asleep. Realizing she had forgotten to turn off the bathroom light, she turned back, and that's when she saw Connor's wallet lying on the closet floor.

The wallet lay open, facedown. She picked it up. About to close it, she noticed a photo: two young boys sitting around a campfire roasting marshmallows. A woman sat next to them. All three were looking at the camera. Lana noticed a cooler near the fire. A jacket had been tossed on top of the cooler. Lana had seen that jacket before. It was an antique green L. L. Bean Anorak.

With the bathroom door locked, Lana held the photo close to the bright lights surrounding the mirror. The CLR monogram glared back at Lana. *Connor Robert Larson,* she mouthed the words to the mirror. The woman in the photo looked to be about 35. Her jet black hair had strands of muted silver and was pulled into a high ponytail, revealing the fine features of a swarthy complexion.

She studied the woman and the boys more closely. The boys had blue eyes and thick, curly black hair. The complexion of one boy was distinctively swarthy; the other boy's was not so much, but still noticeable. The woman was clearly of ethnic origin; her jet black hair and dark eyes reminded Lana of a woman she met at the restaurant where she once worked.

A nervous impulse made her glance at the closed door. She opened the door slowly and placed the wallet on the closet floor, exactly as she found it.

Lana couldn't sleep. She stared at the ceiling as she considered how she would play it. This was the second time they had spent an entire night together. Previously, Connor had always had a reason not to spend the night with Lana: he had an early day, he needed to make some calls, he needed to get back to his office.

Connor lay on his side, breathing softly, his back toward Lana. She quietly slipped out of bed. Their corner room afforded them a view of both the lake and a partial city view. Lana watched the city below as she considered her options.

Lana saw no reason to create a scene. She would not do what a friend of hers did in a similar situation: hire a detective to find out who the woman was. He never really lied to her, well, except maybe a lie of omission. In a few days, Lana would leave Saint Paul, and the relationship would be over.

# CHAPTER 5

# TURNING THE PAGE

### If I May Ask?

Four months after she and Connor met, Lana received her MBA from Macalester. A week later, she passed her CPA exam. The following day, her parents came to St. Paul to help her vacate her apartment.

"I'm surprised by you, Lana," her mother said. "Moving out before you have a place to move to. That's so, so not you."

"Everything I own will fit in my car. Of course, that's after you and Dad haul the rest back to Knoxville. I'll find something. No worries," Lana blithely replied. After her parents returned to their hotel that evening, Lana left her apartment.

She sat on a park bench in front of Old Main on the Macalester Campus. She glanced at her phone and realized she was early. It was a mild spring evening, with a slight breeze that brushed the fragrance off the tulips and daffodils into the air.

Lana contemplated their relationship, wondering if he had managed to keep love at bay. At times, he could be distant—though she had been, too.

Memories surfaced of Connor acting as if there were somewhere else he needed, or perhaps wanted, to be. When Lana asked Connor to meet her on campus, he sensed that their time together would end. And he could live with that. They had become too close, too intertwined.

"Hi, Lana," Connor said as he sat next to her without making eye contact.

"Hi, Connor. Thanks for agreeing to meet me." Lana's businesslike tone set the stage for her next comment. "I think we both know that our relationship needs to end."

"I think you are right. But I have to say, if I had it to do all over, I would." Connor looked into Lana's inscrutable eyes. "You mentioned once that you're not sure where you'll end up. That's gutsy for you," Connor observed.

"You're right. But now with college behind me, I want to be more daring, not give in so easily, and take chances. Or at least try." Lana looked at Connor out of the corner of her eye, waiting to hear his response. But he sat motionless, staring at a dandelion pushing its way up between two contraction joints of the concrete sidewalk. "No more needs to be said," Lana stood as she said it.

Connor stood and faced her. They held hands and slowly walked backward until they could no longer touch.

The next morning, Lana's parents were at her apartment to help her clear her things out.

"Lana, honey, now would be a good time to find a nice man and settle down, don't you think?" Lana and her mother were wrapping glassware with bubble wrap while her father was in the living room dismantling a portable bookshelf.

"You mean someone like Dad?" Lana joked. Her mother gave her an inscrutable glance. Then they both laughed.

"You're not getting any younger, you know?" her mother continued.

"Mom, I'm only 24. It's not like menopause is just around the corner. I know how you want to be a nana, but hang in there." Lana's last remark left her mother with a sliver of hope.

"I know, but—" The crash of the bookshelf tumbling to the floor interrupted Lana's mother's words. They walked out of the kitchen and found Lana's father surrounded by the remains. When he heard Lana and her mother laughing from behind him, he turned and shrugged his shoulders.

"Don't worry. I'll take this back with us and fix it," he said. Lana and her mother looked at each other, each knowing what the other was thinking–Lana would never see that bookshelf again.

Lana and her mother returned to the kitchen as her father went into Lana's bedroom to disassemble Lana's twin bed. Moments later, he stood quietly in the kitchen doorway, waiting for them to notice his Cheshire grin.

When they finally acknowledged him, he nonchalantly announced, "I only have one question." He pulled his arm from behind his back and held up a pair of boxer shorts. "So, whose are these, if I may ask?"

"Maybe I'll be a nana sooner than I think." Lana's mother said as she winked at Lana.

Seeing Connor's boxer shorts reminded Lana that she still had a place in her heart for him: that wasn't supposed to happen.

"Just toss them out, Dad. He won't be needing them anymore," Lana said as she returned the wink to her mother.

They parted ways in the parking lot, Lana heading to who knows where and her parents to Knoxville.

## Lool'vil

Lana ended up in Louisville simply because that's where her finger landed when she randomly opened the atlas her parents had given her. Sitting in the parking lot of her apartment, she placed the atlas on the passenger seat, closed her eyes, and pointed. When she saw she'd picked Kentucky, she giggled at her own spontaneity, started the car, and said, "Louisville it is."

To break up the otherwise ten-hour drive, and to enjoy her freedom, Lana spent one night at a hotel in a Chicago suburb. It was hazy the next morning, and being in no hurry, Lana decided to do some shopping, hoping that the sun would burn off some of the haze. It was only another five-hour drive to Louisville, anyway. As a graduation present, her parents had given her a $5,000 prepaid credit card.

"It's to help you get started," her father had said.

Lana checked out of her hotel and drove to Kohl's department store nearby, where she bought several articles of clothing and two pairs of shoes.

As Lana drove into Louisville, she imagined herself as Mary Tyler Moore driving into a new life in Minneapolis. The show was before her time, but her parents had purchased every season, and Lana had seen most of the episodes over the years.

It was only June, and Lana was already cursing the Louisville heat. She found a chain hotel and checked in for three nights, hoping she would find an apartment by then.

The furnished apartment she found the next day was too good to be true. The brick house, once a single-family dwelling, had been divided into two apartments. Lana was happy to see that it was the second-floor apartment and that it was vacant. The noisy neighbors she had above her in Saint Paul taught Lana to be more selective this time. The apartment had an enclosed staircase leading to it. It was clean, amply furnished, and in a quiet neighborhood. And it had off-street parking.

Lana signed a one-year lease and, by the end of the day, checked out of the hotel and moved into her apartment.

Two days later, Lana saw a want-ad in the Courier Journal for a bookkeeper/accountant for multiple small businesses. She met the qualifications in every area except experience. Applicants were to contact Sally Caitano at Sally's Bar on South Shelby. Lana dialed the number. "Sally's," the voice said.

"Hello. My name is Lana Paulson, and I am responding to an ad in the Courier Journal about an accountant job," Lana said.

"One moment, I'll get Sally." The voice sounded young, and Lana wondered if it belonged to Sally's daughter.

"Hello, this is Sally." They spoke briefly on the phone, and Sally asked Lana to stop by the next day around 3 PM.

The next day, Lana arrived at Sally's early, so she waited in her car until the appointment time. The door was locked when she tried it, but through the window, she could see a woman at the cash register counting money. Lana knocked. The woman stuffed the money into a bag and put it behind the bar.

"Hello, you must be Lana," Sally said as she opened the door. She wore a red silk blouse with black boot-cut denims and had her hair pinned up in a casual updo, held together with a silver comb.

"Yes, I'm Lana," she said, shaking Sally's hand.

They sat at a table, and the interview began. Lana showed Sally her diplomas and certificates, which Sally only glanced at. Sally's probing questions centered more on *who* Lana was, not *what* she was. Lana had a few smudges in her past, but there was no reason to tell Sally about the two times she had been caught for shoplifting when she was a teenager.

"I need someone who is not only competent but also discreet. You'd be working with more than one of my holdings. Where my income comes from would not be your concern. I run the businesses and you do the books," Sally bluntly explained.

Lana was equally direct. "I assure you, I am quite competent for this position. My credentials speak for themselves. I also want to assure you I understand that confidence is a key component in a position such as the one you are offering."

Sally waited for Lana to say more.

"If you wish, I would only do my work here, or at one of your other businesses, and would never take the books or documents off the premises." This time, Lana waited for a response from Sally.

Sally eyed up Lana, not letting on what she was thinking.

Lana sat quietly, pleased with her performance.

"As a formality, I need you to fill out an application. When can you start?"

"Any time. I have no other commitments," Lana phlegmatically replied.

Sally stood and walked into her office to get an application while Lana waited patiently.

*In a short time*, Lana thought, *I found a nice apartment and now a job.* She was never the kind who believed that everything happens for a reason. But she wondered about the day she randomly opened that atlas and, without looking, placed her finger on Louisville. Did her finger land on Louisville on its own?

Sally returned with the application.

"My current accountant has given me a two-week notice. You can meet him tomorrow, right here. Does 10 AM work for you?"

"Yes, of course," Lana replied. "I just have one question. What benefits do you offer?"

"I can offer you health care, a very good plan, actually. But other than that, there are no pension plans or matching IRA contributions. I'll give you something about the health plan tomorrow." Sally started walking to the door, and Lana followed.

"Bring the application with you tomorrow," Sally said while holding the door open for Lana.

## Irregularities

Lana spent three days with Sally's accountant. Immediately, Lana noticed several irregularities in the accounts. Mentioning them, the accountant's response was always the same: "Don't worry, it will all come out in the wash." Lana wondered if *he* had actually given notice or if Sally had asked him to leave.

Once on her own, Lana found even more discrepancies. Sally had at least a half dozen businesses going, some with odd names like Pegasus and Sapphire. Lana thought Sapphire sounded like a strip joint.

The books of all those businesses were a mess. The principles of accounting that Lana knew were incongruous with the accountant's work. It took Lana three months to straighten things out. It was then that she figured out what was going on.

For one, money was coming in from outside sources. When Lana approached Sally about it, her response was, "You're the accountant, figure out what to do with it."

So, Lana did. She saw what the previous accountant had done to account for extraneous monies—he had embezzled it by shifting money between accounts. Sally was content with only seeing the bottom line and never hired an outside auditor.

After six months as Sally's accountant, and following his lead, Lana amassed enough money to buy a new Volvo, which she kept in storage, at least for the time being. She continued her subterfuge until Sally started to take an increasing interest in the books.

# CHAPTER 6

# KITTY

## A Gap Year

Katherine Azalea Barrington was far from the Southern belle her mother had envisioned. Growing up in Alabama, she was constantly being groomed by her mother to be a refined lady, the kind who takes tea at the club, enters azalea contests, and fusses over table settings. Katherine wondered why her mother would want her only daughter to get trapped in an unhappy, meaningless life of martinis, Bridge, and endless charity balls.

As a child, Katherine preferred the company of her father. Early on, he took her with him to the stables and corrals, balancing her on a fence railing while keeping one arm around her. On her seventh birthday, he presented Kitty with her first horse, a Shetland that Kitty called Maple. She soon graduated to bigger and faster breeds and brought home several trophies.

While her mother, Eunice, was proud, she often voiced concerns. "If she ends up bow-legged, she will never get a man," she would say to her husband.

"Katherine, you will never land a husband if you keep beating the boys in horse races. Let them win. Maybe not all of them, just the ones with money, position, and family," she advised Katherine more than once.

Eunice Cynthia Barrington was from the kind of family she wanted her daughter to marry into. She was what others described as *coming from old money.*

Katherine's father, Archebald Barrington III, was described as having *new money.* He and his wife started a home construction business with some of the money she inherited from a wealthy grandmother. Eunice left the management of the business to Archie, while she tended to the social details. He employed several of his seven brothers and was known as a fair but demanding businessman.

But there was one brother he would not employ. His name was Calvin Barrington, and he was Katherine's favorite uncle. While Archebald tried to distance himself from Calvin, Eunice flatly refused to allow him in the house. Nonetheless, he still showed up at family gatherings elsewhere and occasionally met Katherine and her father for lunch when he was in town.

Calvin, or Cal, as his friends and confabulators called him, was commonly referred to as the black sheep of the family. Like his brother Charles, he too was in business, but of a different kind. A more clandestine kind.

Much speculation surrounded Calvin. He had a small shop in a small town just outside of Chattanooga, where he supposedly sold used appliances. It provided a good front for his more lucrative trade, some of which included providing his customers with forged documents. His list of ghost addresses spread into several contiguous states.

As she got older, Katherine was simply fed up with her mother's attempts to mold her into something she wasn't, nor wanted to be. Her father was often at meetings or out of town, and she missed him. She hated that everyone called her Katherine instead of Kathy or Kate. The only person who called her anything other than Katherine was her cousin, Lana, who called her Kat. She hated all the stodgy people her parents entertained, events she was required to attend in the most genteel way. She hated her life. She even hated azaleas.

During her senior year of high school, Katherine was accepted at Auburn University. Her father encouraged her to pursue a degree in business, while her mother suggested nursing. After her freshman year, and still undecided, Katherine declared she needed a gap year.

"A what year?" her father asked.

"A gap year. It's called a gap year. Some take a year off between high school and college. Some travel, some work, some study abroad," Katherine explained.

"And just what would you do in a gap year?" Her father leaned back in his office chair and rested the back of his head in his locked fingers.

"Lana's in Louisville. She's an accountant for a business consortium of some sort. I thought I'd start there. I want to live on my own, though. With my experience as a server at the country club, I should be able to find something," Katherine speculated.

Her father leaned forward and rested his right forearm on his mahogany desk.     "Your mother's going to have a fit, you know. She always does. But with Lana there, she'll be more amenable to the idea. Why don't you let me be the one to tell her? You two already lock horns too often as it is."

Not sure where she'd end up, Katherine contacted her uncle Calvin, who agreed to produce a fake ID for her.

"So, you want to be 21?" he asked. "Any particular date or month for your birthday?"

"How about December 25?" Katherine responded.

"What about a name?"

"Kitty Barr would be nice," Katherine suggested.

"OK, Kitty Barr, you got it. Send me a photo. One that looks like your driver's license photo. I'll do my magic and send—oh, no, that won't work. Your mother would certainly wonder. I'll call you when I have it, and we can meet somewhere. You can buy me lunch."

Two weeks later, the twenty-one-year-old Kitty Barr was ready to start her gap year. With Eunice at a bridge tournament, Archie spirited Katherine out of the house and drove her to the bus station.

"Are you sure you can handle this Michael Kors suitcase all by yourself? Archie asked as he lifted it out of his trunk. "This thing weighs a ton."

"It has wheels on it, Daddy. And besides, I can always find a big, strong male specimen to help me with it."

"Now I *am* worried. You be careful out there. And watch yourself with those big, strong male specimens! I was one of those, once." Kitty chuckled at her father's comment, which was half serious and half lighthearted.

"I suppose if you can handle that powerful Arab you occasionally ride, you can handle anything else." Her father lifted his head in pride and continued, "You do ride that horse like a natural."

He kissed his daughter and whispered, "Goodbye."

Katherine knew her father was trying to be strong for her sake, and that made her admire him even more. She realized that one day their special bond would be strained, but she had always thought it would happen after he walked her down the wedding aisle.

After the bus driver put Kitty's bag into the baggage compartment, her father handed her an envelope. "A little something to help you get started. But if you're not going to study, then you need to find a job."

Archie kissed his daughter again. As many a wise father must have told their daughter time and again, he had one last thing to say. "Remember who you are, Katherine. We all need to make compromises in life, but always consider them carefully. The wrong ones can haunt you for life."

"Thanks, Daddy. I'll remember that." Kitty boarded the bus and waved at her father as it pulled away.

On the bus, Kitty thought about how close she and Lana were growing up, often spending their summers at each other's houses. Lana was older than Kitty, and once Lana was in high school, they spent less time together. Lana's father and Kitty's mother were siblings. But the families became estranged after they settled their mother's sizable estate. Lana's father accused his sister of manipulating their mother into leaving the bulk of the estate to her. And Kitty, knowing her mother as she did, believed it was likely true.

A few days after she was settled in, she would call Lana and reconnect.

## Vera

When the bus finally pulled into Louisville, Kitty rolled her suitcase into the station, used the facilities, and approached an attendant at the ticket counter.

"Excuse me, ma'am, but I am wondering if there is a decent hotel in the area," she asked.

The attendant wondered what type of hotel she meant by decent. Probably one that did not charge by the hour, the attendant surmised, based on Kitty's graciousness and her sapphire earrings, gold necklace, and peach tie-neck poplin top.

"Are you traveling alone, honey?" she asked.

"Why yes, ma'am, I am." Kitty wondered if she should not have admitted that.

"Best not to tell too many people that, especially a man," the attendant advised.

"That's good advice, thank you." Kitty saw that the woman's name was Vera. She figured her to be in her early thirties and could tell by her belabored Southern drawl she was no Yankee.

"Let me tell ya', the first thing I would suggest is that you find a hotel away from this area. You don't want to be on the streets in this neighborhood, especially at night. Tell you what, I'll write the name of a clean and safe hotel that I know. Tell 'em Vera sent you," she proudly suggested with a husky voice; Kitty could smell tobacco smoke on Vera's clothes.

"Be sure to take a taxi, and one from right out in front of the station. Don't hail one from the streets. Too dangerous this time of night. If the driver happens to go by the name of Patch, say Vera sent you."

The attendant handed Kitty a slip of paper with the hotel address. "Now you take care, honey. And welcome to this wonderful city. And if you need anything, you can either find me here, at a bowling alley, or at Sally's, a bar and grill in town."

Kitty thanked Vera and easily found a taxi outside the door. The driver saw her motion for him, and he drove forward. He got out of the cab and put her suitcase in the trunk.

"Where to, Miss?"

Kitty handed him the paper with the hotel's name written on it.

"You wouldn't happen to be Patch, would you?" she asked the driver after noticing his left eye was covered with a patch.

"Why, yes, I am. How'd ya know?"

"Vera sent me."

"That Vera! If she ain't some woman! Talk 'bout gumption! She could talk the hind legs off a donkey. Ain't nobody gonna mess with her though. I mighta known she'd send you to this hotel, her brother owns it. But it's a nice place, in a good part of town."

Kitty enjoyed the guided tour all the way up to the hotel's door. Patch even carried her bag inside. Kitty paid him the fare and added what she thought was a good average tip. She had little experience with tips.

"There you go, Miss. I'll be catchin' up with Vera later on. Tonight's our bowling league night, and let me tell ya', she's a helluva bowler. I'd marry that woman if I could, but my wife, my wife, she'd have something to say about that." He nodded to the hotel clerk as he left the building.

Kitty signed the registry while the attendant checked her ID. He spun the registry around to verify the names matched. He ran over a few hotel policies and handed her a key card. She found her room on the top floor. After setting her suitcase down, she stood in front of the window and admired her view of the Ohio River.

## Sally's

Having skipped lunch, Kitty left the hotel in search of something to eat. After walking past a couple of questionable establishments, she saw the neon sign at the end of the block, Sally's Saloon and Eats. With some reservations, Kitty went in. *Do decent single women do this?* She sat on the first empty barstool.

A few customers at the other end of the bar stared at her for a moment or two and continued their chatter. Soon, a woman came up to get her order. She looked to be in her forties. She also looked like the kind of woman who could handle a rowdy Saturday crowd. The bartender placed a coaster on the bar in front of Kitty.

"I'll have a glass of white wine, please."

Oh, how Kitty wished her mother could see her now, not only sitting at a bar ordering wine, but doing so unescorted. She relished the image of her mortified mother.

"Got an ID, honey?"

"Yes, I do." Kitty took out her ID and tossed it on the bar. Sally picked it up.

Kitty wondered if the bartender was Sally herself. Holding the ID in her hand, the wise and seasoned Sally asked the new customer to state her name. Then she asked for her address. Satisfied, she returned the ID to Kitty.

"White wine, you said?

"A Pinot Grigio would be nice," Kitty mousily requested.

"You got it, Miss Kitty Barr."

As Kitty sat there sipping her wine, she could see her reflection in the mirror behind the bar. She seemed so out of place, so innocent, so vulnerable. The bright Budweiser light on the wall next to her cast a reddish hue on her face. She stared until her imagination distorted her image into something unfamiliar, something unnatural, almost otherworldly.

She moved down the bar to get away from that image.

The juke box was playing way too loud—something about "turning twenty-one in prison, doing life without parole." The song made her feel lonely. Was it too late for her to walk out the door, collect her suitcase, and catch the next bus home?

She pictured her parents as they prepared for dinner. Her father with an expensive Kentucky bourbon, and her mother with a Gibson martini. She wondered what the cook had prepared. Was it steak Dianne? Lobster Newberg? Salmon croquettes? Or Kitty's favorite, Southern-fried chicken, creamy coleslaw, and macaroni and cheese. Comfort food. That's what she needed right now.

Kitty was about to ask about the food service when she heard another customer come into Sally's. He sat three stools away from Kitty.

"Your usual, Robie?" Sally was already reaching into the beer cooler as she yelled the question so the man could hear.

"Yep. Someday I'm going to throw you off course and order something else."

"Nothing throws me off course, Robie. You know that."

She brought the beer down the long, polished wood bar, tossed a coaster down, which would have ended up on the floor if Robie had not caught it.

"There you go, hon. By the way, Kitty, this is Robie, Robie Campbell. You probably gathered that he's a regular." Sally went to the other end of the bar, where she was watching Wheel of Fortune.

"Yes, I'm a regular here. But you ain't, that's for sure," Robie said to her.

"No, I am not," Kitty agreed.

"You new in town? Just passin' through?"

Kitty saw that Robie was a handsome man, with wavy dark brown hair, the kind a woman likes to run her fingers through or grab onto in a moment of passion. Not that Kitty had a lot of memories of such pleasures. She figured he didn't have an office job; he looked like a blue-collar type with the physique to match. He clearly would not have been the type her parents would approve of. And his language was clearly not as refined as Kitty would have heard in her circles back home.

"I'm not sure about anything yet. I might stay; I might move on. If I find a reason to stay, I will," Kitty said with a prolonged devil-may-care shrug.

Robie wasn't sure if Kitty was flirting. He was never good at discerning the subtleties of the art.

"Well, let me be the first to welcome you. Technically, my name's Robert, but most people call me Robie. Mind if I buy you a drink?"

Deflecting what Kitty thought was an advance, she graciously declined. "I'm going to have to decline. My husband, Bubba, is due in a few minutes, and I doubt he'd be pleased to know I let a stranger buy me a drink."

He persisted, "That's odd, I don't see a ring on your finger."

Kitty frowned at the forward comment.

Robie closed his eyes, turned away, and thought, *Man, I'm such a cad at times.* He could just drop it.

He turned back to face Kitty. "I'm sorry. That was uncalled for," Robie admitted, stretching to rub the back of his head with his hand.

"Apology accepted," Kitty replied. She raised her hand to shake his, saying, "It's nice to meet you, Robie."

Robie, taking the hint, grabbed his beer and stood. "Nice to meet you. I hope we see each other again." He went to join a raucous group near the pool table.

Kitty sat behind an empty wine glass. "Why not? What the hell?" Kitty whispered to herself as she ordered another Pinot Grigio.

She pushed her glass forward to catch Sally's attention. Sally knew what Kitty wanted, but asked just the same.

'Yes, same thing. Also, could I see a menu? I'd like to order something to go."

"I hope you're not driving."

"Oh no, I'm staying at a hotel near here."

Sally returned with the wine and the menu.

"Name's Sally. This is my place. Just like it says on that coaster, Sally's. Locals call me Sal, maybe you will someday."

Kitty picked up her drink, raised the glass to eye level, and proposed a solitary toast. "Here's to my mother, Eunice. If she could see me now."

Sally paused and looked back as she walked away. "Something tells me you're being facetious." Sally didn't wait for an answer.

## White Wine for the Princess

Kitty knew she couldn't stay at the hotel Vera had recommended for long. She needed a job and an apartment. She would give Louisville a chance.

She asked the night attendant at the hotel if he knew Vera.

"Of course, everyone knows Vera!" he exclaimed."

"Patch, the taxi driver who brought me here yesterday, implied that she likes to bowl. You wouldn't happen to know where she bowls, would you?" Kitty asked with a perky smile.

"That's a good question. I really couldn't tell you. As far as I know, she bounces around from one alley to another. You could ask her brother, the owner of this place, but by this time of the day, he probably doesn't even know where *he* is." The attendant, with his hand tilted and his thumb and pinky finger raised, imitated someone drinking.

"Patch might know. I'll give him a call." The attendant was a young man in his early twenties and eager to please the woman on the other side of the counter. Kitty's streaked and textured bob hairstyle made her look sassy. Her brown eyes sparkled, as did her perfect smile. When she pulled back her head and flicked her hair, the attendant lost interest in his phone call.

"Hello. Hello. Who is this?" Patch's loud voice brought the mesmerized attendant back to earth.

Kitty walked over to a display case filled with pamphlets and flyers of things to do in Louisville while the telephone conversation continued.

"Patch thinks she's got the night off from bowling," the attendant called out to Kitty. "He thinks she's probably at Sally's shooting pool." The young man behind the desk offered his services as an escort for the evening in an effort to flirt. "I'd love to escort you, but, as you can see, I have to work. Maybe next time?" he proposed with a wink of his eye.

"Maaaaybe," Kitty taunted, her coy smile punctuated at both ends with delicate dimples on her pixie face. With a glimmer in his eyes, the young man's mouth dropped open, but not a sound came out.

"Anyway, Sally's is just down the street, a couple of blocks on your right." Kitty didn't tell him that she already knew that.

Patch was right, Vera was at Sally's, shooting pool and winning almost every game.

Kitty approached Vera as she skeptically watched her opponent try a bank shot.

"Hi, Vera. Remember me?" Kitty's voice bubbled with enthusiasm.

"Why, of course, honey. From the bus station. Can't say that I remember your name, though. Hang on a sec and watch this winning shot." Vera chalked up her pool cue. After sizing up the table, she took her shot.

The eight-ball bounced off the side of the table and casually rolled over to the corner pocket Vera had designated as her target. Breaths were held as it slowly approached the pocket. All eyes were upon the black ball as it teetered on the edge of the pocket. Thunk. It dropped in. Vera returned her pool cue to its case, dusted off her hands in victory, and walked over to Kitty.

"Kitty, my name's Kitty."

"I'll be. Nice seein' you again, Kitty. Got a last name too?" Vera wasn't much for formalities—pool halls, bowling alleys, and bus station lobbies were her bailiwicks.

"It's Barr. Kitty Barr."

"You old enough to *even* be in here?" Vera brushed some chalk off her bowling shirt as she gave Kitty a questioning look.

"Yes. "I'm 21." Kitty beamed.

"Well, you're a young 21, I'd say. Let's grab a drink." Vera headed for the bar and elbowed her way through the boisterous crowd.

"Sally, a beer for me, and—what did you say you were drinking?" Vera turned to find Kitty trying to politely wend her way through the crowd.

"Make way, folks," Vera commanded the crowd. "Let the young lady through. She's with me." Vera might have been Charlton Heston parting the Red Sea. But without a staff.

"I'll have a white wine."

Vera rolled her eyes as she turned back to Sally. "The princess would like a white wine."

They looked for a table, but all the tables were taken. At a corner table, a woman sat alone, working on her laptop. Kitty hesitated as Vera approached the woman, staying a few steps behind.

"Hi, Lana. Mind if me and Kitty join you?" Vera asked.

"Of course, please do." Lana closed her laptop and gestured to the open chairs. Lana froze when she saw Kitty.

"Kat, is that you? It is, isn't it?" Lana waited for confirmation.

"Lana, yes, it's me." Kitty squealed in delight. Lana stood, and the two hugged.

"You look different. It's your hair. You always wore it long and often in a single braid. But look at you! You look so smart and cheeky!" Lana and Kitty were still holding onto each other's hands.

"I heard you were living in Louisville. I was going to call you as soon as I got settled in. I'm taking a gap year."

"But, but, you should have called me when you first arrived. You could have stayed with me." Lana's furrowed eyebrows made it clear that she was either bewildered or offended by Kitty's actions.

"That's just it. I wanted to do this on my own," Kitty explained. "I was going to call you any day now." Vera watched the exchange with a curious look on her face. "Oh, Vera, Lana is my cousin," Kitty explained. Lana hugged Kitty again. "No worries, Kat, have a seat. I'll get a drink so we can celebrate." Lana walked behind the bar and made herself a drink.

"Oh, so Lana must tend bar here," Kitty surmised.

"No. But she is Sally's accountant and business manager," Vera clarified.

"But she went behind the bar and made her own drink." Kitty seemed baffled as she said it.

"Welcome to Sally's, Kitty. Lotsa stuff goes on 'round here. This is a good place to keep your mouth shut. Except to drink, of course."

Kitty thought that Vera and her uncle Cal would make a good pair, but they were both married already, at least so far. "I think Lana's been here for about a year now, maybe even longer," Vera added.

"So, how is it that you two know each other?" Lana asked as she set her drink on the table and sat down.

"We met at the bus station," Vera answered. "I knew right away she was out of place. Not many people who take the bus wear designer clothes and expensive jewelry. And they certainly don't talk so pretty."

Lana turned toward Kitty. "Being in the company of Vera can open a lot of doors, including some you'd be better off not entering."

Vera shot Lana a glance. "Now just what do you mean by that?" she asked in a poorly executed response of indignation.

"I tell ya' Kat. Vera's either at the bus station, bowling somewhere, or here. Sometimes, she even goes home." Lana took a sip of her gin and tonic. "But what you don't want to do is cross her."

Vera's shoulders rose, and she set her head high.

"Oh, by the way, Lana, I go by the name Kitty now."

"OK, Kitty, bring me up to speed." Lana put her elbows on the table, locking her fingers below her chin.

Kitty and Lana rattled on about their past exploits, family gossip, and their futures.

Vera, who had basically disengaged from the bantering, downed the remains of her beer and redirected the conversation. "So, Kitty, what are your plans for now? If this is your gap year, aren't you supposed to be studying in Europe or volunteering for the Peace Corps, or something like that?" Vera thought for a moment, then added, "Do they still even have the Peace Corps?"

"I'm sure my mother would love to tell her friends that her daughter is studying in France. But I wanted to taste life at the ground level, meet people with other backgrounds, see what it's like in the real world," Kitty explained.

"You picked the right place," Vera stated. "And the right people. You can't get any more real world than here, at Sally's."

"I think that's what my father wanted me to do, too. At first, I was surprised that he agreed to go along with my plans. He comes from a humble background, and I think he wanted me to have a dose of reality. So, reality, here I am." Kitty slapped the edge of the table to underscore her resolve.

"Kat, I mean Kitty, you might just be in the right place at the right time," Lana suggested. "I know Sally is about to run an ad for a waitress for the restaurant side. She wants to try opening for lunch. Plus, she has apartments, two of them, above the bar, and both are vacant."

Trying to take it all in with a blank look on her face, Kitty said nothing.

"There you go, kiddo. Better act fast, Sally waits for nobody," Vera advised.

"Oh, yes, I will. This sounds too good to be true," Kitty squealed as she looked back and forth between Lana and Vera.

"I'll go tell Sally that I may have found her a new employee." Lana stood as she said. She took one more sip of her drink and left.

Since Lana didn't see Sally in the bar area, she figured she must be in her office in the back. Instead of going to the office through the crowded bar, Lana slipped out the front door and walked around the building toward the back alley. When she saw a van parked in the alley, she hid behind some lilac bushes to watch.

The back door of the bar was held open with a large rock as a man inside the back of the van was handing boxes to Sally, who was taking them inside. The boxes weren't marked. But Lana had seen unmarked boxes in the back room before—Sally was either buying off-market liquor or stolen liquor.

Lana waited until the van was long gone. She then went back into the bar and worked her way to Sally's office to tell her about Kitty.

## All In a Day's Work

The next day, Kitty went to Sally's for the interview.

Sally unlocked the door, and they sat at a table where Sally had an application and a pen ready for Kitty.

Kitty had barely sat down when Sally dove right in, "I need a waitress for the restaurant. And I need one now. Are you interested?"

"Yes."

"Have you ever had a job before?"

"Yes, during the summer I worked at a local country club as a server."

"Oh, yes, of course, as a *server*," Sally emphasized the last word. "I'm going to start serving lunch in the restaurant area in about a week. I can't guarantee forty hours a week right off the bat. But I'm hopeful."

Sally pointed to the application. "Why don't you fill that out while I tend to other matters?" Sally left the table.

When she returned, Kitty had long completed the application and was looking at her iPhone.

Sally sat down. "One thing I'll tell you right now. No staring at your phone when you're working for me. When you're on break, fine. Otherwise, keep it with your belongings in the back. That clear?" Kitty nodded, observing that Sally wasn't as refined as the people at the country club.

"Also, Lana said you need an apartment. I've got two upstairs. Both furnished and vacant. Interested?" "

"Yes, I am," Kitty replied.

"Let's go." Sally headed for the door as Kitty just sat there in neutral. "Hey, are you coming to see the apartment, or not?"

*Surly*, Kitty thought, *that's what Sally was.* She remembered the word from a vocabulary test in high school.

"I'll show you the nicest one first," Sally said as she unlocked the door marked 1A.

The apartment was nowhere near the comforts Kitty was accustomed to on her parents' ranch. But it was, at least, better than her hotel. The kitchen was small and had a two-burner stove—not that Kitty would cook very often, anyway.

The bathroom was also small and very basic. Kitty pictured her bathroom at home, which was spacious and furnished in a fashion that a Hollywood leading lady would approve of.

The living room and bedroom were both roomy. Kitty sat on the bed and pressed on the mattress to assess its condition. She looked around the room and decided she'd have to apply her makeup and fix her hair in the bedroom instead of the tiny bathroom. It would have to do. If this is the nicer of the two apartments, Kitty thought, then she didn't even need to look at 1B.

"Yes. I'll take it," Kitty cheerfully declared, inwardly congratulating herself on finding both a job and an apartment in one day.

They worked out the details, and Kitty moved in the next day.

## A Different Crowd

Because many diners preferred eating at the bar, Sally's had just five booths and six four-top tables, which could be pushed together for larger parties. There were no tablecloths or ornaments on the tables, except for the condiment organizer, which, other than the typical items such as ketchup and mustard, held three types of hot sauce.

It didn't take Kitty long to find out that, for the most part, diners at a country club are different from diners at a bar and grill. True, country club diners can be demanding, and if they had one martini too many, they could be loud and overbearing. But Sally's was something else.

For one, the pace was faster. Most diners were in and out, rarely lingering to talk about the stock market and golf scores like they did at the country club. No longer was Kitty serving steak and seafood; it was mostly burgers and fries. Sally's did offer other specials, though, ranging from comfort foods like roast beef with mashed potatoes and gravy to Southern specials like fried chicken with collard greens and cornbread. As Louisville sat right on the Mason-Dixon line, Sally's catered to southerners and northerners alike.

The smart and crisp uniform Kitty wore at the country club was a far cry from Sally's policy of "pretty much anything as long as it's clean, in good condition, and covers most of your flesh."

But it was the comments that mostly ruffled Kitty's refined, graceful style of waiting tables. Most of the comments were meant to impress fellow diners, so Kitty brushed them off with a smile. Other times, though, Kitty felt ill at ease, wishing she could have a comeback. After a few feckless attempts to deflect the unwanted comments, Kitty gradually built a glossary of snappy retorts.

"Hey, Kitty. How 'bout you and me getting together and raising us some kittens?" one diner asked.

"Why, that's very romantic of you, Billy Bob. But the only thing you know how to raise is hell."

"Evening, Miss Kitty. Let me take you away from all this. I can give you a life of luxury." It was Gus, surrounded by his buddies.

"Why, Gus, I thought you'd never ask. Just one thing, though, you're about as useless as a screen door on a submarine." While Gus' buddies had a good laugh, he didn't.

"Lookie here, aren't we the lucky ones tonight?" the cowboy said. "Such a pretty young thing you are. Should I pick you up after work, or do you want to meet at my place?"

"Just be patient. I'll bring you some crayons and an age-appropriate coloring placemat when I return with your drinks." Tex was not amused, but his homeboys hooted loudly as they stomped their feet and slapped the table.

Soon, those same men offered Kitty their protection.

"Kitty, if that guy over there is giving you trouble, just let me know," Tex said.

"If anyone starts giving you guff, Kitty, you call me over," Billy Bob said as he smashed his fist into the palm of his other hand.

Gus had a different approach. "I know people, Kitty, people who could convince anyone to be nothing but a gentleman in your presence."

Soon, Kitty was adroitly navigating her way around Sally's like a pro, deflecting even the raunchiest of taunts and raking in tips that she never saw at the country club.

## Bubba, My Foot

With her elbow on the table and her head precariously cradled in her open hand, Kitty's eyelids drooped as she stifled a yawn. Vera was lost in a game of pool that had drawn the attention of several patrons at Sally's. The excitement of her gap year was waning. She missed her friends, her parents, and her horse, Maple. *What would they all be doing right now?*

Vera finished the game and sat next to Kitty. "Honey, we gotta find you a man. You're such a pretty young thing. Any man would be lucky to have you in his bed. Or should I say in his kitchen?" Vera had a much less congenial way of phrasing her concerns for Kitty's marital status than Kitty's mother did.

"Let me buy you a white wine. Loosen you up a bit. In the meantime, go into the lady's room and splash some cold water on that gloomy face." Vera went to the bar and motioned for Sally. Sally and Vera had a brief conversation, and Vera came back with a wine for Kitty and a beer for herself.

When Robie came into Sally's fifteen minutes later, Sally waved him down to tell him his aunt Vera was there and she wanted to see him.

Robie grabbed a beer and made his way back to the pool. When Vera saw him, she waved him over excitedly. Another woman was sitting with her, but Robie could only see her back. He kissed Vera on the cheek, and she introduced him to Kitty.

Kitty knew who he was but acted like she didn't. Robie did the same. The three of them made small talk and, with Vera's handiwork concluded, she excused herself to share her success with her co-conspirator, Sally.

Seconds later, Robie turned to Kitty with a playful smile. "I just knew you weren't married. And when you told me your husband's name was *Bubba*, I mean, really. Next time, try a name like *Robie*."

The way he said his own name, with a masculine, sexy timbre, incited a flutter of excitement that Kitty had rarely felt before. She hoped he didn't notice the flush on her face.

After a bit of small talk, Robie leaned in with a half-smile. "So, Kitty… would your husband—Bubba, was it?—mind if I asked you out to dinner sometime?"

"Bubba wouldn't necessarily have to know," Kitty responded lightheartedly.

"How about tomorrow night?" Robie's eyebrows rose as he leaned in, casually resting his forearm on the table. His bold enthusiasm was uncharacteristic of his usual clumsiness around women.

He braced himself for a rebuff. Robie's forwardness took aback Kitty, as any Southern gentleman would never have been so bluntly presumptuous. She was inclined to put him off, but this was Kitty Barr and no longer Katherine Barrington.

"I suppose that would work. I do have the night off," she said.

They agreed that the evening would be casual, so Kitty wore her Versace stone-washed denims with a white Veronica Beard turtleneck. Her black Eileen Fisher crisscross sandals caught Robie's attention when he met her at Sally's. Kitty thought it would look, as her mother would say, unseemly, to have him come up to her apartment—she still hadn't shaken off some of the proscriptive practices of her genteel past.

Robie opened the passenger door of his truck and, as Kitty gracefully stepped in, a pang of apprehension distracted him—was he dating above his rank?

"You can close the door now, Robie," Kitty modestly suggested.

As he hesitantly walked around the back of the truck, he paused when he saw his reflection in the driver's side mirror. His eggshell white short-sleeve poplin shirt was good enough for him. As were the blue jeans from Kohl's. He did splurge on the Eastland boots, though, and hoped Kitty would notice.

As they drove away, Robie asked Kitty what she was in the mood for. "I don't eat out very often," he confessed, "but I do know of a lot of good restaurants."

"How about we do Mexican?" Kitty suggested. "I'm in the mood for some enchiladas." Robie, who also had a craving for enchiladas, surprised Kitty when he responded, "Yo, también."

"I'll tell ya' what. I know just the place. It's called Limón y Sal," he suggested.

Robie related some history of Louisville on the drive to the restaurant, some of it true, some of it lore. Kitty especially enjoyed the story of Hogan's Fountain in Cherokee Park, where, as legend had it, the statue of Pan goes for a stroll on nights when the moon is full.

Kitty glanced out the passenger window and saw a half-moon. "Too bad there's not a full moon. Otherwise, we could go over to that park and have a stroll with Pan."

Robie laughed at Kitty's sense of humor. *Or was she serious?* he wondered. "I never even understood the significance of the statue," Robie admitted.

"Pan was one of the Greek gods. He was the god of shepherds and flocks," she explained. "There's more to the story, but that's all I can remember. We had a unit on Greek Mythology in high school. Interesting stuff."

Kitty felt so at ease with Robie. He was a good listener, he had a good sense of humor, and he was a gentleman.

Robie, on the other hand, wondered again if Kitty was out of his league. Granted, she only worked as a waitress and lived in an apartment above a bar, but the signals he picked up on led him to believe she was much more refined than he was. After their meal, they decided to have a nightcap at Sally's.

Sally's was quiet, which is what they both hoped for.

Sally waited on them herself. "Why, good evening, you two." Sally greeted them as she would any other customers, playing it cool as she suppressed any hints that she might have had a hand in bringing them together.

"We went out for Mexican food," Kitty said.

"I see. What can I get you?" Sally asked.

"The usual," they said in tandem.

Sally hummed her way down the bar with a crafty grin on her face. After she served them a beer and white wine, she left them alone and joined two customers who were shaking dice at the opposite end of the bar.

"Aren't they so cute together?" Sally cooed.

"Who?" They both asked at once.

"Robie and Kitty. They're the only other ones here," Sally snarked.

Shrugging off Sally's sarcasm, the woman responded first. "Don't get any ideas, Sally. The last time you played matchmaker, you hooked Annibel Lee up with an actuary from an insurance company. But, yes, they do make a nice couple. I don't know Kitty very well, but Robie is a nice catch. In fact, if I weren't married...."

Her husband cut her off. "Ha, ha, my dear and loving wife of many years, you're old enough to be his mother," he scoffed as he rolled the dice. "Box cars!" he yelled.

Kitty and Robie began to spend more time together. He would take her out to eat once in a while, or to a movie, and they both enjoyed their mutual affection. Kitty sensed Robie's hesitation to move things to the next level of intimacy but didn't want to sabotage their relationship by being impatient.

At first, Kitty left Sally's when her shift was over. But as she got to know the customers better, she would sit at the bar and have a glass of wine before heading upstairs. Gradually, she mixed comfortably with people who were no longer only customers.

When she started hanging around people Robie labeled as shady, he warned her to be careful. "Kitty, some of these people are unscrupulous. They are petty thieves and swindlers. Some have police records, and they are being watched," he explained. "I worry that you will either become a victim of their wiles or get sucked into their way of life."

*Did I hear him right?* Kitty thought. *Did he just use the words unscrupulous and wiles?*

Kitty was moved by Robie's concern, but didn't know how to respond. She knew she had lived a sheltered life, one surrounded by a supportive family, ample financial resources, and little contact outside her social class. His caution felt protective, something she only ever felt from her father.

# CHAPTER 7

# FOR OLD TIME'S SAKE

It was a year ago that Lana and Connor had said their goodbyes. With her job at Sally's and having Kitty in town, Connor was far from Lana's mind. His call caught her off guard.

"Hi, Lana. It's Connor. Got a minute?"

The truncated way Connor jumped into the conversation gave Lana pause. *What could he possibly want? And after more than a year?*

"Lana, you there?"

"Yes, sorry, I got distracted by a stray dog trying to cross the street in traffic. I'd like to pull over and help the poor thing, but there are cars on both sides of me. Oh, wait a minute. It looks like someone is putting a leash on the dog. Obviously, I'm in my car. What's up?"

"I need to see you. There's something urgent I can't take care of myself, and I'm hoping you can help."

Lana threw back her head with a muted sigh of annoyance. "So, what is it?"

"It's too much to talk about over the phone," Connor explained. "Can we meet somewhere to talk about it? It could mean a nice chunk of money for you. And it's strictly legal."

"I don't know, Connor. What kind of time are we talking about?" The driver behind Lana tapped his horn, signaling that the red light they were stopped at had turned green.

"Lana, need I remind you of the big favor I did when you were at Macalester?"

She agreed to meet him at the Embassy Suites in Peoria, Illinois, two days later. "But this is strictly business, Connor, nothing else," Lana emphasized before ending the call.

They met in a quiet area of the lobby and dining area. Connor explained the situation, and Lana, with her chin cradled between her thumb and forefinger, listened without interruption.

Lana remained silent, her expressionless face revealing nothing as she watched the staff prepare for the evening social over Connor's shoulders. Connor turned to see what she was watching. When he turned back, he knocked his paper coffee cup off the table. They both glanced at the coffee on the floor.

"Apparently, it wasn't full," Lana observed.

"I'll tell them about it when we've finished our business," Connor said as he leaned in. "Lana, I need your help. Please."

She stared down at the table, avoiding his eyes—those magnetic eyes that had always drawn her in, that could still pull her into things she wasn't sure she believed in. But something in his voice stopped her. He had said *please*—softly, earnestly, with a humility that didn't sound like the Connor she remembered. Then his hand reached across the table, warm and steady, resting gently on hers.

"For old time's sake?" he inveigled. "It's my money to begin with. I'll even guarantee you a minimum of $20,000, even if the safe is empty."

Lana wanted to move on from her current job, and soon. Sally had become increasingly interested in the books. And when Lana went into Sally's office to drop off a report, she noticed the business card for an auditor on her desk. *This could be the catalyst I need,* she thought.

"I wouldn't be surprised if my mother kept an accounting of the money in her diary. Or included a clue to where she kept her book-keeping records." Connor shook his head. "I tell you, she was a stickler for keeping records. Anything that dealt with money or finances, she took extraordinary precautions."

Lana leaned forward and nodded.

"OK, Connor, I'll do it. But I won't go alone."

Connor slowly pulled his hand back as he considered her stipulation. "I guess I can understand that. Who do you have in mind?" he asked.

"My cousin Katherine, who now goes by Kitty, is doing a gap year. She's in Louisville now but is looking for some adventure. This might appeal to her."

"That's fine. I really don't care how you do this, as long as you keep it as low-key as possible." Connor said. "But don't be surprised if my aunt Edna shows up. She and my mother never got along. Actually, neither of them got along with anybody. Our family reunions were carefully organized to keep them apart as much as possible."

Lana's phone chimed, so she excused herself and found a quiet corner in the lobby.

While she was gone, Connor thought about his aunt Edna. Yes, she was a force to be reckoned with. He recalled one incident at a reunion on the farm, around the time he was seven. The family had grown into a multitude of aunts, uncles, cousins, and in-laws, making it easier to keep Roberta and Edna apart.

Edna said, "Hi, Connor. Come over here and sit next to your aunt Edna," patting the seat of the empty lawn chair next to hers.

"How old are you now, Connor?" Edna asked.

"Seven." He proudly responded.

"That's a fun age to be. I bet you get to do a lot of exploring around the farm, don't you?"

And that was the hook that brought Connor into Edna's web.

"You wanna see somethin', Aunt Edna?" Connor's eyes opened wide as he jumped out of his seat.

"Why, I most certainly do. Lead the way, and I'll follow. But no running."

Connor showed his Aunt Edna his secret hiding spot inside a group of lilac trees, his initials that he had carved into the outhouse, and the small garden nearby.

"What an interesting garden," Edna muttered with a stony look on her face. "I don't even know if I even recognize some of those plants."

"It's my mother's special garden. That right there," he pointed with his foot," is something called Belladonna. I'm not supposed to touch it, though. C'mon, Aunt Edna, I got something to show you in the house, too. "

"Isn't your mom in the house?" Edna asked.

"Not now." Connor pointed to the windmill. "She's over there with my dad."

Edna followed Connor into the house and down the stairs.

"See that?" Connor pointed to an old trunk. "That's where my mom keeps her secret diary. But it's locked."

"Who's down there?" Roberta's voice thundered down the stairs.

"It's me, Mom, and Aunt Edna."


Lana returned to the table, interrupting Connor's thoughts.

"That was one long call," Connor commented.

"The issue is that you get the money out of the house before we sell it, which, hopefully, is soon," Connor explained. "Once you have the money, leave the house and stay at a nearby hotel. Just leave a note on the table at the farmhouse so I know where to find you."

"How long do you think this will take? Lana asked.

"I'm not sure. Most likely, a few days," Connor guessed.

"I suppose I should stay at the farmhouse," Lana suggested.

"Yes, good idea. Tell people you're thinking about moving to Gailsprings. Also, just to err on the side of caution, if we need to communicate, let's keep it to a minimum and use vague language. And if you bring your cousin in on this, I suggest you two do the same."

Lana's phone rang again, and she left the table to take the call. When she returned, Connor was gone. On the table was a hand-drawn map of the Gailsprings area with a notation on the side: Sometimes GPS doesn't work in remote areas.

# CHAPTER 8

# BRINGING KITTY ON BOARD

## A Troubled Kitty

It was a breezy and mild Sunday autumn morning as Kitty and Lana strolled along the Ohio River in Riverfront Park. The shimmering waters of the Ohio meandered between Kentucky and Indiana on its journey to the Mississippi River, defining a border it had carved out many years ago.

At that time of day, walkers, joggers, and bicyclists mostly shared the park. But soon, as it was Sunday, that would all change. It might have been a muskrat plunging into the protective waters, or possibly fish jumping high, but the splash was close enough to startle the two cousins. As they continued, Kitty and Lana separated to let an oncoming dog walker with three dogs pass through.

Kitty looked at the river and longed to send her worries downstream and watch them as they slowly drifted away and were swallowed up by the mighty river. "Lana, let's sit down for a minute. I need…I need to talk to you about something."

Lana could see in Kitty's troubled face that something was eating at her. They found a picnic table and sat across from each other.

"Lana, I'm in a real jam. I'm almost out of money, and now Sally tells me she may have to cut my hours." Kitty envied a small group of noisy birds as they playfully darted from one place to another. She turned her attention back to Lana. "She claims she's losing money on the noon lunches. I asked about the bar area, but she said she may be making cuts there, too."

Lana knew all too well that Sally was making even more money than when Lana first started working as her accountant, but said nothing. *Something else must be at play.* Lana told herself.

"After my freshman year at Auburn, I realized I wasn't ready for college. And now, I'm only a few months into my gap year, and everything's falling apart. All I have in my life is you and Robie. Oh, and Vera too." Kitty wiped the tears off her cheeks with her fingers. "But, now, if what I heard is true, you gave Sally notice and will be leaving."

"It's true. I was going to tell you this morning."

Lana was confident that whoever replaced her could never find any evidence of her wrongdoing. But she wanted to get out before it was too late. Besides buying the Volvo, Lana had stashed over $300,000 in an offshore bank account and kept nearly $100,000 in cash, most of which she left in the safe at her apartment in Louisville, where she intended to return once her mission was over. She arrived in Gailsprings with $10,000 in cash.

Lana remained silent as Kitty studied the ants as they darted around the concrete below the table.

"Kitty, this is going to sound strange, but I think I might have a solution."

Kitty quickly turned to Lana with a hint of recovered hope on her face.

"You and I were always close growing up. We were more like sisters than cousins," Lana continued.

"Yes, that's true. And it's great to have you back in my life again. You've done so much for me here." Kitty reached across the table to place her hand on top of Lana's.

"But, before I say any more, I need to check on something. I should know by the end of the day." Lana had to think things through before she could make a decision. "Let's meet at Sally's tonight around six. It's build-your-own-sandwich night."

"Sounds good. I could use a free meal," Kitty cheerfully agreed.

They both stood, and Lana leaned over to hug her.

## Lana to the Rescue

Sunday evening at Sally's was a special night that drew in many customers. The spread Sally put out varied from week to week. The hot beef sandwiches were a big hit and usually came with potato salad. Sally dedicated one Sunday a month to pizzas. The biggest crowd pleaser, though, was Sally's pulled pork sandwiches with hushpuppies and coleslaw. More than once, customers suggested she should bottle her secret sauce and put it on the market.

"I got enough irons in the fire," was her standard reply.

Lana and Kitty sat with their sandwiches in front of them. When Kitty took a bite of her pickle, some of the brine dripped onto her shirt. She brushed it dry.

"So, Lana, what's the plan? Your idea?" Kitty picked up a potato chip but waited for Lana to reply before putting it in her mouth.

"Now, this is going to sound crazy, but just hear me out," Lana said, sliding her chair closer to the table and leaning in. Kitty put the chip in her mouth.

"You remember me talking about Connor, right?"

"Yes, it's too bad you two never made it past casual sex, even though you were apparently satisfied with just that. Who knows? Maybe you two will reconnect," Kitty speculated.

"He recently contacted me. He needs help getting some money from a safe in the basement of his family home. They think they have sold the house and farm and are likely to close at the end of September." Lana watched as Kitty wiped the mayonnaise off her cheek and then washed down her first bite with a Diet Coke.

"And?" Kitty asked with a shrug.

Lana slid her chair closer to the table and lowered her voice. "Apparently, his mother kept a diary over the years. Connor believes that either the combination to the safe is in the diary or it contains clues on how to find the combination," Lana explained.

"Why can't Connor just go through the diary himself?"

They both saw Sally approach their table. "Kitty, I could use you. Can you finish your sandwich and help out? I know it's your night off, but—"

Kitty interrupted her, "Sure no problem. I'll be finished soon."

When it was safe to talk again, Lana continued, "That's what he had planned to do. But at the last minute, his company sent him to Brussels."

"Isn't there someone else who can do it? Kitty said, brushing some crumbs onto the floor."

"No. That's the thing. He believes his mother wanted him, and only him, to have the money. He wants me to go to his hometown, stay at the house, and go through the diary."

"Okay. But where does that leave me?" Kitty asked, her hopeful mood shriveling into uncertainty.

"He is paying me to do this. But I don't want to go alone. Why don't you come with me? I'll pay you good money to help me." Kitty perked up when she heard "'good money."

Kitty tilted her head and looked at Lana out of the corner of her eyes. "How long would we be gone?"

"Only a few days," Lana responded with a dismissive wave. "Once we have the money, I'll keep it until Connor returns. Then, I plan to head west. Which is why you need to drive to Gailsprings, too."

"But, I don't have a car," Kitty exclaimed.

"I'll rent one for you. No cost to you. I will guarantee you at least $10,000, maybe more."

"And where is this Gailsprings?" Kitty shot a curious glance at Lana while holding the second half of her sandwich in mid-air.

"In Wisconsin," Lana replied.

"In Wisconsin?" Kitty raised her voice in alarm. "Isn't it cold there?"

"Not this time of the year. No," Lana explained. "It will be a beautiful time to see the fall colors. And besides, this is your gap year; your opportunity to go to new places, take on a challenge, make a little cash." Lana shrugged as she delivered an abridged version of what she wanted Kitty to do.

"But what about Robie? What should I tell him?" Kitty asked in a melancholic voice.

"The same thing you tell everyone: a family emergency. And besides, your absence just might jar Robie into asking you to marry him. I know he wants to, and this might be the impetus he needs."

*The impish smile on Kitty's face was answer enough,* Lana thought; *she's in!*

Lana laid out the logistics of her plan as Kitty finished her meal and moved to her lemon cookie.

# CHAPTER 9

# THE MISSION BEGINS

**September, 2021**

When she pulled into the driveway and caught her first glimpse of the old farmhouse, Lana hoped she had the wrong address. She put her car in reverse to have a second look at the mailbox on the desolate county road. *Yes, this was the place,* she lamented.

Pulling back onto the gravel driveway, she slowly edged her way toward the battered farmhouse. She heard a sharp screeching noise and rolled down the window. As she craned her head out the window, she looked up and saw the blades on an old, rusty windmill spinning, but no longer pumping water for the livestock. A shrieking howl pierced the otherwise tranquil setting and sent chills down Lana's spine.

Lana blew her horn in case there were squatters inside or an unfriendly animal nearby. She pressed the horn again, this time holding it longer.

Convinced that it was safe to get out of her car, she slowly opened the door and stepped out. She brushed some donut crumbs off her white gauze button-up shirt and put her keys in the pocket of her rolled-up blue boyfriend jeans. Her mauve breathable slip-ons crunched on the coarse gravel of the driveway like eggshells scattered on stone. The wind mussed her fine blond hair. Reaching into the car, she retrieved a butterfly-shaped Jennifer Behr Caria gold barrette to hold it in place.

She climbed the slanted driveway as if drawn by gravity and ghosts, her steps slowing as she took in the tired house.

Years of neglect had turned what Lana imagined was once a stately home into something that now looked abandoned and forgotten. What little paint still clung to the house was chipped or discolored. Some shutters were missing, crooked, or barely hanging on. The sagging roof reminded Lana of an old horse she had once seen while driving by a farm in rural Tennessee. Several shingles were missing, and others had curled. She hoped the roof didn't leak.

She rounded the corner of the distressed house and approached the back door. The door was locked, which brought a shred of relief to Lana's uneasiness. The key was under the rubber mat in front of the door. Once she unlocked the door, she opened it inch by inch.

"Anybody here?" she called out. "Hellooo!"

As she stepped into the kitchen, she winced as she heard the floorboards creak below her feet. But it was the fetid odor that stopped her in her tracks. The house had been closed against the summer sun for nearly two months, leaving the microorganisms to culture as they would in a petri dish.

Lana stuck her head out the back door and sucked in all the air she could hold. Darting to a kitchen window, opened it as far as it would go, sticking her nose close to the window screen. She drew another deep breath.

The second window she tried to open wouldn't budge. Frustrated, she ran back outside, leaving the back door open behind her, gasping for air as she bounced down the four steps. Her steps slowed as she approached the car to grab her suitcase, but she stopped short, squinting at the pitiful house. The thought of staying even one night, let alone three or four, made her hesitate. She left the suitcase in the trunk, unsure if she would need it at all. Gravel crunched beneath her feet as she shuffled across the driveway and into the dewy, unmowed grass. At the edge of the yard, beside a weathered picnic table, she paused. Slowly, she turned in place, surveying the property with wary eyes.

The moribund remnants of a once living farm brought a sad look to Lana's face as she compared it to an abandoned graveyard. The worn fence posts that once bore the tension of barbed wire stuck out of the ground in all directions, like bony arms reaching from their graves toward heaven. The outhouse from long ago protruded above the tall grasses, an anonymous headstone marking the death of a farm. Not far from the outhouse were the remains of a burned-down barn, a soulless pyre of fiery rage. A dog barking in the distance mimicked a lonely trumpet wailing a prolonged version of Taps.

Pushing the sepulchral imagery aside, Lana found respite in the remoteness of the setting. She watched the surrounding fields of corn as the wind nuzzled their leaves, the bright mid-summer green now splattered with the light brown of autumn. An aged oak tree guided Lana's eyes to fluffy cumulus clouds that lazily drifted across the cerulean sky. The distant sound of a tractor brought back memories of how her mother used to hum her to sleep as a child.

Lana sat backwards on the bench of the discolored picnic table. She leaned her back against the table, sliding her elbows behind her to rest on the top of the table. Her thoughts turned to Connor Larson, the youngest son of the family, who once lived on the farm. From what he had told her, she could almost hear the wind whispering voices from the past: a mother reading to her son, a father talking to his cows, brothers crossing the line from teasing to belittling.

Feeling Connor's presence, her mind drifted away with the clouds as she recalled that weekend in May, over a year ago, when their relationship came to an end.

## No One Lives Here Anyway

So, there she was, sitting backward on a picnic bench in rural Wisconsin, preparing to take a considerable amount of cash out of a safe in the basement of the vacant Larson family home.

Lana stood and stretched as she watched a school bus stop at the driveway across the road. She saw the bus driver look at her as he opened the door to let a young girl off the bus. After he saw that the girl had safely crossed the road in front of the bus, he drove off. Lana turned her attention to the house, slumping her shoulders in exasperation. Her lower lip vibrated as she released an exasperated puff of air from her lungs.

Lana returned to the kitchen. It had aired out some, but her nose still wrinkled at the stale odor that lingered.

She looked around the eerily quiet room. One of the chairs lay on its side. She set it upright and slid it under the table. A vintage meat grinder precariously clung to the top of the counter. Lana grabbed what was left of the wooden handle and tried to whirl it back to life. The ratchety grinder sputtered, the gears stubbornly defying any attempt to make a complete rotation with the handle. Some cupboards were missing doors, and others hung open. Lana could see several cans and boxes of commercial food products. *She wouldn't go hungry, at least,* she reassured herself.

She moved to the dining room and turned on the light switch, but the room remained dark. She raised the stained vinyl shade covering the window, releasing a cloud of dust that fluttered in the beam of sunlight as it spilled in through the cracked window. Lana opened the window and shooed away the dust particles with a magazine on the table.

The dining room table was covered with piles of old catalogs, magazines, books, and a red teapot. The one chair at the table had a pale yellow sweater hanging over the back. The china hutch teemed with collectibles of all sorts. Lana, whose parents collected antiques and had some knowledge of their value herself, noticed several pieces of Hull pottery, what appeared to be a complete set of blue Nordic china, and an engraved wooden box that she suspected held a set of sterling silverware. She tried to open one of the doors on the heavy mahogany piece, but it was locked. So were the other two.

Next, she went into the living room. A multicolored Afghan throw hung over the back of a lumpy, overstuffed couch. The recliner was covered in stains and left in an open position. The wooden rocking chair sprang to life as Lana pushed the back of it with one finger. After unlocking the heavy oak front door, she tugged on the ornate knob, the stubborn door resisting her until it gave in with a whoosh.

The bathroom door was partially open, and Lana needed to pee. Opening the door slowly, she peeked around the edge of it as her eyes darted around the room. She flushed the stagnant water and lined the seat with toilet paper before sitting down.

There was a bar of soap on the sink, which she was thankful for. The small medicine cabinet above the sink had a mirror on the door. After checking her hair, Lana stared at the mirror, tempted to open the door and see what was inside the cabinet. *Why not? No one lives here anyway.*

And that's when she heard a car door slam.

## Wally Simonson, G.P.D.

Lana stood sideways behind the open front door, peeking through the cloudy beveled glass window. Her agitation rose when she saw a police officer approach the front porch. He rapped on the rickety metal door with his knuckles. *Clang. Clang. Clang.* She could see his squad car parked next to her car.

Lana opened the front door wider, sidled around it, and crossed the porch to the screen door. "Yes. Can I help you?" Lana asked as she quietly locked the screen door.

"Good afternoon, ma'am. I'm Lieutenant Wally Simonson. I'm with the Galesprings' law enforcement department. I just received a call about a car parked on this vacant property." He showed Lana his ID.

"I see. I'm Lana Paulson, and I'm a friend of Connor Larson. He's letting me stay here until I can find something more permanent, not to mention suitable."

"How do you know Connor?" he asked.

"We met in the Twin Cities. We share the same profession." Lana replied.

"And what profession might that be?"

Lana knew the officer was screening her. "We both have degrees in business administration. He works at 3M. He's told me a lot about this place. That story about his father burning down the barn is bizarre, but apparently true." Lana was sure she had just passed the test.

Could I see some identification?" Officer Simonson asked.

"Yes, of course. Hold on, I'll get it." Lana retrieved her ID from her purse and returned to the porch. She unlocked the poorly hung screen door and opened it slowly, provoking the hinges to snap in annoyance. She handed the officer her ID.

After returning her driver's license, the officer fixed a steady gaze on the interior of the house and said nothing. Lana turned around to see what he was looking at.

"Is, um, everything alright?" Lana asked, drawing him out of his trance.

"Oh, no, nothing's wrong. It's just that this house—this house holds a lot of memories, and it's almost like I can feel some of them now," he mused.

"Then you knew the Larsons?" Lana raised her eyebrows in affirmation.

"Everyone knew the Larsons," he paused. "Or at least knew of them. Good day," he abruptly ended the conversation and turned away. Lana's eyebrows narrowed as the officer's sudden departure sparked her curiosity, making her wonder if he was fleeing more questions.

The officer stopped and walked back to the screen door, this time noticing the several tears on the screen.

"Let me know if you need anything. Keep these doors locked at all times. You might want to close and lock all the windows, too." He glanced at the filthy window to his left, barely able to see the thread-bare curtains that hung at a slant.

"It's late September, so the nights are starting to cool down. I also suggest you leave both the front and back outside lights on, at least at night. Also, leave an inside light on all night."

If Lana wasn't already apprehensive about staying there, she was now. "Are you trying to tell me it's not safe for me to stay here?" Lana pricked up her ears, hoping he would advise her not to.

"No, nothing like that. It's just that I've caught some teenagers hanging around here at night, doing what teenagers do. They wouldn't harm you, but if they see the lights on, they'll find somewhere else to drink beer, smoke, and learn firsthand about the facts of life." He reached into his shirt pocket and pulled out a small card.

"If you like, here is my card with my contact information." Lana opened the door wide enough to take his card. As he turned to leave, Lana called out. "Excuse me, Officer Simons."

He turned to face her. "Actually, it's Simonson."

"Sorry, Officer Simonson. But does news always travel this fast around here? I mean, I've only been here for half an hour." Lana held her mouth open as she waited for his reply.

"Yes, ma'am, it does," he said. "It sure does. You know, now that I think of it, Gracie Sanderson has a house for rent in town. It's a lot nicer than this place, and safer too." He offered to text Lana the contact information later if she was interested.

"That would be great," Lana said as she waved away the cobwebs on the front door. She gave him her phone number, and he left.

Lana immediately went up to the second floor of the house to check the windows. She paid little attention to the furnishings as she bounced from room to room with unflinching determination, stopping only to wipe the perspiration on her forehead with the back of her hand. With the windows secured, she returned to the lower level, grateful to be in the airy rooms she once avoided.

Lana headed to the bedroom on the main level, resigned to spending the night there. The bed was fully made, but she had no intention of climbing under the covers. *There's no way I'm getting in that bed,* she thought. Remembering a linen closet just outside the room, she was relieved to find clean sheets, blankets, and pillowcases inside. She stripped the bed without hesitation, tossing everything into a corner, then remade it with fresh linens and fluffed the pillows. Still feeling the tension coil tighter inside her as night settled in, she went to the kitchen in search of something warm and soothing—anything that might help her unwind.

She found an unlabeled bag of what, at first, she thought was weed. *Just what she needed,* she thought. She opened the bag and took a gentle whiff of the contents. It was chamomile tea, homegrown chamomile tea. She remembered Connor mentioning that his mother grew, as he put it, "weird stuff."

Remembering the red teapot in the dining room, Lana filled it with water and stuffed a handful of the mixture of buds and leaves into the teapot.

With her hands wrapped around a warm mug of tea, Lana went into the living room. She ran her finger along the frame of the beveled glass window while admiring the craftsmanship of the solid oak door. She swung the door back and forth in a vain attempt to limber the bone-weary hinges on the door. Once the door was locked, she pulled on it just to be sure it was secure. Taking Wally's advice, she turned on the outside light.

While trying to get comfortable on the lumpy overstuffed couch, Lana spotted the old wooden rocking chair. She placed her tea on the table next to the chair and slowly rocked as she stared at a crack in the wall in front of her. The rhythm of the rocking chair and her fixed gaze on the crack lulled Lana back in time, to the day after their last night in Chicago.

## So Now What?

It was a beautiful spring Sunday morning, and the sky above the city was a deep sapphire blue. Breakfast had been awkward as they both avoided any mention of the night before. The silence continued as they left the city, each in a world of their own. Lana broke the silence once they crossed into Wisconsin.

No longer dealing with traffic, Connor casually drove with his left wrist hanging over the top of the steering wheel, freeing his right hand to sip from his University of Minnesota coffee mug.

"Connor, there's something I have to tell you." They glanced at each other. "And I guess the best way to do it is to be frank. Connor, I'm pregnant." Connor returned his coffee to the beverage compartment in the console and placed both hands on the steering wheel.

"Are you sure?" he asked.

"Yes. My doctor confirmed it." Lana replied.

"How long have you known?"

"For a couple of weeks. I was going to tell you last night, but the way things—" Lana let Connor finish the sentence, if only in his mind.

They drove in silence for half an hour.

"So, now what?" Connor asked. "Are you sure it's mine?"

"Well, it certainly is not an immaculate conception."

"But I always used a condom."

"Sometimes that's not enough."

"So, again, what now?" Connor briefly raised both hands from the steering wheel in surrender. "I think there's only one choice. And I think it's best for both of us. An abortion."

Over the next few miles, Lana let that sink in, into both of them.

"But that costs money, money I don't have." The roar of a passing semi was a momentary distraction from the tenor of the conversation. Lana counted the mile markers as they sluggishly went by.

"Then I guess it's up to me," Connor conceded.

## A Minor Delay Subhead

Lana didn't notice that she had stopped rocking until her memories faded away. She could see how the shadows from a disappearing sun had moved across the living room floor, revealing undisturbed dust mites in his path. The dull orange glow in the house reminded her of the old sepia-tinted photographs that her father brought out on occasion.

She took a sip of her once-steaming cup of tea, the lukewarm tea doing little to shake off the chill that shivered down her spine. Although she had never been prone to the suggestibility of ghosts, goblins, and monsters, there was no way she would go down into that basement alone after dark. She finished her tea, read for a while, and checked her phone one last time.

She was concerned to see that Kitty had called and left a message— they had agreed to limit contact. She played the message:

"Hi, Lana. It's Kitty. Minor setback. Arriving a day late. Will explain later." Lana was relieved that Kitty had left such an innocuous message, one of little value to anyone but her.

The first night at the house was fitful. Lana's eyes darted from corner to corner in the dark room, prodded by the creaking and cracking sounds of the house settling in for the night. Even though Lana told herself they were nothing but branches, the scraping sounds on the outside wall elicited images of fleshless fingers slashing their way through the fragile plaster. She pulled the bed coverings tighter around her neck and shoulders until she finally drifted off, safe in her cocoon.

# CHAPTER 10

# SETTLING IN

## Coffee and a Smoke

Lana was never happier to see the sun rise on a Monday morning, even though she was dead tired and could easily have slept two more hours in her own bedroom.

Coffee. She needed coffee. The coffee cup she had brought with her the day before was empty, and the sight of it made her even more desperate. She saw an old percolator on the counter and searched the cupboards for a container of coffee. All she found was some tea; that would have to do. As the tea was steeping, she lit a cigarette and savored the first inhale.

As it was a pleasant morning, Lana decided to take her tea and cigarette outside. The wind from yesterday had died down, and the blades on the windmill stood silent. In a flash, a sense of déjà vu washed over Lana. She wasn't sure what it was, but something had triggered the feeling.

She had spent many summers on her grandparents' farm in Kentucky growing up, but their farm looked nothing like this one—it was a happy place, a tidy place, well-maintained, not like this one at all.

Once her head cleared, she made a decision—she would not spend another night in that house. If the house for rent that Officer Simonson mentioned didn't pan out, she would find a hotel.

She snuffed out her cigarette with her toe on the dewy grass. It was time to go down to the basement. As she opened the basement door, the fusty cold air rose to greet her, like captive spirits ascending from an ancient crypt. She stepped back with a grimace of disgust on her face, fanning the air in front of her nose with her hands. She returned to the kitchen to get her iPhone in case she needed to use the flashlight app or call if she somehow got stuck in the basement. *But who would I call?* she thought. Imagining the door closing while she was in the basement, something she'd seen in many movies, Lana put a chair in front of the open door.

With her flashlight app, Lana directed the beam at the stairs. The woefully steep and narrow steps had the sinister look of a stairway to hell. Lana was thankful to see that there was a handrail, even though it was wobbly. She took each step slowly and deliberately, pressing her toes on each one to check its sturdiness. Once she made it to the last step, she turned and looked up at the open door. She wanted to run back up the stairs and slam the door shut, but she was there for a reason, a very good reason, and she wasn't about to back out now.

She easily found the trunk right where Connor said it would be. She then went to the basement window to find the key to the trunk. Upon seeing the window covered with cobwebs, she imagined that the concrete ledge below would be covered with filth, and possibly even animal droppings. There was no way she would reach up and run her hand along the concrete ledge.

She looked around the basement, hoping to find a solution. She spotted an old broom and used it to brush away the cobwebs and clear off the ledge. The sound of a key hitting the floor never came.

Lana threw the broom at the trunk, throwing her hands up in exasperation as she swore at it. She trudged up the stairs in defeat, letting out a thankful sigh when she reached the kitchen, now an oasis of freshness compared to the dank basement.

In desperate need of some coffee, Lana hastily grabbed her purse, keys, and phone and left the house. There was little traffic on the road as she drove into Gailsprings. Not expecting to find a local bakery, Lana's face lit up when she saw the sign: Mae's Bakery and Coffee. There were three other customers in the bakery, so Lana got in line, eyeing up the array of freshly baked pastries and breads. When the first person in line turned to leave, the clerk said, "Thanks, Gracie. See you next time."

*Gracie–that was the name the police officer had mentioned*, Lana thought. Considering that Galesprings was a small town, and Gracie was not a common name, Lana took a chance.

"Excuse me," Lana caught the woman's attention as she walked by. "I'm sorry to interrupt, but you don't happen to be the Gracie who had a house for rent?"

Gracie leaned back slightly and arched her eyebrows in both surprise and concern. "Why yes, I am," Gracie replied as she sized up the stranger.

"I'm sorry. I didn't mean to startle you." Lana's voice softened into a tender apology. I'm Lana Paulson, and I'm a friend of Connor Larson's. He is letting me stay at their farmhouse for a few days." Lana wasn't about to tell Gracie that she would likely only be there for a few days, fearing that she wouldn't rent to her. Lana would take the hit for a couple of months' rent, not to have to spend another night on the gloomy Larson farm.

"The thing is that the house is in such a state of disrepair that I really need to find something else. And fast," Lana emphasized.

"Yes, I can imagine," Gracie gasped. "I've never been inside that gloomy place, thank God." Gracie turned her gaze to the ceiling as she offered her gratitude.

Lana continued. "Yesterday, a police officer stopped by to check out the place after receiving a call from someone."

"Oh, I bet that was our Wally," Gracie remarked. "He's such a nice man. Even when you break the law, not that I ever have, mind you," Gracie assured Lana.

"Anyway, he suggested I contact you about the house you have for rent. The Larson place is deplorable. I just cannot stay there alone." Lana's jaws tightened as she shook her head with resolute determination.

"If you're interested, you could come over this afternoon," Gracie suggested.

"Yes, I'd like to. The officer said he'd text me your phone number, but never did."

"Yes, that sounds like Wally. He gets pulled in many directions. People call him for the dumbest things. One time, someone called him because the door to their mailbox was open. Can you imagine that?" Gracie tsked. "But seeing a strange car out at the Larson place, I mean, that would get anybody's attention. The things that went on out there...." Gracie shook her head and left it at that.

"Hold on a sec." Gracie took a pen out of her purse to write down her address. Realizing she had no paper, she tore off a portion of the paper bag that held her donuts. She placed the bag between her knees to free her hands, careful not to smash the donuts. After writing something on the scrap of paper, she handed it to Lana. "That's my address and phone number. Please call before you come." Gracie retrieved the bag of donuts that dangled from her locked knees.

"Yes, of course. Thank you," Lana said, putting the information in her purse.

"I'm not going home right now, but in the meantime, if you want to drive by at least, please do. At any rate, let me know if you want to see it." Gracie's charming smile faded as the bell on the door of the bakery jingled. Lana watched as Gracie and the man who had just entered overtly snubbed each other, wondering what that was all about. *Small towns,* she told herself, she'd seen that on TV shows.

"Ma'am, I believe you're next." The woman in line behind Lana said as she tapped Lana on the shoulder.

Lana flinched at the gesture, pulling her shoulder forward. "Oh, sorry," Lana replied as she approached the counter.

Noticing that there were places to sit in the bakery, Lana ordered a large black coffee and a sumptuous chocolate eclair, a three-napkin treat.

Lana thought it would be nice to have the comforts of a home again, if even for only a few days. Connor had suggested that Lana try to make it look like she was planning to settle in Gailsprings.

"Make it look like you're planning to stay, even though it should only take you a few days to decipher the clues in the diary and get the money," he had suggested. "It's a small town, and people get suspicious."

However, Lana had no intention of spending more time on the project than necessary. She did, however, understand that living in a house in town would make her more visible and make her presence less suspicious.

## Midwest Nice

After she left the bakery, Lana drove by the house that Gracie was renting. Finding it suitable, at least from the outside, she called Gracie and set up an appointment for 1 PM that afternoon.

When Lana arrived at 12:55 to view the house, she found that Gracie wasn't home. She parked on the street and got out of her car, leaning against it as she enjoyed the fall colors. A few minutes later, a man walking his dog stopped on the other side of the street.

"She's not home," he said. "I saw her leave about twenty minutes ago." Sensing another prolonged conversation, the man's dog plopped down on the warm pavement.

"You're not her daughter, I can see that. Her granddaughter, maybe?"

"No, I'm not family. I'm here to look at the house she has for rent." Lana shaded her eyes with her hand to get a better look at the man.

"Of course, Sonia's place." He pointed to the house across the street from Gracie's house. She doesn't live here anymore. No, that's for sure. Her husband died some time ago, and she's lived here alone until Gracie somehow figured out a way to get her to move into assisted living."

Lana graciously smiled even though she felt uncomfortable with the gossip.

"Some of us who know Sonia don't think she was that far gone to need assisted living. Gracie tells a different story. We've heard Gracie plans to put the place up for sale. Nice place, too."

The weary look on Lana's face and her lack of response put an end to the idle gossip. "You thinking of buying it?" the man asked.

"Not at first, at least, but who knows? I'm just renting it. It's furnished, and that's what I'm looking for."

"New in town, I'm guessing?" he probed.

Lana took a moment before answering the question. *Was this small-town America? Is this what Midwest Nice was all about?* she thought.

"Yes, I am," Lana acknowledged.

"How nice for both of you. You get to rent a furnished place, and Gracie gets to pocket the money. And when Sonia does pass on, Gracie gets the house, too. Those two sisters never got along. How they ended up living across the street from each other—"

"I'm sorry to interrupt," Lana said when she saw a car approaching. "But that must be Mrs. Sanderson coming now."

"It is," he affirmed as he gently tugged at the leash of his dog, who apparently was used to lengthy interruptions on their morning walk.

Gracie was wearing a floral cotton dress with a white lace collar. Her solid pink snap-on earrings, her pink sweater, and her matronly demeanor led Lana to reconsider the impression left upon her by the neighbor.

Gracie went into her house and emerged with a key in her hand, and they crossed the street together.

"What, if I may ask, brought you to Galesprings?" Gracie asked Lana.

"I needed to get away from a bad relationship. A friend from my college days suggested this might be a good place to get a fresh start."

"Oh, yes, you did mention Connor Larson. And to think you even spent one night in that house. How spooky!" Gracie declared. "How is it you know Connor?"

"We met on the campus of Macalester College, where I earned an MBA, a master's degree in business administration. I am also a CPA, a

Certified Public Accountant." Lana hoped she hadn't insulted Gracie by explaining what those letters meant. Still, she wanted Gracie to be aware of her credentials, easing any possible misgivings about renting to a stranger.

They continued the tour inside the house. At one point, Gracie stopped to ask another question. "I know I really am not supposed to ask this, but do you happen to be a woman of faith?" Gracie enquired.

"Why, yes, I am," Lana hoped Gracie wouldn't ask for clarification.

"If, by chance, you are a Lutheran, I'm a member of a very welcoming church. You wouldn't be Lutheran, would you?"

Lana was unchurched and had no idea what the difference was between a Lutheran and a Catholic, or any other denomination for that matter.

"Good gosh, I don't know how you could have guessed." Lana tittered in an attempt to add some levity to Gracie's discovery. But Lana had never been a giggle-girl, and her efforts came out awkwardly staged.

"We have a church dinner coming up soon. Maybe you'd like to help out. I can introduce you to some of the church ladies. It would be a good way to meet some of the many good Christian people in our community," Gracie suggested with a broad smile.

"Oh, I don't know," Lana said with a skeptical tone. "What kind of dinner?" Lana's mixed message didn't dissuade Gracie from persisting.

"It's a smorgasbord," responded Gracie.

Lana admitted to Gracie that she didn't know what a smorgasbord was, and Gracie cheerfully told her it was like a buffet with traditional Norwegian and Swedish dishes. When Gracie rattled off the names of some of those dishes with a semblance of Norwegian pitch and intonation, Lana was curious and agreed to help.

"So, I'm assuming it's just you then? Gracie surmised.

"Just me," Lana replied.

"Yes, it's just me now, too." Gracie breathed a wistful sigh as she glanced out the window at her house. "My husband passed on years ago."

With sympathetic eyes, Lana leaned closer to Gracie, inviting her to go on.

"He went out to the back yard to prune some roses. I called him in for lunch, but he never came. I went out and there he was. Those old snippers were still in his left hand when I found him. He was left-handed, you know."

"That must have been awful," Lana dolefully responded, hoping the story would end there.

"It was," Gracie sighed. "There he was, sprawled out on the lawn. Evie, who lives next door, heard me scream. She came over and called 911. Fortunately, I remembered to grab the snippers before they hauled him away. I used to have so many beautiful roses, but not anymore." Gracie trailed off as Lana stood by, speechless.

Again, Lana was surprised at the candor of the people she had met so far. *Is everyone like this?*

"I guess the place is yours," Gracie finally announced. "But I do need the first month's rent and a deposit of two months' rent up front." Lana was amused by Gracie's savviness, as if she had been a landlady all her life.

Lana grabbed her purse and withdrew a substantial amount of paper currency secured by a rubber band.

"Oh, my!" Gracie placed her open hand on her cheek. "That's a lot of cash to be carrying around. I was expecting a check." Gracie's eyes ballooned as they remained fixed on the cash.

"I understand. I just haven't had the time to open a checking account," Lana explained.

"I'll have to go back to my house to write out a receipt. I'll be right back." Gracie was out the door before Lana could suggest she make out a receipt right then and there. She then continued to browse around the house until Gracie returned.

She looked out the kitchen window and saw a clothesline in the backyard. She found it odd that there was still laundry hanging on the line. She shook her head, unable to imagine that someone who needed assisted living would need it so suddenly that they wouldn't have time to bring in the laundry. A black crow landed on the clothesline. Lana frowned as superstition clouded her thoughts.

Gracie returned with a receipt book and sat at the kitchen table, motioning for Lana to do the same.

"Before we close this deal, I need to tell you something," Gracie solemnly said. "You see, this house really belongs to my older sister, who is now in assisted living. She lost her husband a few years back. She thinks she'll be coming home, but the doctors say otherwise."

Gracie sat down at the table and opened a receipt book. "She wants me to rent the place out. Her husband didn't leave her much when he died. She was so lost without him; totally dependent on him. I've tried to help her financially, but I'm in no position to offer more than I do."

"How sad," Lana sighed faintly.

"But if a miracle should happen, and I've been praying, and she can return, you would have to leave."

Gracie waited for Lana to respond, afraid Lana would back out of the deal.

"I would, of course, return some of your money if that did happen." Gracie wrote the date on the receipt. "That is the Christian thing to do, don't you know."

Lana handed Gracie $800.00 in cash, and Gracie gave her the receipt. "Let me know if you need anything," Gracie said as she walked away. "Oh, and by the way, help yourself to anything in the cupboards and refrigerator."

"Why, that's very generous of you." *Or your sister,* Lana thought.

Gracie turned back to face Lana. "Oh, I almost forgot. If you would like to help us out tomorrow, come to the Gailsprings Lutheran Church around 2 PM. It's easy to find. It's right on Main Street," Gracie assured her.

Gracie left the house, pleased to have recruited additional help for the smorgasbord. The money was nice, too.

After bringing her suitcase and the clothes she had on hangers into the house, Lana decided to drive by the farmhouse before nightfall—certainly Kitty would be there by then. When she picked up her phone, she saw that Kitty had left a message: "Running late. Will explain," was all it said.

Deciding there was no need to drive out to the farmhouse, Lana drove to a supermarket and bought a turkey sandwich and some potato salad. Lana yawned through most of the meal and decided it would be an early night for her. As the sun set on Gailsprings, Lana welcomed the arrival of nightfall, unlike the night before. With her eyelids sagging, she surrendered to the hushed stillness as it lulled her into a restorative nothingness.

# CHAPTER 11

# KITCHEN DRAMA

## The Apron

As Gracie had predicted, Lana easily found her way to the church and down to the church kitchen in the basement. Gracie met her at the Dutch door that led into the kitchen, and all eyes were on her as they entered.

Gracie beamed as she said, "Girls, this is Lana. She just moved here, and I recruited her to help today."

The women in the church kitchen all stopped what they were doing to greet Lana, some with words, others with nods. Lana, who felt out of place already, mustered a feeble "Hi" as she clung close to the door.

At age 34, she was obviously much younger than the other women. Clearly, she was not dressed for the event. Her white square-neck T-shirt drooped casually over her acid-washed denim jeans. Her two-inch red slingback pumps were noticeably out of place in a working kitchen where sensible flats were the norm. Realizing what she was up against, Lana was thankful she had gone light on makeup.

Some of the women wore casual slacks with floral or solid pastel blouses, some with ruffles, others unadorned of frippery.

The older women mostly wore modest dresses, and floral patterns were obviously the theme of the day. Lana was the only one not wearing an apron.

Lana's long blond hair was pulled into a casual, messy bun, with strands dangling along the sides of her red Swarovski cat eye glasses. The other women either had gray hair or had done something to conceal it. There were several perms in the kitchen as well.

As Gracie put on the apron she kept in the kitchen closet, someone entrusted Lana with filling the salt and pepper shakers for the tables. Lana could hear the ladies dithering around the kitchen as they discussed the final arrangements and shared stories about their husbands, children, and grandchildren. The chatter was light and the mood congenial.

Even though the women did their best to make her feel welcome by glancing at her and pausing, inviting her to jump into the conversation, Lana remained quiet.

Here she was, she thought, as out of place as an atheist at a tent revival. To begin with, the only times she had ever been in a church were either for a wedding or a funeral. Having no husband, children, or grandchildren, she had nothing to add to the chatter.

Of course, she could change the subject to something more akin to her skills; she could casually mention the principles of fiduciary accounting, or the Securities Act of 1933, or maybe ask if there were many Certified Public Accountants in town. She decided on option number three. Not only would that be the perfect segue to tell the ladies that she was a CPA, but it would also strengthen the ruse that she was in town to stay. But Lana missed her chance.

"Girls!" A disembodied voice called out, drawing little attention. "Girls!" This time, the forceful voice echoed throughout the kitchen. All eyes abruptly fixed on a stout woman with a determined yet self-satisfied look on her face. With the Kenmore gas range as a backdrop, she waited for a cue.

"What now, Edna?" someone dismissively bellowed.

Edna took the cue. "Girls. I have an announcement to make." She stood tall, took in a deep breath to add thrust to her voice, and exclaimed, "I will not be making the lefse this year." Edna scanned the kitchen with challenging eyes, offering no explanation.

When it came to lefse, Edna Stern held center stage. But then again, she usually did, no matter where she stood. A portly woman with a no-nonsense demeanor, Edna carried her head high at all times. Her piercing brown eyes could make a Sumo wrestler cower and back away. Whether she was blessed or cursed with a fiery shock of wavy red hair that begged to be either cut, styled, or permed was a matter of one's perspective, but it never went unnoticed.

Of course, others knew how to make lefse, but Edna's took first place at the county fair for as long as anyone could remember.

Many wondered what her secret was for making the traditional Scandinavian flatbread, which consists of potatoes, flour, heavy cream, salt, and sugar. Her griddle was no different from any other. Nor was her lefse any thicker or thinner than usual.

When asked about the recipe, Edna claimed she kept the family recipe in her safe at home. Or, it was securely locked in a safety deposit box at an undisclosed bank. Or, the recipe was written in Norwegian, so they wouldn't be able to read it anyway. Her favorite response when someone asked for the recipe was, "Over my dead body."

Years later, when she passed away at the age of 97, her children had the recipe etched on her headstone—in compliance with her wishes. Yes, Edna Stern was known for her lefse.

The other ladies stared at Edna in silence, anticipating something more. And they got it. The coup de grâce. With all eyes still on her, Edna adeptly untied her apron from behind her back with a dexterity that rivaled Houdini breaking free from handcuffs.

Suddenly, the apron was airborne. The women watched as it floated down to the kitchen floor with a gentle thump. It was Edna's favorite apron. She made it herself, out of durable cotton with a 200 thread count. It was a practical apron, spared of frills, decorative borders, and words like "World's Best Grandma" or "My Nana Cooks."

Instead, a kitten playing with a spool of yarn adorned the apron. It was an orange Persian, lying on its side, set against what Edna described as Carolina blue. The ball of yarn was red. She embroidered it herself.

Silence fell upon the kitchen as the other ladies stared at the apron on the floor, dismissing any symbolism Edna might have intended. They pretended to believe she was serious this time. Edna had played the scene just as she had rehearsed. She knew she was no Rita Hayworth in Salome, but the prop was appropriate to the setting, and it made for good stagecraft. The apron was washable anyway. She wondered, though, true to many performances in life, did her audience see a comedy or a tragedy?

"But Edna, why didn't you tell us earlier?" several ladies asked in unison.

"This is Tuesday, and the smorgasbord is tomorrow," someone pointed out.

One was even more direct. "My God, Edna, why didn't you at least tell us a few days ago? What's a smorgasbord without lefse? You know, Edna, it's no wonder people say what they do about you."

The earlier sociable atmosphere of the kitchen ebbed as a wave of uneasiness washed over it. The only sound came from a distant lawnmower.

Lana watched the scene unfold and wondered what people said about Edna. With her head down and an empty salt shaker in her hand, Lana rolled her eyes upward to furtively watch the drama play out. Trying to watch the scene unfold while still filling a salt shaker, Lana accidentally knocked a cap on the floor. The tinny bounce of the metal cap on the hard kitchen floor drew glances from around the kitchen. Lana could feel her face turning red as she froze with a vacant stare. She finally bent over to pick up the cap. But the cap had bounced under the large wooden work table. She would need to get on her hands and knees to retrieve it. Once under the table, Lana wanted to just stay there until everyone left. She knew there would be no graceful way to crawl out from under the table while the women watched her awkward maneuvers.

Edna recused Lana from the spotlight, giving her a chance to remove herself from under the table unnoticed. Once again, with the spotlight back on the leading lady, Edna launched her closing act. "There, I've said my piece." With her lips pressed tightly together, she scanned the kitchen one last time, with a squint that dared anyone to say more. With that, she exited stage left.

But as she walked away, Edna felt unfulfilled by her unimaginative exit. *She might have done more,* she thought. *Maybe turned back and said something, pushed something or someone out of her way, or cursed in Norwegian.* But it was too late now. In high school, on the stage in the gymnasium, she fancied herself a Bette Davis, even though it was nothing more than Our Town.

The ladies focused on the abandoned apron, some wondering aloud if Edna meant it this time. Nobody could see the smirk on Edna's face or the spring in her otherwise altered gait as she climbed the basement stairs toward the door. The ladies stood quietly, expecting the outside door to slam. But Edna did not oblige them.

A chilly rain greeted Edna as she came out of the church, a rain she cursed because she had forgotten her umbrella in the church kitchen and had no intentions of returning to get it. As for the apron she left behind, she would send her husband, Lester, to fetch it.

Lana stood speechless. She only agreed to help with the annual church smorgasbord because her new neighbor and landlady, Gracie, had asked her to. Now she questioned what she'd gotten herself into.

She moved onto the sugar bowls with meticulous caution after noting that an image of the church had been etched into the glass of each one.

## A Wet Hen

When Edna arrived home from the church, she stood in the kitchen, dripping rain onto the once fashionable avocado-green linoleum floor. Her husband, Lester, entered the kitchen for his mid-morning coffee and saw the puddle forming around his wife.

Lester was a thin and frail man in his late seventies. Incongruent with his otherwise pasty appearance was the fact that he had managed to hang onto a full and luxurious crop of black hair. He had retired from something, but nobody ever remembered from what. If challenged to list his daily physical activities, he would likely include watching television, solving crossword puzzles, and shuffling his way into the kitchen for coffee and cookies.

"Where's your umbrella?" he asked in his usual deadpan nasal way.

"In the church kitchen," Edna brushed aside his question with a detached response, void of any emotion that would disclose her discomfort. "I didn't know it was raining until I left," Edna explained as she grabbed another kitchen towel and dried her hair.

Lester wasn't sure he wanted to know the answer, but pressed on. "Why didn't you go back and get it once you saw it was raining?" Lester's off-the-cuff question, along with its condescending undertone, caused the muscles in Edna's face to tighten as she drew a deep breath, ready to pounce on anything that moved. "This is a cold rain, the kind that causes colds, sinus infections, and pneumonia," Lester warned.

"Thank you, Doctor Stern." Edna's flippant response dripped with derision, her tone as sharp as a barber's razor. "Grab me another dish towel." Lester listlessly trudged his way across the kitchen as if he were crossing the Great Divide on foot. He shrugged when he reached the sink.

"Try the drawer under the toaster," Edna said as she closed her eyes and shook her head in annoyance. Lester shuffled across the kitchen with a sigh of imposition, found a towel, and tossed it to Edna. The carefully folded towel unfurled in mid-air and gently wafted to the floor.

"Would it have hurt you to bring the towel over to me?" Edna's huffed question went unanswered.

Shaking her head in disgust and with a scowl on her face, she snatched the clean towel from the floor.

Unable to hold back any longer, Edna regaled Lester with an enhanced replay of her recent performance, with a damp towel as the prop for the apron. "Now those so-called Christian church ladies will have even more to gossip about," she added as a postscript.

"I suppose so," Lester muttered mechanically as he opened the cat-shaped cookie jar and took out an oatmeal-raisin cookie to go with his coffee.

"So, you left your apron on the kitchen floor? That's your favorite apron," Lester flatly reminded her.

Lester's insistence upon making Edna look foolish set the scene for her damsel-in-distress comeback. "Maybe you can go get it for me," she responded as she looked at him with puppy dog eyes. "And don't forget the umbrella," she whimpered.

Patty and Paige, Edna's two Persian cats, watched the exchange from under the kitchen table and cautiously emerged to investigate the remaining few drops of water on the floor. Edna climbed the stairs with a puzzled look on her face and paused on the landing before the final steps. Was it satisfaction or disappointment she was feeling? she asked herself. *Why had nobody, not the church ladies nor Lester, asked why she would not make the lefse?*

## What's Lefse?

Long before Edna arrived home, the church kitchen was a buzz as the ladies exhausted what they had to say about Edna, some using language seldom heard in a Lutheran church kitchen.

"I hear she and Lester are having a rough time these days." Lana didn't know who said it, but she wondered if they meant financially or in terms of relationships.

A woman at the sink washing dishes turned her head and, speaking over her shoulder, addressed Lana's unasked question.

"If you mean in terms of money, there's no problem there," she confirmed. "She came out like a bandit after her first marriage." The sound of the lawnmower had stopped, so everyone could hear. The only sound was the ticking of the kitchen clock, marking the passage of time, even as it stood still. Jaws dropped and postures stiffened as the ladies focused their attention on the woman at the sink.

Quizzical smiles spread through the kitchen, tacit prompts for the woman to elaborate. She turned away from the sink and began drying her hands with her apron.

"As it turns out, Edna first married a man with money, and they—"

"A man from the area?" someone interjected.

"No, from out of state, I forget where. Anyway, as I was saying, they lived in LaCrosse until she found out he was a womanizer. Edna sued for divorce and got a nice chunk of money."

The lingering stares told her they wanted more, as much as they could get. "But after buying a new Cadillac every year for the past thirty-some years, I would imagine much of that is gone." Still hungry for more, the ladies continued to ignore their preparations until the sizzling sound of something boiling over on the stove caught their attention.

"That's all I know," the woman acknowledged with an apologetic shrug. "Sorry."

"My, my. Isn't that something?" someone jeered. "I guess Edna can keep a secret after all, but only if it's about herself."

"Let's see if Edna shows up for the smorgasbord tomorrow." Another woman said as she tossed a freshly peeled potato into a stock pot of cold water on a nearby counter, causing water to splash onto the floor.

"Anyway, thanks to that woman, we'll have to make the lefse ourselves," the woman next to Lana gruffly announced. "We'll have to make it tomorrow morning, right here, in this kitchen. Not that we haven't done enough already." The woman did her best to elevate the impact of Edna's slight.

"And what's with that melodramatic apron scene?" someone asked as she walked over to pick up the apron. She wiped up the splash of water on the floor with the apron and hung it with a clothespin on a makeshift clothesline between a hook above the sink and the hot water heater.

"I've known Edna since first grade. She'll make some lefse, mark my words," Gracie Sanderson predicted as she continued putting coffee cups on a cart.

Minutes later, Ruth spotted Edna's umbrella hanging on the doorknob. She glanced out the small basement window and saw raindrops descending on the glass. "I see Edna forgot her umbrella, and it's raining. I bet she couldn't bring herself to come back and get it. She'll be soaked through and through by the time she walks those five blocks." Even though the concept of Karma isn't an integral component of Lutheran theology, the prospect of it playing out in Gailsprings on a rainy Tuesday brought unstated joy to the women in the church kitchen.

Things quieted down momentarily until Lana jolted the group with what would have been a benign question on another stage. "What's lefse?"

Shocked faces and muted gasps were followed by implicit suspicions that Lana wasn't even a Lutheran. The perplexed looks on their faces made Lana feel like she was about to be scolded for not studying for a vocabulary test.

"Why don't you come back tomorrow and see?" It was the same woman who wiped the kitchen floor with Edna's apron.

Lana, again wondering why she was even there, hesitantly indicated she'd try. A couple of the ladies offered to bring in their lefse griddles from home, and three others agreed to bring their potato ricers. Once the other tasks were settled, the ladies finished their deeds for the day, gathered their belongings, and turned off the lights.

The brigade was just about to leave the church when Lester walked up. With a colorful array of umbrellas in all sizes, they all greeted him at the same time, sounding much like the church choir, slightly out of tune. He recognized all of the women except one, a younger woman who had scrunched under Gracie Sanderson's transparent umbrella.

Without greeting the group, Lester, who was also under an umbrella, declared with an inward smile, "I'm here to pick up Edna's umbrella and apron."

Lester was used to cleaning up after what he called—and only to himself and others—Hurricane Edna. Many times, he had smoothed ruffled feathers, masterfully undone the damage, and atoned on her behalf. It was just easier that way—for both of them.

"You know how she is," was his standard line.

Ruth responded. "The apron's hanging near the sink, and the umbrella is still hanging on the doorknob on the kitchen door. I'll wait for you to return so I can lock the door."

The small crowd dispersed in all directions, some toward their cars and others down the sidewalk. Gracie escorted Lana to her car and then scurried to her own car, even though she finally had the whole umbrella to herself.

## The Customary Casserole

After she left the church, Lana drove by the farmhouse again.

Lana drove by slowly, but not too slowly, to look suspicious. She made a U-turn and drove by again. She pulled off onto the narrow shoulder of the country road, readjusting her rearview mirror to watch for traffic. Through a copse of box elders, she could see that the blue car had Tennessee plates. *Could this be some of Connor's family?* She decided to drive on, hoping that the blue car would be replaced by a red one soon.

Soon after she arrived home, there was a knock on her door. Lana went into the dining room to peek around the curtain to see who it was. She saw a man with what she guessed to be his son. Lana opened the door. "Yes?"

"Hi, I'm Kyle Tyson, and this is my son, Josh. We live in the brick house behind Gracie's. We saw her showing you the— I'm sorry, where are my manners? I hope we didn't interrupt anything."

"Oh, you're not interrupting at all. It's nice to meet you," Lana regretted her response, dreading another drawn-out account of someone's life. Kyle wore a Milwaukee Brewers T-shirt and a solid red baseball cap, which he had on backward. Josh was also wearing a T-shirt, an esoteric design that had writing on it that Lana couldn't understand.

He also wore a red cap backward. Josh was carrying something wrapped in a towel.

"My wife Evie made a casserole for you to welcome you to the neighborhood." Kyle pointed to the dish his son was carrying. "I'm sorry, I didn't catch your name."

"I'm Lana Paulson."

Josh stepped in front of his father and proudly presented the casserole to Lana. "It's got tater tots on it," he proudly announced as she took it from his hands. "It's pretty good," he said. "Except for the green beans, he complained with a turned-up nose.

"How thoughtful!" Lana gushed. She wasn't sure if she'd ever eaten a tater tot before, but decided not to ask. "Mmm, it sure smells good." Lana hadn't eaten since breakfast.

"What brings you to our fair city?" Kyle was a long-time resident of the Galesprings area and just had to know.

"You know," Lana cocked her head slightly and tightened her gaze. " I just wanted to get out of Louisville, you know, start a new life. It's a long story." Lana left it there, and so did Kyle.

"Have you lived here all your life?" Lana asked Kyle.

"I was born in Minnesota, but we moved to Galesprings when I was five. My parents found jobs teaching at the high school," Kyle replied as he swatted away a persistent mosquito.

"It certainly is a beautiful area." Lana looked around as she commented. "It seems so peaceful."

Josh, bored with the adult conversation, quietly walked back toward his house.

"But, you know, I have a couple of concerns you might be able to help me with. I'm wondering about the law enforcement presence here in the area. You see, I live alone, and would feel better if I knew whom to call in case of an emergency. Sheriff? State Patrol? Town police?"

"For one, you'll rarely see a state boy on our city streets. You mostly see them on state highways and Interstates. There is a county sheriff and some deputies. But since you are technically within the city limits, you should call the local police. Wally Simonson is the chief and a good friend of mine. Would you like the phone number?" Kyle pulled a pen out of his T-shirt pocket. "I tell you, these pocket tees are the best. I'm lost without a shirt pocket."

"I've already met Wally and have his number."

"Then you're in good hands. Hopefully you'll never need to call him," Kyle said as he handed the pen to Lana.

"But that's your pen," Lana pointed out.

"I know, but it has the name of the accounting firm I work for. You never know when you might need to do business with us. Keep it."

"You probably won't need to call Wally anyway, this being a pretty safe neighborhood. You might want to be a bit more vigilant on Halloween night, though," Kyle cautioned. "We keep our outside lights on all night. Mostly the usual stuff: smashed pumpkins, toilet papering, and some screaming banshees."

At Lana's startled look, he added, "Just kidding about that last bit." Kyle didn't know if Lana was playing along or was genuinely alarmed. Maybe she was just unfamiliar with the word banshee. "Well, anyway, enjoy the casserole, I always do."

The smell of the hot dish was making her salivate. "Thanks again," Lana hollered after she swallowed.

She set the casserole on the dining room table, took her phone out of her purse, and dialed Kitty's number. It went to voicemail. "Where are you?" Lana asked.

# CHAPTER 12

# LET THE FEAST BEGIN

## It Needs a Little Something

It was the third Wednesday in September, the traditional date for the church dinner at Galesprings' Lutheran Church in southwestern Wisconsin. Lana surprised some of the ladies when she arrived this time in a subtle floral midi cotton dress and basic white sandals. Her hair was pulled back into a crisscross ponytail held in place by a gold barrette. Her fine gold tennis necklace, along with her delicate sapphire earrings, added a touch of simplicity to her look.

Gracie was the first to comment. "Lana, you look absolutely perky. That dress is perfect for you."

Then Ruth joined in, "Lana, you look radiant. If you're looking for a husband, tonight might be your lucky night."

"Not looking! Definitely not looking!" Lana vehemently confirmed, shaking her head.

"That is a nice dress." Edna managed to admit in passing. "And those glasses look nice too, she called back as she walked away." She met Ruth at the kitchen sink and mumbled, "Better than those god-awful red ones from yesterday."

Soon, the church basement would be full of hungry Lutherans, and maybe a couple of Methodists or Episcopalians as well. When Lana first saw the piles of lefse, she pointed to it and innocently asked,

"What is that?" The ladies in the kitchen all gave Lana an odd look. Then they gave each other a concerned look. A Lutheran who doesn't recognize lefse?

Remembering that Lana did not show up to help make the lefse, Someone broke the silence. "Why Lana, that's lefse."

Lana asked, "How is it made? What's in it?"

Ruth responded this time. "There are variations of the recipe, but basically it's potatoes, flour, lard or butter, salt, sugar, and sometimes cream."

A third voice took it from there. "The boiled potatoes are put through a potato ricer, mixed with the other ingredients, rolled into a thin pancake, and cooked on a griddle. You might think of it as a Norwegian flatbread."

"What's a potato ricer?" Lana really had no idea.

One of the ladies turned to a cupboard, took one out, and showed it to Lana, showing her how to use it.

Gracie, Lana's landlady, who had just joined the group, explained how to eat the lefse. "We usually put butter on it, roll it up, and eat it like that. Some people put sugar on it, too. Try some."

Lana took a flat sheet of lefse from the pile of yet-unrolled lefse on the large table in the church kitchen. Someone slid the butter dish to her. Someone else handed her a butter knife. Lana carefully spread a thin layer of butter on the lefse and was about to roll it up when Edna interrupted.

"You probably want to use a bit more butter," Edna suggested.

Lana hadn't seen Edna, who now stood there with her apron tied tightly around her waist, where it would stay for the duration of the evening, never touching the floor. Lana added more butter, rolled it up as instructed, and took a bite.

The butter oozed onto her lips, and she had to lick them off as the ladies watched for her reaction.

"Soooo?" Edna asked. "I made that batch myself."

Even though Lana found the lefse bland and in need of a spicy filling, she told them what they wanted to hear. "I like it. I'll have to get the recipe from one of you," Lana said, trying to sound sincere.

Several ladies in the kitchen offered to bring in their recipes, jubilant that there was hope for Lana after all. With a puzzled look on her face, Lana couldn't figure out why Edna would even be there after the kitchen episode.

## If Gracie Should Talk

With minutes to go before the doors would open for the first sitting of the annual smorgasbord, the woman fussed around with last-minute details.

"Just like that, people are living out there, out there at my brother's old place. How do we know they ain't squatters?" Edna asked before sliding a piece of the ham she was slicing into her mouth. She quickly devoured it and washed it down with coffee. A buzzing timer interrupted Edna and distracted her audience, giving Edna a chance to snatch another piece of ham.

Once the timer was off, she continued. "They got Tennessee tags on the blue car out there. I'm not sure what kind of car that is, one of those foreign jobs, I think," Edna guessed. "As for people, all I've seen is a young man in his early twenties picking apples. Outlaws, maybe. Looks suspicious, if you ask me!"

But no one ever did. No one ever needed to. Everyone who knew Edna knew where they stood without even asking. Nothing was ever sugar-coated in Edna's world; it was just raw, unedited blather.

"Edna, what on earth are you going on about now?" Ruth asked. She and Edna tolerated each other as best they could. Some said their animosity toward each other went back to high school, when Ruth showed up at the prom in all white and Edna spent a good part of the evening making snide remarks.

Others said it was the time Edna spent a bit too long under the mistletoe at the Elks club Christmas party with Ruth's husband,

Wally—everyone knew Edna and Wally had dated in high school. And some claimed that Edna held a grudge since the time Ruth gave Edna's son a 'D' in English class.

"My brother's old farmhouse. Try and keep up, Ruth," Edna sneered. Lana recalled Connor's comment about his aunt Edna, but until then, she hadn't made the connection. "My brother died years ago, and recently his spooky wife, Roberta, died. Their four boys have the farm up for sale. But I know it's not them out there. I know their cars," Edna explained as she put the cover on the Nesco, picked it up, and nodded toward the closed kitchen door that led to the dining area.

Lana took the cue and held the door open. The ham was now at the very center of the buffet tables, where, according to Edna, it belonged.

Edna returned to the kitchen with little concern that the topic of conversation might have changed. "I drove out there this morning. I saw a young man who looked to be around seventeen or eighteen. But there was no way I was going to stop to see who it was. Not with the way things are going these days!" Edna shook her head and drew her lips together as tight as she could. "Every time I call Connor, I get some strange message about being unable to place the call as dialed."

Lana didn't mention that she, too, had seen a car at the farmhouse she now knew once belonged to Edna's brother. She just listened, carefully, aware that news travels fast in a small community and easily blends with gossip stoked by both vivid imaginations and sheer boredom. Fortunately, Gracie had been drawn away by an incident at her sister's assisted living facility and wasn't there to connect Lana with the house.

Still nibbling on her lefse, Lana considered what might happen if Gracie should, at some point, casually mention her connection to Connor to Edna, or anyone else, for that matter. Edna certainly would want to know more. *What if she contacted one of Connor's brothers?* she asked herself.

"But still, we need to find out more about them," Edna persisted. "Who are they? They might not even be from Tennessee for all we know. I don't think I even know anyone from Tennessee, and I doubt if my brother ever did either. Why are they here? That's what I'd like to know."

Edna was looking squarely at Ruth Simonson, whose husband, Wally, was the chief of the town police force, a force that included two other officers and a part-time female administrative assistant whose filing skills were mostly applied to her fingernails.

After Ruth remained silent, Edna was more direct. "Ruth, did your husband say anything about that? Did anyone go over to the place to, ya' know, sleuth around?"

Ruth responded with a theatrical shrug as she slid even more butter into the Rømmegrøt. That was Ruth's specialty and her contribution to the event, and she made sure it stayed that way. Nobody made the rich and velvety pudding the way she did, anyway, so her position remained unchallenged. The hierarchy and roles in that church kitchen were as fixed as law. They only changed in the wake of a death, a life-altering event, or a dramatic departure.

Pouring herself a cup of coffee, Edna made a suggestion. "Someone needs to tape down the cord to the floor from the Nesco so nobody trips over it. As for me, I need a break."

A telepath in the area might have picked up on a chorus of, "yes, we need a break from you!"

But Lana's mind was elsewhere. *What's all this about a young man with that blue car?*

## Butter, Butter, Butter

By five o'clock on Wednesday, the long-awaited annual smorgasbord at Gailsprings Lutheran was laid out on long tables. At the head of the first table were the plates, utensils, napkins, and water glasses; the coffee cups and butter dishes were already on the tables. Then came the piles of thickly sliced ham. The ladies knew it would go fast, so they had prepared more in advance. Several bowls of mashed potatoes enriched with butter and cream were second in line. Those first in line watched as the dollop of butter eased its way into the steamy mountain of white bliss.

Next came a Nesco filled with meatballs smothered in rich brown gravy, a gravy so smooth that not a single lump of flour could be found amid the meatballs.

With the foundation loaded onto the plates, the line moved to the side dishes. The large bowls of squash, corn, and carrots started the sides, with generous dollops of butter that the first diners in line snatched for themselves.

As for salads, there was coleslaw, of course, but that was it; a Caesar salad, a seven-layer salad, or a Salade Nicoise would be in clear violation of traditional standards. There were platters of freshly sliced tomatoes, some red, some yellow; platters that would need constant replenishing. And then the lefse, accompanied by both butter and sugar.

But at the end of the L-shaped configuration of the three serving tables was the grand finale: Ruth Simonson and her Rømmegrøt. She never let anyone serve themselves, as it had to be rationed out. Of course, the minister and his wife got a few drops more, as did some of the church board members, but not all of them. Ruth kept one eye on the dish that held the extra melted butter ready to drizzle on top of each serving if one wished, and they always did. She allowed the guests to spread their own butter but was never hesitant to reprimand someone who took too much.

Ovo-vegetarians would find slim pickings at a Norwegian smorgasbord.

The church basement could only seat a limited number, so people took numbers and ate when their numbers were called. Children ran throughout the church, exploring corners, closets, and even venturing into the bell tower—prohibited places on the Sundays when watchful eyes kept them in check. Some of the waiting carnivores were gathered in the parking lot, smoking and talking about the weather and the crops.

# Edna Stern, P.I.

With the event in full swing, Edna launched her plan. She would wait until Ruth's husband, Wally, who would surely show up any minute, was well-fed and sipping his coffee. She would then move in for a chit-chat with the chief.

Intentionally passing through the tables with an empty pot of coffee, so as not to have to pause to pour, Edna homed in on Wally as he entered the basement to get in line for the food. She buzzed around the basement and kitchen as if she were accomplishing something. Wally was wiping his eyeglasses with the paper tablecloth when Edna descended into the empty chair to his right, this time with coffee in her pot.

"Why, Waldemar, I didn't even see you come in. And since when have you needed glasses?" Edna had to start with something; she couldn't just get to the point.

"About two years ago." He knew Edna wanted something. Edna always wanted something. And when she did, she approached the mission with the zeal of a lonely barber awarded the opportunity of cutting disheveled dreadlocks.

"So, I suppose you know all about what's now known as the 'apron affair,'" Edna would ease into the real purpose of her probe.

"Yeah, I heard all about it that same day, and so did most of the town," Wally snickered." I understand that the other church ladies had to come back the next day to make the lefse."

"They got nothing else to do, anyhow. I ended up making some, after all. You know how I am."

"Yes, Edna, I know how you are. So, Edna, what's really on your mind tonight? I haven't seen your husband, Lester, here yet. Is he coming?" Edna skipped the second question in favor of the first.

"It's our old farm. It appears someone is living out there, in that vacant house, and it's not one of us."

Wally pulled a toothpick out of his shirt pocket and slipped it between his lips. "Yes, I know all about it, Edna." He knew that would not satisfy her.

"Here's the thing, some of the other church ladies and I were wondering about what's going on out there. I'm thinking we might just organize a welcoming committee, pay them a visit, maybe bring a pie. Good time of the year for apple pie. Maybe even get Ruthie to—"

Wally slid the toothpick to the side of his mouth, securing it between his teeth as he spoke. "I gotta tell ya' Edna, I don't rightly know much about the more recent developments. I went out there myself a couple of days ago. Met a woman who seemed to know quite a bit about Connor and his family." Edna warmed up Wally's coffee, finally emptying the pot so she could go off duty. "But that woman was going to try to rent Gracie's sister's vacant house."

"Ya, that Gracie, she's another one I don't trust. She's always so sweet and

hoity-toity. And the way she always acts so piously. Ha!" Edna's mouth opened wide as she brought forth a throaty scoff.

"I'll try to get out that way tomorrow, depending on how things go." Wally stood, took one last gulp of his coffee, and left. Edna turned in her chair, throwing her arm over the back of it as she watched Wally work his way down the long tables. *Depending on how things go? What could possibly happen in Gailsprings on a Thursday in September?* she wondered.

Despite the dustup about the lefse, the church ladies had indeed rallied and had managed to make enough of it to go around. By the time the last dish was washed and dried, the leftovers divided up, and the floor swept, the ladies sat down with a heavy sigh. One more year, and the event was over. Ruth overheard Edna whisper to those sitting near her. "If there was a bottle back there tonight, I could use some right now." Ruth realized she could, too.

But Edna could not let it go. "I'm still thinking about that house, you know, my brother's old place. Most of you remember my brother, Karl, the one who was slowly poisoned to death by his wife, Roberta. She was a strange one, that woman. She was a witch, and I mean that in the literal way. She was always growing strange plants and herbs." Edna's accusations were preposterous but not surprising to the group.

"I brought it up to Waldemar tonight. He says he might go out there tomorrow." Edna's gaze fixed on Wally's wife, Ruth. "Ruthie, honey, why don't you see what you can find out. And let me know."

Ruth was so tired she could only muster a half-hearted nod, and that was only to get out of that church basement and away from Edna.

# CHAPTER 13

# A COUNTRY DRIVE

## The Purse

The morning after the smorgasbord, Lana was up early. She ate a quick breakfast and drove out to the farm. Distracted by her thoughts about the wrong car, the turn off for the country road came up fast. Lana snapped on her blinker, hit the brakes, and sharply veered to her left. Lana's purse on the passenger seat tumbled onto the floorboard, but she ignored it as she tried to maintain control of the car. The prolonged honking of the horn from the driver behind her gradually faded away as the two cars went their separate ways.

With the farmhouse less than a mile ahead of her, Lana stopped the car on the side of the road to compose herself. The contents of her lavender Louis Vuitton shoulder bag were all over the floorboard mat. She'd deal with it later.

She continued the short distance to the farmhouse, still slightly shaken by what had happened. When she approached the farm, she saw the same blue car. But this time she saw a young man standing next to it. As she was already driving more slowly than usual, she saw no need to slow down anymore and catch his attention. She continued another mile and made a U-turn. When she drove by again, the young man, who was getting into the passenger side of the car, gave her a perfunctory wave. Lana thought she saw someone sitting behind the steering wheel, but wasn't sure if it was a man or a woman.

On her way back into town, a sleek black car approached at high speed. As it passed, she glimpsed the driver—a woman with striking red hair.

When Lana got home, she opened the passenger door to retrieve her purse and belongings. She picked up the address book she bought at the Art Institute of Chicago. There it was again, another reminder of Connor. Next to the address book was the Czarina crystal barrette she thought she'd lost. She picked up her iPhone 6, made sure it was working, then scooped the remaining items into her bag and went into the house.

## Edna's Tackle Box

That same morning, Edna stayed close to her phone, expecting a call from Ruth any minute. By late morning, when she could wait no longer, she called Ruth.

"No, Edna, I forgot to ask him. He's been so busy, what with all that's been going on around here. I was just on my way out. I'll let you know, though. Bye," Ruth abruptly dismissed Edna and could imagine the look on her face, not to mention the words that would come out of her mouth.

Edna stared at her phone with the peeved look on her face that Ruth had predicted. Not only did Ruth have no information, but her comment about Wally "being busy with all that's been going on" had left her dangling. *Did she mean what was going on at the farmhouse?* Edna thought.

Edna stuck her head into the living room. "Lester, I got some errands to run. Need anything?" Lester sat in his recliner, sipping coffee while watching a news channel.

"Nah, I'm good," he grunted.

Edna grabbed the old fishing tackle box that she had repurposed into a crime investigation kit, got into her new black Cadillac, fired up the engine, and sped out of town, brazenly daring local law enforcement to stop her. Not that any of them would even want to stop her for such a minor offense, since it would only lead to more grief than the fine would be worth.

As Edna approached the farmhouse, she saw a blue car pull out of the driveway. She quickly pulled the sun visor down and spun it around to the left. She took her foot off the gas and let her car slow down as she watched the tiny blue car disappear into the horizon in her rear-view mirror.

Edna would have to work fast. She carefully scouted out the area, looking for any farmers in the nearby fields, someone who would see her or recognize her car. Edna Stern wasn't scared easily, but she was cautious.

She pulled onto the unpaved driveway and sat in her car for a few minutes. She blew the horn three times. No one came out of the house. She blew it again, louder and longer.

Nothing.

Edna got out of the car and knocked on the screen door, which led to the front porch. Convinced that she had the place to herself, she went back to her car, grabbed her phone for the photos along with her repurposed investigation kit. She was about to go around to the back door when she heard the distant sound of an approaching vehicle.

## Dame Yegg Edna

Kyle Tyson was about to leave the house when his wife, Evie, called down from the upstairs hallway. "Kyle, why don't you stop off at that apple orchard on your way home. The one that sells apple cider and pumpkins. I can't remember the name of the place. Get two gallons. Josh loves it."

"I don't remember the name either, but I know the place you mean, it's just beyond that old Larson place. Good idea. It should be a pretty drive now that the leaves are turning." Kyle grabbed his keys and was out the door.

He would not have paid any attention to the Larson house, which he had passed many times in the past, but the bright sun reflecting off a car mirror caught his eye. He slowed down. He had recently seen a car there, but this was a different car. This one had Wisconsin plates, and it wasn't blue. And he knew who that black Cadillac XTS belonged to.

Fortunately, Edna had heard the truck approaching and had managed to duck behind an abandoned yet redolent manure spreader. Peering around the manure spreader, Edna saw the truck slow down. She pulled back and held her breath.

When the truck sped away, she headed straight to the basement, descending the questionable stairs slowly. Once on solid ground, she directed her flashlight beam around the entire basement and easily found the metal trunk she was looking for. "Ha!" she scoffed when she discovered that the trunk was locked. "Don't worry, I'll have you open in a jiffy."

Edna opened her crime-investigation kit. She had been waiting for the opportunity to try out the 28-piece lock-picking kit she had her grandson order for her last Christmas. When she told her grandson that she had been a yegg in another life, he said, "An egg?"

"No, silly, a yegg, y-e-g-g, someone who breaks into safes."

"Ya, sure, Grams, whatever you say," he responded as he clicked the 'buy now' icon. Edna claimed she could pick the locks in the US Mint— if she only knew where it was. Edna had already practiced with the lock-picking kit on some doors at home. But this was the real thing, she gleefully told herself.

With her skillful manipulations, Edna had the trunk unlocked in no time. She flung the lid open with her right foot, releasing an army of dust particles and the smell of a used clothing store. Knowing she had no time to waste, she removed the clothes by the armful, tossing everything onto the floor. When she pulled out the last item, a floral dress, she finally saw what she was looking for: a diary.

Resisting the temptation to leaf through the diary, Edna left it where it was. She took a photo of the unopened diary, stuffed the clothes back in, slammed it shut, gathered her belongings, and got out of there fast. She only needed to know if the diary was still there.

Edna passed the same blue car on her way back into town.

When she got home, Lester asked where she had been; her response rolled off the tip of her tongue. "I went for a drive in the country. I wanted to drive by that pumpkin patch we used to take the kids to, you know, the one out by the Larson farm. Just reminiscing, that's all."

"And you didn't pick up some apple cider?" Lester moped.

# CHAPTER 14

# FALLING INTO PLACE

## She Could Have Left a Note

Friday had started warm and breezy, but soon low clouds brought a light, chilly rain. This time, Lana told herself she would be more attentive to her driving than she had been the day before.

She drove by the house slowly, hoping she might draw someone to a window, or an open door, anything to move things along.

Within a few feet of the driveway, Lana heard a thud, and her car began to shake. Lana stomped on the brake. "Damn!" She slammed the palms of her hands against the steering wheel. She dragged her purse onto her lap and frantically searched for her phone. One by one, she pulled out objects and threw them on the passenger's seat. No phone.

An image flashed before her eyes—her phone on the kitchen counter, fully charged by now.

The knock on the passenger window startled her, as her eyes had been on the side rearview mirror.

"Something wrong, ma'am?" the young man asked.

Lana didn't move as she pictured herself walking onto the set of a Hitchcock movie: an old farmhouse, a lone woman gets a flat tire, it's raining, a man comes out, his name is Norman.

"Are you alright? Are you hurt?" The rain was dripping from the young man as he stood there, his arms wrapped around himself in the shivering cold. He wished she'd say something. "Do you need an ambulance? A tow truck?" he shouted through the steamy glass of the passenger side.

Lana turned to see that he was a young man of about seventeen with blond hair and blue eyes. She empathized with the young man as he stood patiently in the cold rain waiting for a response.

She rolled the window down an inch. "I'm sure I have a flat tire," she finally replied.

The young man could hear both frustration and hope in her response. "Yes, you do. It's the back tire on the driver's side. I'll tell you what. Why don't you just come on into the house? I'll go back inside, get my rain gear, and change that dang tire for you."

Lana's uneasiness about who was living there was slightly assuaged by the young man's polite yet casual soothing language. "

Lana looked in the rearview again, her desperate eyes squinting in search of an oncoming car. "I'd like to, but I'm all alone."

The young man picked up on the uneasiness in Lana's voice. "It's ok, ma'am. My aunt, well, she's really a cousin, is inside. She sent me out to help. I'm Virgil. She told me to invite you in for some hot coffee."

With her misgivings somewhat palliated, she closed the window, grabbed her purse, keys, and umbrella, and followed Virgil into the house. The back door opened with a bang as Virgil flew into the kitchen to get out of the rain. Lana stood on the steps leading to the back door, briskly fanning her umbrella in and out as Virgil held the door open.

"Just what you thought, Aunt Kitty, a flat tire," Virgil said as he sidled past Kitty, transferring some of the residual rainwater onto her robe. Kitty just brushed it off with no comment as there was something more crucial to deal with.

Lana froze at the sight of Kitty. Her eyes glanced at Virgil. She sensed something wasn't right.

Virgil, sensing the awkward stiffness of the two women as they stared at each other in silence, broke in. "Is there, um, something wrong? Do you two—do you already know each other?" Virgil glanced back and forth between the two with a puzzled look on his face.

"As a matter of fact, we do. This is my cousin Lana, who happens to be your second cousin, too. I told you about her on our way here," Kitty explained.

Lana, still unsure of the situation, shot Kitty a dazed look of bewilderment.

"Lana, this is Virgil. He's our uncle Calvin's grandson. He says he has never met you. He's why I'm late. I had to swing by Chattanooga to pick him up on my way here."

Lana's furrowed brow told Kitty that Lana was still uneasy at the situation. "And then, just before I rolled into Chattanooga, that car you rented for me died. Something about a blown gasket. Cal had the car towed to the local lot and then set me up with a different car. And here we are."

"Uh, Virgil," Kitty crossed her arms in front of her. "Are you going to change her tire or just stand around here wasting time?"

Virgil sprang into action, digging through closets in search of a raincoat. In the meantime, Kitty poured Lana a cup of coffee and the two talked about the weather at the kitchen table. Moments later, Virgil appeared in the kitchen with a shapeless army green raincoat that drooped over his shoulders like a dark frown on a circus clown's face.

"I'm going to need your keys, ma'am. Or did you leave them in the car?"

Lana handed him the keys.

"Virgil was barely out the door when Lana let loose.

"What the hell is he doing here?" Lana hissed at Kitty.

"Virgil has had a rough life. His parents are drug addicts, and he has been living with Cal and his wife. Virgil's parents said they wanted him back living with them, but Cal doesn't like the idea. When I told Cal I was planning to visit him on my way back from Wisconsin, he asked me to pick up Virgil on my way here so he wouldn't be around when his parents came to pick him up. I couldn't say no. You know what a softy I am."

"I may have met Virgil years ago, but I would never have recognized him now. What did you tell Virgil?" Lana asked.

"That you were planning to buy an old farmhouse and renovate it, and you wanted me to help plan the renovations." By Lana's sly smile, Kitty saw that Lana was satisfied.

"But, Kitty, I left you a voicemail two days ago. Why didn't you respond?"

"I lost my phone. Yesterday, we went into town to buy Virgil a pre-paid phone, hoping we could find my phone when he called me. But we didn't. We were just about to go into town to buy me a new phone when you showed up." Lana slid her empty coffee to Kitty for a refill.

As Kitty returned the cup to the table, she took a less defensive tone.

"You know, Lana, you could have stopped anyway, despite the different car. You could have said you were lost. And not only that, you could have left a note on this table telling us where you were. And another thing, there is no way I would stay here alone. You should be glad Virgil's along." Kitty was on a roll.

"You're right about everything you just said," Lana acquiesced. "I stayed here one night and that was enough, so I rented a furnished house in town."

"I'm sorry about the delay; I truly am," Kitty whimpered.

"Actually, it's no problem. We have plenty of time. In fact, I'm enjoying my quiet life here in Gailspring. Sally can be a loose cannon at times, and she runs her businesses on a whim." The two women continued their conversation until they heard the back door open.

"Tire's changed, ma'am." Virgil declared as he triumphantly marched into the kitchen, dripping water from the ill-fitting coat. Kitty threw a towel at him. "And Virgie, please wipe up the floor too."

The subterfuge continued. But Lana and Kitty were eager to end the drama. Lana thanked Kitty and Virgil. She reached into her purse, took out a twenty-dollar bill, and slipped it into Virgil's hand.

"Probably wanna get that tire fixed soon, ma'am. The spare is still good, but you never know."

Lana would heed his advice. She certainly didn't want to get another flat tire soon.

## A Cog Named Virgil

Now that Lana knew Kitty was in place, they could begin their mission. The problem, though, was finding time to work when Virgil wasn't listening. They needed a strategy, and Lana had worked out a couple of options. Lana stopped at the farmhouse the morning after the flat tire incident. Instead of going around to the back door, Lana knocked on the door of the front porch.

"Hi, Lana," Virgil greeted her through the screen on the porch door as he unlocked it. "Judging from what I've seen, you two have quite the project ahead of you. This place is in baaaaad shape."

"Who is it?" Kitty yelled from the kitchen, where she sat at the table doodling while she waited for the oven timer to ring.

"It's Lana," Virgil called back.

"Bring her into the kitchen," Kitty yelled.

Virgil escorted Lana into the kitchen. The savory aroma of a baking pizza evoked an audible growl from Virgil's stomach. "It's almost ready," Kitty assured him. Kitty motioned for Lana to sit down. But Lana walked over to the stove instead. She opened the oven door to check on the pizza.

"I do know how to make a pizza, Lana. I mean, really," Kitty rolled her eyes as she again motioned for Lana to join her at the table.

"Call me when it's ready," Virgil said as he disappeared into the living room.

Each with a cup of coffee and a glazed donut, Kitty and Lana were free to talk.

"What you told Virgil about renovating this farmhouse was good thinking. When he's around, we should pretend to be doing just that. I doubt he'll be suspicious if we go into the basement." Lana reasoned. "Just let me know when he's not around. I saw the new fishing pole leaning by the door. I expect he plans on fishing. Or do you?" Lana joked.

Kitty ignored the comment as she retrieved the slightly burned pizza from the oven, noticing that the timer was still set at 25 minutes. After she set the pizza on a large cutting board, she opened several drawers in search of a pizza wheel.

"Kitty, if you're looking for a pizza wheel, I doubt you'll find one in this old farmhouse. Use a knife, for heaven's sake. I'm getting hungry," Lana proclaimed.

"This pizza's for Virgil and his fishing buddy. They'll have it down in no time." Kitty envisioned a tomato-smeared cardboard tray abandoned to the flies on the picnic table outside. "And then they'll be off fishing somewhere. Come back in a couple of hours."

With a half-eaten donut in her hand, Lana stood. "For now, I have to get going. I have some shopping to do."

"How about bringing some lunch back with you? Kitty requested. "A rotisserie chicken would be nice. With a couple of sides," Kitty added.

# CHAPTER 15

# DIARY PAGE ONE

## Dinner and a Diary

Lana returned around noon with the chicken and was glad Kitty approved of at least one of the two sides.

"Honestly, Lana, I mean, who gets a side of mixed vegetables? They're probably from a can anyway." Kitty crinkled up her nose in disgust as she fought to cut a leg off the chicken.

"Here, Kitty. Give me that knife," Lana commanded. "You obviously have never carved a chicken before." Kitty handed Lana the knife and licked her fingers as Lana skillfully removed the legs and wings, and then started on the rest of the bird.

"Let's eat on the picnic table outside," Lana suggested. "It's a beautiful fall day, and if we're going to be in that dark basement all day, I say we get some sun and fresh air first."

Kitty only nodded in agreement, her mouth full of potato salad. They sat at the picnic and reminisced.

"Remember the time you snuck two of your mom's cigarettes from that fancy cigarette case?" Kitty recalled. Lana threw her head back in laughter and responded. "I don't think it was the smoke that alerted your father to us behind the stable; it was us hacking away."

"What was hilarious was when my father offered us each a cigar!" Kitty's laugh faded quickly as a pall of melancholy clouded her face.

"I miss him," Kitty murmured. "And I can't believe I'm saying this, but I miss my mom too. Am I doing the right thing, Lana? What do you think?" Kitty tugged at her earlobe as she waited for Lana's response.

"I think you are. And I think your father was right in supporting you. I think you and Robie have a good thing going, just don't rush into anything if you're not ready." Both Kitty and Lana looked up as a flock of noisy Canada geese announced both their arrival and departure.

"I'm not a clairvoyant," Lana continued. "But I think your so-called gap year will better prepare you for life. I think it already has," Lana concluded.

Lana snapped on the basement lights, not expecting the brightness that now filled the area. Sensing Lana's surprise, Kitty explained. "I had Virgil put some more light bulbs down there. He took them from the upstairs bedrooms."

Kitty thought it best not to tell Lana that Virgil had shown interest in the trunk.

"I checked the window ledge when I stayed here that one frightful night. That's where the key was supposed to be. But it wasn't."

Lana approached the trunk, bent over, and grabbed it by two corners. Inching it out until there was enough room for Kitty to get behind it and push.

"Kitty, hop behind this thing and help me slide it out so we can take a better look."

Kitty squeezed in between the trunk and the concrete wall and began pushing. Once they had the trunk in the center of the room, Lana signaled Kitty to stop.

"You know, I don't think this is even locked. The cover seemed loose when we moved it." Lana examined the lock as she said it. "Someone's broken into this trunk. And whoever did it must have done it after Connor's mother died because Connor told me the trunk was locked."

Lana opened the lid and drew her palm to her forehead. "And to think I could have been working on this all along," Lana's lips tightened, and her eyes closed as she reproached herself with a self-deprecating bow of her head. "I didn't even bother to see if it was unlocked."

Kitty stood in front of Lana and put her hands on Lana's shoulders. "It's fine, Lana. You didn't know. It's not like we do this kind of thing for a living. We'll get it done!"

"I know, but still—"

"Enough already," Kitty cut her off. "If Connor's not due here until two or three weeks from now, then there's no real hurry."

"This trunk is full of nothing but old clothes," Kitty observed.

"Not for long," Lana replied as she removed a dark gray skirt from the trunk. "How about it, Kitty, want to try it on?"

"Ewwww!" Kitty crinkled her nose as she said it. Lana tossed it to the floor.

"Maybe this is more suited to your taste." Lana held up a black shift.

"Is there a funeral somewhere?" Kitty responded. "Toss it!"

"And get a load of this. It was a lime-green leisure suit from the early seventies.

"Don't tell me she made her husband wear that hideous thing. My oldest brother's wife is always trying to get him to wear the latest styles, some almost as bad as that thing." Kitty pointed to the leisure suit. Thud. It hit the floor.

"Oh, my, my, my, look at this." Lana held the black lace bra to her chest.

"Oh lah lah!" Kitty sang. "You know, Lana. That looks like it would fit you. That's probably been in that trunk since their honeymoon." Onto the pile it went.

The fashion show banter continued until Lana pulled out a brightly colored floral dress, causing both of them to drop their jaws in disbelief.

"How odd," Kitty observed. "The most beautiful piece is near the bottom. And that's about your size, too."

"It makes you wonder." Lana squinted her eyes and cocked her head. "Did Connor's mother stuff this dress away long ago? Is this symbolic of her life?"

"I'm not sure, Dr. Freud," Kitty joked.

Lana reached back into the trunk and pulled out an article of clothing that was still in its package. She tossed it onto the floor.

"Look, Kitty!" Lana exclaimed.

Kitty approached the trunk, looked inside, and pulled out the final object.

"It's the diary!" Kitty screamed. "We have it!"

But Lana's eyes were on the article of clothing that she had just tossed on the floor.

"What is it?" Kitty asked.

"It's a pink christening gown." Their moist eyes met as they both assumed the same thing.

"Lana, you don't think—"

"I don't know, Kitty. It might have been Roberta's."

"But it's still in the package," Kitty whispered.

They stood in mournful silence as they processed the absurdity of finding joy and sorrow nanoseconds apart. Finally, Kitty ascended the stairs with the diary in hand. Lana followed.

Kitty poured a glass of water for both of them.

They sat at the table until Lana broke the silence. "Connor said to look for clever clues buried inside mundane passages. He suspects there will be at least five clues. He doubts the clues will lead all over the farm, but instead will be limited to the basement."

"So, what exactly are we looking for?" Kitty asked.

"The combination to the safe," Lana replied.

"I didn't see a safe down there." Kitty shook her head as she said it.

"We'll have to find that, too. Let's get started with the diary," Lana suggested.

"Page one, first entry," Lana solemnly announced.

*October 7, 1974*

*I, Roberta. I had a diary as a child and to this day have no idea what happened to it. So, I am going to try again and, just like before, I am likely never to know what will happen to it. This will be my long sought after distraction from the woe that has beset this farmhouse. But more on that later.*

*The breezy and warm autumn day beckoned me to launder the bed sheets and hang them outside in the fresh air. Of course, using the dryer is more convenient, but with this lovely breeze, the sheets will dry just as fast and capture the scent of nature.*

*Karl left immediately after breakfast, announcing he would be in the fields all day. It behooves me to admit that, despite his irksome ways, he is a hard worker and a diligent provider for his family.*

*Unfortunately, when Karl left the house, he saw the cows had breached the fence and were wandering about, munching away on the vegetation they had long coveted. The boys were still asleep, so I left the house to help him herd them back into the corral. I swear he cares more about those cows than me.*

*I never blamed all those people who protested that war in Vietnam. I fear it is a lost cause, and those who sacrificed their lives will have done it for naught. But at least the crook finally resigned. President Ford pardoned him, of course, saying our long national nightmare is over. But will that nightmare be replaced by a dream?*

Lana slid the diary over to Kitty so she could read the next entry.

*October 11, 1974*

*Last night's storm was fierce, not to mention unusual for this time of year. It is always unnerving when the tempestuous winds cause the branches on that old oak tree to eerily scrape the side of the house. The sound evokes a scene from a horror film, a creature clawing with bony fingers, trying to get inside. Karl slept through the tumult as I sat on the front porch watching the ominous clouds roll over the landscape. I find numerous metaphors in storms: the impending destruction, the cleansing effect, the serenity after it has moved on.*

*Karl and I had a heated discussion before the real storm moved it. As usual, it centered on our finances. We live a frugal life, as many farmers do, so he thinks we should have more money in the bank than we do. At his insistence, I showed him the bank documents, which I have to admit do not reveal a substantial accumulation of wealth. He has a mindset that I am hoarding money.*

*At first, his innuendos that I am stashing money out behind the old outhouse were jovial. He sees me out there since that is where I have my special garden. Lately though, his innuendos have morphed into accusations.*

The next several entries were brief and mostly about daily life. But, more and more, Roberta was adding commentary on larger events.

*August 30, 1979*

*That's a real mess over there in the Middle East. That Saddam Hussein sounds like a deranged and narcissistic megalomaniac. Ernest turned three last week. I expect he'll be our last; three are enough. At least for now. I just started reading Joan Didion's* Slouching Toward Bethlehem.

After reading several more mundane entries and sliding the diary back and forth, Lana and Kitty decided to sit next to each other and skim and scan, jumping over commentary on daily life. Fortunately, there were several gaps in the diary, some weeks apart.

## A White Wedding

"This is getting interesting," Kitty observed. "As we now can connect bits and pieces to find a coherent narrative. So, Roberta's parents had believed she was marrying below their place in society?"

"Yes, it sounds that way," Lana agreed. "Her parents were financially well-off, and Karl was—how did her mother put it again?"

"A poor farmer," Kitty replied. "How condescending! And this business about having a modest wedding, as her mother said, so as not to embarrass the Larson side."

"I do have to agree with her mother, though," Lana said. "So, what if tradition had it that she wasn't supposed to wear white at the wedding? Of course, times were different then."

"It sounds like Roberta's mother was a progressive woman," Kitty observed. "Did you see what she said about it being fine for the men to have all the adventures they want, but when it comes to us women, it's a different story?"

"No. I must have skimmed over that," Lana admitted. "But this is all gossip and leads us nowhere. Let's move on."

## As Time Goes By

It was Kitty's turn to read. She read aloud several entries and paraphrased others.

"These next few entries deal with the birth of Ruben, their second son. He was born on Christmas Day in 1974," Kitty continued, paging through the entries.

"Here's something from February of 1976," Kitty said as she brushed away the drop of tea she had spilled on the page.

*We are snowed in. Karl's outside now, plowing snow with his truck. He'll then milk the cows and come in for breakfast. And knowing him, he'll be off plowing snow for some of the neighbors. He tells me he doesn't make any money doing that, but I know he does. I sometimes wonder if he is doing more than just plowing snow. He still is a handsome man, and there are plenty of widows out there, not to mention unfaithful wives. I've heard there is some gossip going around about his shenanigans. Karl can still be affectionate with me at times, but it rarely leads to anything more.*

*The snow started yesterday, just after supper. The lights flickered on and off, so we got out some candles. Fortunately, we didn't lose power. At least we wouldn't freeze since we still have a wood-burning stove in the living room.*

*I am listening right now to Barbra Streisand singing 'The Way We Were'. It's such a beautiful song. I especially like the line, 'What's too painful to remember, we simply choose to forget.' If only it were that easy to simply choose to forget.*

"At least we will be out of this state when it snows," Kitty questioned her prediction before she had finished it.

"Of course, this being Wisconsin, who knows when it might start snowing." Lana had been to Wisconsin before and was no stranger to snow.

Kitty had seen snow before, but nothing like she imagined after reading the last entry. Kitty slid the diary to Lana, who slowly paged through, hoping to find something of use. Lana took over the diary, paging through years of entries as Kitty prepared some iced tea.

"Here's something from November 7, 1980," Lana finally said.

*Ruben is growing fast. He's such a good baby. Matt loves to play with him. But I have to keep a close eye on him. At five, he can sometimes get a bit too aggressive. Karl can't get enough of*

*Ruben. For the first time since our firstborn, Karl has learned to change a diaper.*

*I have been following the Iran hostage situation in Tehran. From what I understand, colonial powers have exacerbated many of the problems facing that part of the world, arbitrarily setting borders without any regard to ethnicities.*

"Whoa! It seems to me that Roberta likes to keep up with things. I bet she felt isolated on this farm," Lana paused after the comment. "I sort of feel sorry for her." She leafed through subsequent pages, sipping tea as months in the journal went by.

*August 9, 1981*

*Now that I think back, it didn't take long for me to find out how controlling Karl is in his passive-aggressive way. I have to admit it gets to me sometimes. He continues to express his displeasure at my joining a writers' group at the public library. I never graduated from UW-Madison. Life got in the way. Or was it stupidity? I enjoy the writing group and would hate to have to drop out. I told Karl not to worry; I'm not writing about him. There's too little to write about him, anyway! It doesn't hurt him to stay home with Mathew one night a week. At least I take Ruben with me to the library. He usually sleeps through.*

*Finally! That's all I could say when they announced Sandra Day O'Connor was appointed to the Supreme Court. Maybe we'll see more women on the court over the years.*

*I started Truman Capote's In Cold Blood. I've been meaning to read it since 1966, when it was popular, when I met Karl.*

Lana and Kitty both enjoyed reading about Roberta's life, but they had a clear mission and needed to keep moving.

"This is all very interesting," Lana remarked. "But maybe we can come back and read more about Roberta's life later on. Kitty agreed. Lana continued thumbing through entries about the weather, the corn harvest, and neighborhood gossip while Kitty doodled on the margins of a Chinese take-out menu.

"Wait!" Lana's abrupt exclamation brought Kitty's thoughts back to the farmhouse. "What's this? Listen to this, Kitty!"

*August 18, 1981*

*Just as I expected. I'm pregnant.*

"What?" Kitty dropped the pencil as well as her jaw. Is that it?' Lana turned the page.

*September 21, 1981*

*Karl said nothing when I told him.*

"Go on, Lana," Kitty encouraged from the edge of her chair.

*September 23, 1981*

*He keeps asking me about the money I inherited after both my parents were killed in a car crash in South Dakota. I've told him many times that it wasn't that much since I had to split it with my two living brothers. He's checked out the house, but now he thinks I've hidden some money in the barn. Why would I hide money in the barn? I swear the thing's going to burn down one of these days. The wiring in it is so out of date. He'll never find the money, anyway. He hasn't said anything about the safe. I think he has forgotten about it. But if he does, I'll tell him to go to the basement and check it. Big night tonight, final episode of MASH.*

Lana took off her glasses and massaged the bridge of her nose.

"Want me to take over?" Kitty asked. "How about we just take a break. Step outside, maybe." Lana agreed.

Kitty sat on the tire swing, spinning from side to side. Lana reached for a branch on the apple tree and pulled it down. As she twisted one apple to set it free, two fell to the ground. She swooped them up, rubbed both apples on her top, and gave one to Kitty. The crisp and juicy apples, along with the cool afternoon breeze, were precisely what the two of them needed.

Back in the kitchen, Kitty flipped through a few more pages. "Nothing much here," she whispered as she moved on to the next page.

With their first day of reading the diary fading into Friday evening, Lana made a startling discovery.

"Lana, Lana, look!" Kitty spun the diary around and slid it in front of Lana. "Some pages have been torn out of this diary!" Lana ran her finger along the frayed remnants in the crease of the book. "Yes. You're right. Though it's hard to tell just how many pages she—Lana raised her eyebrows—or someone else tore out."

"Well, I do declare!" Kitty's polished voice and long-honored Southern mannerisms always brought a smile to Lana's face. "This is an added mystery."

"What I suspect," Lana posited, "is that Roberta wrote some things down that she later regretted and tore them out herself. Possibly something about her pregnancy."

"How about we keep searching another time? Virgil will be here soon, and you should be out of here before he returns." Kitty said as she stood to look out the window. "But come back tomorrow morning. Virgil was invited to go camping with the Boy Scouts. They leave early tomorrow and will return late Sunday afternoon. We should be able to accomplish a lot this weekend. Let's start around nine tomorrow." Lana agreed.

# CHAPTER 16

# IF THIS BASEMENT COULD TALK

## Connor's Corner

Roberta Larson rarely let any of her children go down into the basement. "It's too creepy, and I don't want you having nightmares. Besides, there's not much down there for you kids anyway, unless you like spiders, rats, and snakes."

But as Connor got older, he had a reason to go down there. It was his secret, his private spot, under the stairs. He stocked it with a few blankets and a few magazines he got from some of the boys at school. This was where he first discovered the joy of gratifying himself. He tried to time it to coincide with his mother's schedule of activities, usually when she was in the kitchen, preparing a meal or wrapped up in a book. But sometimes he had to take a chance.

It was late on a Saturday night, and Connor hoped his parents would go to bed soon. Once he heard the TV go quiet, he waited until he felt the coast was clear. His three brothers were out of the house until later.

He crept down the stairs in his stocking feet with the lights off and found his way to his private spot under the basement stairs. He dug out some magazines and read them using a flashlight, and began. Connor was about to reach the point of ecstasy when the basement door opened, and the light went on. With the moment ruined, he slid back as far as he could, turned off the flashlight, and tried to control his breathing.

He could see his mother, but she could not see him. She walked over to an old trunk Connor had seen more than once. He had even tried to open it only to discover it was locked. His mother had her diary in one hand and something else in the other hand, something too small for Connor to see. He realized it was a key when she inserted it into the trunk and opened the lid.

She took some old clothes from the trunk and piled them on the floor. She was about to put the diary in the trunk, but stopped. She opened the diary and stared at it for a few seconds, then read the entry aloud. "Finally, he's dead." She turned to the next page and read the entry aloud again. "And buried." Then she put the diary in the trunk, returned the clothes, and put the key on the ledge of the basement window. Thinking his mother was about to go up the stairs, Roberta turned and walked over to the wall opposite Connor.

He scrunched in even farther.

She painstakingly slid a table covered with a bed sheet and piled high with old blankets to the side and placed her purse on top. It was the first time Connor had seen the safe. He could see her hand spinning back and forth and assumed it was a combination safe. Once the safe was open, she grabbed a sock from inside the safe, reached into her purse to retrieve a wad of money, and stuffed the money into the sock. After she closed the door, she spun the dial on the safe, grabbed her purse, walked up the stairs, and turned off the light.

Connor sat alone in the dark; his mood was gone. He knew the entry was about his father, but had so many questions. *Why would she write finally? Did his father want to die? Was his mother counting the days, hoping he would die soon? Why would she want him dead?*

Connor knew the answer to his last question. He waited a few minutes and quietly crept up the stairs. He opened the door slowly and only wide enough to get a sense of the situation. Seeing nothing but darkness, he turned his ear to the opening. The humming of the refrigerator was all he could hear. There was nothing else for him to do but go to bed.

# CHAPTER 17

# A CLUE

## Safe and Sound

Lana stopped at the Saturday farmer's market before meeting Kitty. She bought some sweet corn and some fingerling potatoes. When she arrived at the farm, she found Kitty sitting in the tire swing, spinning around and around with her iPhone on speaker mode. Lana recognized Robie's voice in the background.

Kitty's back was facing Lana as she approached. They were talking about Sally. When Kitty spun around and saw Lana, she quickly changed the subject.

"I know, I miss you too. I should be back in a couple of days."

"I got a surprise for you when you get here." Robie almost sang the words.

"Oh, a surprise. I love surprises, well, most of the time at least." They ended the call with I love you.

Kitty and Lana went inside and headed for the kitchen, which they now called the reading room.

"Kitty, can't you clear off this table?" Lana asked as she picked up a plate containing a half-eaten burrito and handed it to Kitty. "I need some elbow room. And I don't want to sit next to a bean burrito." It had already become apparent to Lana that Kitty's housekeeping skills were rudimentary at best, as for most of her life, staff saw to such matters.

Lana scanned several pages without reading anything aloud while Kitty moved a few items from the table and tried to find room for them on an already crowded counter. But that changed when Lana blurted, "Oh, my God, what have we here? Listen to this!" Lana was now standing, holding the diary with the reverence of a rabbi cradling a Torah. With an ethereal voice, Lana read the entry.

*June 30, 2002*

*"Safe and sound and blanketed down. Numbers are posted, not easily found."*

"What? That's it?" Kitty irritably asked. "Read it again."
Lana repeated the entry.
"What is the date of the entry?" Kitty asked.
"June 30, 2002," Lana replied.
"Let's go. We're going down." Lana scooped up the diary and headed for the stairs.
"I think 'blanketed down' is the key phrase here," Lana concluded. They both began their search for blankets.
"Look at this, Lana, under these stairs. Look at those blankets and old magazines. You don't suppose someone once slept down here." Kitty gave Lana a frightful glance as she said it.
"Connor said he tried to avoid his parents as much as he could. Maybe he hid down here," Lana said. "But I highly doubt that Connor would have slept down here. He likes his creature comforts now, and I bet he did back then, too," Lana reassured a still bewildered Kitty.
They removed the blankets, shook them out, but saw nothing.
"These are girly magazines," Kitty blithely said as she thumbed through one of them.
"I guess we now know what Connor did down here," Lana chortled with a mischievous wink.
Kitty kicked the blankets back under the stairs, so as not to have to touch them with her hands.

"What's that?" Kitty chirped as she pointed to something she'd never seen before.

"That's an old-fashioned wringer washing machine. They ran the wet clothes through the wringer before they hung the clothes up to dry, usually on a clothesline," Lana replied.

"How primitive!" Kitty concluded, picturing a maid as she transferred the wet laundry to the dryer. Still puzzled by the workings of the washing machine, Kitty tried to roll the wringer with her index finger.

## Ta-da

"I'll tell you what, Kitty. How about if you go to the left and I'll go to the right, and we can keep on circling the entire basement from the outside to the center?" Kitty consented to the strategy.

"But be careful," Lana warned. "Watch out for broken glasses, hidden wires, and rusty or sharp objects." Lana paused. "Not to mention snakes, rats, or mice."

Kitty froze, wrapping her arms around herself as her expansive eyes circled in all directions.

"Don't worry, Kitty. Snakes and rats are more afraid of us than we are of them."

"Speak for yourself, Lana. Let's get this over with and get the heck out of here," Kitty shuddered. "This place gives me the willies." Kitty brushed imaginary cooties off her arms and legs as she said it.

After searching for a few minutes, Lana said, "Kitty, over here. I got something."

Kitty bounded over boxes and wove through other hazards as she eagerly welcomed the opportunity to edge in close to another human being.

"What?" Kitty saw nothing of interest.

"Well, what do you see? Lana asked.

" I don't see anything." Kitty narrowed her eyes while she tried to zone in on a detail she was missing.

Lana stood by an old table that sat against the west wall of the basement. A large blanket hung over the table, and a pile of old blankets and quilts lay next to it.

Finally, seeing what appeared to be table legs, Kitty ventured a sketchy guess. "Could be a table covered with something, a blanket, maybe."

"Are you ready, Kitty?" With eyebrows raised, Lana eagerly awaited Kitty's response. Kitty scrunched her face together, "Ready for what?"

Lana pinched the center of the blanket where it hung in front of the table. "Ladies and gentlemen. Now, for your viewing pleasure," Lana announced as she slowly pulled up the front of the dark blue blanket—a velvet curtain rising on a Broadway stage.

"Oh, geez! Honestly, Lana. Do you have to be so dramatic?" Kitty groaned.

"Kitty, help me move this heavy steel table," Lana pleaded with a strained face from trying it alone. Once the table was moved, Kitty finally saw the star of the show.

"It's the safe!" Kitty exclaimed, throwing out her arms as if she were going to hug it.

Lana crouched as she moved closer to the cast-iron relic object that stood in front of the scarred basement wall. She ran her right finger over the spiral gold trim that accented the square York Safe & Lock Co. creation, imagining that the safe itself would be worth some money.

The T-shaped door handle was silver, as was the dial. Two thick, formidable hinges secured the heavy door to the safe, two armored sentinels challenging unwanted intruders. The safe was held off the floor by four metal wheels that protested loudly when Lana tried to move it.

"This is a thing of beauty," Lana whispered in awe.

## Something Vaguely Familiar

"Well, I would say the part about 'safe' has been solved. And I bet numbers means the combination," Lana deduced. "But posted? As in a letter, maybe?"

They both continued looking around the basement while repeating the word *posted*.

Kitty lifted an object from the floor. It looked like an alien spaceship. "What's this contraption?" she asked as she held it up for Lana to see.

"That's an old hair dryer. There should be a hose and a plastic bonnet nearby. That is, if you're in need of a hair dryer." Lana heard the object hit the floor and concluded that was Kitty's response.

"The only thing I can come up with is that there are posts down here, holding up the floor above. Could that have something to do with it?" Lana thought aloud.

"It's better than anything else we got, I'd say." Kitty started circling the basement, looking at the posts. "I see markings on a few of these posts. This one's got Connor's name on it. And that one over there by you has a name on it, too."

Lana turned to look closer and then began walking around. "These posts have names etched into them, too," Lana observed as she rubbed her fingers over the names. "These are chalk markings and must be their children's heights over the years."

"Posted? Numbers?" Kitty was onto something. "Etched? Could Connor's mother have etched the combination into one of these posts?" And then they heard the front door open. They ran up the stairs two at a time and came face to face with Virgil at the top of the stairs.

"What were you two doing in the basement?" Virgil shot them a puzzled gaze. He had a feeling he knew Lana from somewhere, but couldn't quite place her. *Why was the woman whose tire he changed visiting Kitty?* "Well?" Virgil's eyes moved between the two as he waited for an answer.

Kitty responded, "I just wanted to show Lana that trunk you have your eye on down there. She knows a lot about antiques. She thinks it's beyond any attempt to refurbish it without a great deal of expense."

"But how is it you two—"

"Thanks for inviting me over, Kitty. I hope we can get together again sometime," Lana said as the screen door slammed behind her.

"What happened with the camping trip?" Kitty asked Virgil.

"I got it wrong. It's next weekend. When I showed up at Jason's house, they were all having breakfast, he explained. "They had a good laugh and invited me to join them. Jason's dad then offered me a day job helping around the farm."

"That was neighborly of him," Kitty dryly replied, realizing that Virgil wouldn't be gone all weekend.

"They want me over again tomorrow. If that's OK with you."

Kitty hid her relief. "I suppose."

## He Really Did That?

The next morning, Lana left her house and drove out of town to the sound of church bells ringing in every direction. She pulled up close to the back door of the farmhouse and found it locked. Knocking gently, thinking Kitty was probably in the kitchen, she waited, then knocked again, this time louder. Still nothing. She descended the steps and pushed her way through a patch of cottony milkweeds. In front of the kitchen window, she cupped her hands around her eyes and peered inside. Seeing nothing, she retreated, brushing milkweed floss from her sweater.

Lana went around to the front of the house and banged on the battered screen door. When she saw that the door was ajar, she walked through the porch and into the living room.

"Kittyyyy, Viiirgil, it's Laaana," she yelled just as Kitty was coming into the room, holding a stack of clothes.

"Kitty, where have you been? I've been knocking and yelling for I don't know how long?" Lana complained.

"I was upstairs going through some closets. I need some warmer clothes. I found several flannel shirts and this sweatshirt I'm wearing. Of course, none of it goes with my things. And I've never heard of the designers Croft and Barrow. I just want to be warm, that's all. What's in the bag?"

"I brought some sandwiches for lunch. You should put them in the refrigerator."

Lana followed Kitty into the kitchen, where Kitty put the sandwiches in the nearly empty refrigerator. Lana sat at the table, and Kitty grabbed the diary.

Kitty solemnly opened the diary, as if it were the Torah, as if it contained all the answers to all the questions that plagued mankind.

"Come on, Kitty, lose the melodrama," Lana impatiently suggested.

"Well, Lana, you're not the only one who appreciates a little drama," Kitty smirked.

Kitty opened the diary and paged through a few entries before something caught her eye.

*September 15, 1995*

*The crazy old fool did it, he burned down the barn. Fortunately, he had the good sense to put the animals out to pasture. He said he found some money in the barn and that was proof enough that I was hiding money there. So, he burned down the barn because if he couldn't have the money, neither could I.*

*I watched it burn from the steps on the back of the house. Connor saw the whole thing from his bedroom window. Imagine a fourteen-year-old boy having to witness such an event!*

*A car pulled into the driveway soon after the fire started. It was Wally's squad car. He must have been patrolling the area. He got out of his car and walked towards Karl, who still had that red can in his hand. The entire scene was eerie as the flames churned into a thunderous vortex, spewing out sparks that either fell to the ground or disappeared into dark. The crackling of the flames was occasionally interrupted by the plaintive moans of the barn defenselessly surrendered to the ravenous blaze like a row of crashing dominoes.*

*But it was his face, Karl's face as he looked at me, a dichotomy of spite, one side illuminated in orange and the other side black as the night. Karl yelled something at Wally, which I gathered was a threat because Wally backed away slowly. By then, the fire department arrived.*

"What? He burned down his own barn?" Kitty asked in disbelief. "I've seen what's left of it but never imagined that Karl did that himself. Poor Connor, imagine having to witness something like that."

"He told me about that one time," Lana recalled. "What surprised him the most was his mother's indifference to the whole thing. Of course, since Karl set the fire himself, the insurance wouldn't pay anything. That's when Connor finally realized he needed to get off that farm as soon as he graduated from high school."

They quickly thumbed through several pages of the diary, now more adept at wading through minutiae. Kitty halted the process when they came to what she thought might be something important.

*October 10, 1998*

*We got sad news today, well, I did at least. My parents were both killed in a tragic car crash yesterday. They are still working on the cause of the crash, so that's all I know so far. They were on their way to visit my father's brother in South Dakota. Too much death in this family. First, my oldest brother, David, died from leukemia. He was only fourteen. Then Lennie, my favorite, was killed in a hit-and-run accident in Des Moines. My parents were devastated by his death. Well, so was I. It was my only living brother, Willard, who called me about the accident. He's still in Wyoming. He and his son Willy, who is an attorney, will see to the arrangements. We'll deal with the estate issues when I get there. Karl says he can't go to Wyoming with me because of the harvest. Just as well, I'd rather go alone, anyway. I've decided to take the bus. I wish I could make it a one-way trip.*

"Lana, let's slow down and follow this story. It might lead to something important." In an effort to humor an increasingly apathetic Kitty, Lana flipped the page to the next entry and read it aloud.

*October 11, 1998*

*I leave for Wyoming in two days. I can't wait to get out of here, to get the hell out of here. I now only have Connor in my life as his siblings have lives of their own.*

*October 15, 1998*

*I got back from Wyoming two days ago, back to Karl and the misery he sows. I tried to stay away as long as I could but knew I would have to return sometime. So here I am. While I was gone, he got into it with the Amish family down the road. It bugs him that they go around in horse-drawn carts. He'll often speed up as he passes them and lays on the horn. Apparently, they followed him home this time and suggested that what he does is dangerous, not only to him, but to them as well. The fact that they remained calm and respectful bugged him more than the fact that they even stopped. I can just imagine him raging at them.*

*Actually, I don't have to imagine. I've seen it many times. He is never physically violent with me because he knows I can handle myself. Now he has been following me around, asking about my inheritance. I told him it hasn't been settled yet.*

*I see they finally freed those prisoners in Iran. It was a gift to Ronald Reagan, some say. Could be.*

Lana stuck a napkin between the pages and closed the diary. "Kitty, we need a break."

They sat at the picnic as they ate the steamed sweet corn and roasted fingerling potatoes seasoned with fresh rosemary Kitty had found in the garden the day before. Neither was in the mood for conversation, so they quietly enjoyed the sounds of the farm, at least for the most part.

"I am so sick of that screeching thing spinning around back there. If I had my druthers, I'd turn the damned thing off." Kitty complained.

"Kitty, it's a windmill. You don't turn it off. You climb up it and oil the gears."

Kitty reeled back and gave Lana the bewildered look of a lost person in a foreign-speaking country.

Back at the kitchen table, Lana continued what had become a laborious drudgery for the two treasure hunters.

"Why didn't that old biddy just put the money in a safety deposit box, or something, and give Connor the key? I'm getting worn slap out." Kitty followed her moan with the longest yawn Lana had ever heard.

Suddenly, Lana blurted out. "Kitty, listen to this!"

*"Down and up, cozy and warm, right down here, on the farm.*

"And there's no date."

Lana slid the diary across the kitchen table for Kitty to read the passage. After a minute of processing the passage, Lana grabbed the diary, stood up, and started for the basement. Kitty painstakingly pushed herself out of the chair and stumbled behind Lana.

Once in the basement, Lana read the clue again. "So, now we are down. Do we go back up? Are we supposed to go back up again? Maybe there is something along the stairway." Lana led Kitty back up the stairs, both looking around for something, anything. But there was nothing. They went back down to the basement.

Kitty read the clue again. "So, we're down again. Is that old woman toying with us? Now what?" Kitty let out a gasp of air and dropped her shoulders in defeat.

"Down and up. I wonder if we should be looking upward, toward the ceiling," Lana wondered aloud. They began walking around looking above the messy basement, which was festooned with cobwebs, littered with rodent droppings, and cluttered with a lifetime of detritus.

Suddenly, Kitty stopped. "Lana, look over here."

Lana went over to where Kitty was pointing—to a wooden beam in the far corner of the basement.

"It looks like a bunch of numbers." Lana was excited. She took her phone out of her pocket and pressed the flashlight app.

"It's instructions on how to open the safe. But it's only one set. Safes usually have at least three sets, maybe four. I used to help my dad open his safe, which never really had much in it except for important papers." Lana explained.

"My father has a wall safe, probably more than one," Kitty said. "Who knows?"

"Kitty, run upstairs and find some paper and a pencil."

All Kitty could find in the kitchen was the take-out menu from a local Chinese restaurant. They would have to write the numbers in the margins, alongside her doodles and the circled numbers of her choices.

Lana wrote the numbers on the menu, then they walked over to the safe, and Lana tried the numbers. Just as Lana expected, they needed more.

"Cozy and warm." Kitty had it memorized. They began to look around once again. "Lana, this is getting tedious."

"Kitty, this is your gap year. Be adventurous! Cozy and warm, I think I have it. You check the hot water heater, and I'll check the furnace area. Be sure to look carefully and go over everything more than once."

Lana was scanning the furnace and its surroundings when she almost ran into a shelf of empty pickle jars close by. She stared at them, amazed at how many empty ones there were.

"Wait a minute, Kitty. Come here. I might have something," Lana cried.

"It's a pickle jar, Lana. You called me over here for a pickle jar. An empty one at that?"

"It may seem empty from where you stand, but it's not. There's a wad of paper inside." Lana removed the paper and smoothed it out.

Kitty watched impatiently, eager for it to be the rest of the combination.

"It's another set of numbers and instructions. But we still need more. Did you find anything around the hot water heater, Kitty?"

"No, but I wasn't done looking." They both went over to the water heater and searched the area from different angles. Nothing.

"Kitty, these old farmhouses originally burned wood for heat." Lana thought out loud.

"Earlier, I saw a door that looked like it might lead to another room," Kitty recalled. "It was behind, humm, let me think. It was behind that tall shelf over there, next to that, that, whatever that metal thing is sticking out of the wall."

"That's an old coal chute. Let's move that empty shelf and see what's behind it." Lana suggested. They opened the door and found a vintage pot-belly stove.

Lana opened the door where the wood or coal would have gone. "Kitty, open your flashlight and shine it in here." Nothing.

Lana tried the lower door, where the ashes would have collected. Kitty shone her flashlight into the dark area. "There's something in there," Lana said. She reached in and took out a sheet of lined paper from a third-grade handwriting class. Written in crayon and with some of the characters backward, they discovered two more sets of instructions.

With four sets of instructions, Lana was confident they had what they needed to open the safe.

## Permutations

Neither Lana nor Kitty had any idea of the correct order of instructions, which was necessary to open the safe.

"Kitty, let's go upstairs. I got an idea," Lana announced as she headed for the stairs.

"We need a clean sheet of paper and some scissors, Kitty. Have you seen anything like that around here?" Lana said as she shuffled through a stack of papers on the kitchen counter.

"I think I know where we might find some paper. In Roberta's desk, in the bedroom." Kitty bolted out of the kitchen to verify her hunch.

"Check for some scissors too," Lana hollered.

Kitty returned to the kitchen, paging through a spiral notebook with a pair of scissors dangling on her thumb.

"This must have been a notebook for one of the Larson boys. It looks like notes from a history class," Kitty observed.

Lana tore a sheet of paper out of the notebook and cut it in quarters the long way. "Ok, Kitty, now read me one set of instructions at a time, it doesn't matter in what order, but go slowly." Kitty wasn't sure what Lana's strategy was, but she went along.

"Here's the first one," Kitty said. "Turn right, stopping when fourteen comes the fourth time to mark at the top of the dial."

Kitty repeated it, Lana read it back, and then continued until they had four strips of paper with four sets of instructions.

"Now's the hard part," Lana forewarned, and she waved for Kitty to follow her into the basement.

Once there, Lana prepared Kitty for the next step. "This might take a while. I'm not sure of the order of these sets of numbers," Lana explained. "Find something for me to sit down on. Also, something for you."

Kitty retrieved the wooden crate from earlier and then spotted an old wooden floor stereo speaker. She flipped it on its side and kicked across the rough basement floor with little concern for the particleboard that housed the speaker.

Lana chose the speaker since it was a bit lower than the crate. "Now relax, Kitty, and don't distract me. There are various permutations at play here."

"Perma...whats?" Kitty asked.

"Permutations. It means the variations in which a set of numbers can be ordered."

"Thanks for the lesson, Hypatia," Kitty remarked.

Lana turned her attention from the safe to Kitty. "I am impressed you know who Hypatia is, Kitty."

"I did an extra-credit report on her in a high school math class. I needed all the extra credit I could get in that class. I was more into art, English, and history. And horses and boys. In that order."

Kitty slid the crate closer to watch as Lana tried various permutations while keeping an ear tilted toward the dial. She sat on the crate, twining her hair with her fingers as Lana spun the dial, their twirling motions in sync. *Click.* Their unblinking eyes met as the grin on their luminous faces widened.

"Go ahead, Kitty. You do the honors."

Kitty blew on her fingertips and rubbed her hands together with a fiendish sneer on her face. She leaned in and edged her right hand toward the handle, as if the handle might be hot. Finally, she grabbed the handle and steadily turned it one trifling millimeter at a time.

*Thump, Thump. Thump, Thump.* The pounding in her ears was all she could hear. Her eyes grew wider as her lips grew tighter. *Snap.* The door disengaged from its frame. Kitty dragged the door open, as one would on a heavy door on a large safe at Fort Knox.

"Bravo!" Lana applauded. "Three cheers for Kitty. Two for opening the door and one for the best supporting actress role in a basement drama."

Kitty stood and bowed. "I'd like to thank—"

Their unrestrained laughter was fueled by the relief of finally accomplishing their goal.

## A Stocking Discovery

"Socks?" Kitty cried. "Socks? All this work for a pile of socks?" Kitty's outburst made Lana laugh.

"Let's have a look," Lana calmly suggested.

Lana grabbed one sock and felt that there was something inside it. "This sock is stuffed with something." And she was right. It was stuffed with something, and that something was money, bills of several denominations, but mostly of C-notes.

"Kitty, flip over that crate. And find another container, a box, whatever. Anything to help us carry this money upstairs."

*This was so Lana,* Kitty thought, *always in control.*

Kitty squealed in excitement as she hustled around the basement until she found a box of books. She dumped the books on the floor with no regard for them.

"I'll be right back," Kitty called out as she headed for the stairs. When she came back down, she was wearing a pair of latex kitchen gloves.

"No way am I going to touch those filthy socks," she declared. "Here, I brought a pair for you." She held the pair of gloves out to Lana.

"Too late, now," Lana held up her dusty hand, spreading her fingers wide.

The two worked in tandem as they removed the socks, turned them inside out, and tossed the bills into the box and crate, high on a euphoria that comes when anticipation finally reaps its reward.

The empty socks were cast aside and accumulated next to the safe.

"It's hard to tell, but this looks like a lot of money. Why she hid the money in socks is beyond me. But thank you, Roberta!" Lana was picking up the pace as adrenaline pulsed through her bloodstream.

"Yes, thank you, Roberta Larson!" Kitty echoed Lana's gratitude. "What a woman! Stashing all this money from her husband. And now it's ours, well, not all of it."

"Well, that's it, that's all of it," Lana surmised, slapping her palms together. "But just in case, let's take one last look." Lana got down on her hands and knees and felt around the inside of the safe. As she lifted herself off the floor, she saw something sticking out from under the safe.

"I found something, Kitty."

Lana held up the large, sealed envelope. Since it was not addressed to anyone in particular, she opened it.

"My, my. What have we here?" she asked as she removed several sheets of paper from the envelope.

"What is it?" Kitty asked.

"It looks like sheets of clues. Yes, that's what it is. This must be some, if not all, of the clues Connor's mother gave him for his treasure hunts." Lana handed a few sheets to Kitty.

Lana set the envelope on top of the safe, grabbed the crate filled with money, and started up the stairs. Kitty grabbed the cardboard box that held the overflow. They climbed the stairs with the spirit of pirates, ready to present their treasures to their faraway king. They stopped before reaching the top. Kitty peeked around the door.

"The coast is clear."

"We might need a calculator," Lana announced as they approached the reading room.

Kitty searched for her iPhone until she found it under the sofa. Lana organized the bills by denominations.

Fortunately, Roberta had bundled the hundred-dollar bills into packets of fifty, binding them with paper strips she had cut from brown paper bags and glue. Those alone totaled $700,800.00. After sorting out the other bills, Lana counted them while Kitty watched in suspense, her tongue jutting out between her teeth. Kitty wrote down the total.

"I think we should count it again," Lana suggested.

Lana counted the money again but came up with a different total. After another try, which matched the second total.

Let's go with that," Lana suggested.

Kitty emphatically announced the results aloud. "$1,248,000."

"Let's put the money back in the safe and lock it," Lana proposed. They went down into the basement and tucked the money back into the safe. Lana closed the door and gave the dial several spins.

"There," Lana said. "You have the safe, and I have the combination. And neither of us can do anything without the other."

"Did you get those lines from a movie or something?" Kitty asked, partially in jest. "They sound like a Hollywood script. And besides, neither of us has any reason to mistrust the other."

They ascended the stairs slowly, believing it would be their penultimate climb.

"Lana, I have some leftover Chinese in the fridge. Care to join me?"

"I don't mind if I do!" Lana emphatically accepted the offer.

Kitty prepared the food, and Lana set the table. The afternoon sun was low, and it cast an eerie glow through the kitchen windows. Kitty turned on the kitchen light to mitigate the effect. They nibbled slowly at their food and spoke very little.

"You know, this house creeps me out. Especially when Virgil's not here." Kitty said as she expertly rolled Mu Shu Pork into a lettuce wrap.

"Believe me, I know what it's like. At least you have Virgil. I had to spend an entire night here by myself," Lana reminded Kitty.

"I'm just scared, Lana," Kitty's voice cracked. "Scared of this, this creepy basement, this house, and what happens, what comes next. I'll be in limbo when this is over."

"Relax, Kitty. When we're done here, you can go back to Robie. He'll ask you to marry him, and you'll say yes. Granted, he's not the polished Rhett Butler type, but he is a gentleman, and he won't run out on you."

The lettuce wrap slipped through Kitty's fingers as she started to cry. Lana slid the napkin rack across the table. Kitty dabbed her eyes with a napkin, noticing the dark smudges on it when she finished.

"Kitty, lean over the table and let me take care of that mascara on your face." As Lana wiped Kitty's face, Kitty recalled something from their past.

"Remember when you raided your mom's makeup bag and gave me a full makeover? She said I looked like a hooker. But I was too young to know what that meant." They both burst into hearty laughter.

"What was worse is that when I got home, I asked my mother what a hooker was," Kitty howled, sparking even more boisterous laughter. After the laughter died down, Kitty's eyes drifted into a dreamy million-mile gaze into space.

Lana let the silence be.

"I hope what you said about Robie is true. And yes, I will say "Yes. Katherine Azalea Barrington Campbell. Katherine Campbell." Kitty returned to earth. "Thanks for cheering me up, Lana."

"No problem. I just hope you don't start writing your new name over and over on notebook paper in pink ink, dotting your 'i' with a heart," Lana bantered with a roguish grin.

"As if?" Kitty rolled her eyes.

Kitty looked at the teapot-shaped white plastic kitchen clock on the wall.

"Lana, you should get going. It's late, I can clean up the kitchen."

Lana put on her coat, grabbed her purse, and started walking away.

"But be careful driving home, Lana. Virgil says that this is the time of the year when deer pop out at night. In fact, where is he? I would think he'd be here by now." Kitty looked at the clock again, went over to the window, held the curtain back, and looked out.

"Don't worry, Kitty. I have the impression Virgil can take care of himself," Lana affirmed.

On the drive home, Lana concluded that her future would likely be less romantic than Kitty's and even more uncertain.

# CHAPTER 18

# KITTY COMES CLEAN

It was a sunny Monday morning, and Kitty was alone. Virgil wanted to go fishing one last time before he took the bus back to Chattanooga later that morning. Lana stopped for a brief visit and was happy to hear that Virgil would leave soon.

"I can't stay long today, Kitty. I need to pack for our departure. You probably should, too," Lana suggested.

"Finally, I can get out of this hell-hole," Kitty asserted.

"I'm driving to LaCrosse today. One of the wheels on my large suitcase broke off. I needed a new suitcase, anyway. So, I'll see you tomorrow," Lana informed Kitty on her way out the door.

While Lana was saying goodbye to Kitty, Edna was cleaning up the lunch dishes when she glanced at the calendar on the kitchen wall.

"It's been five days now, almost five days, and still nothing from Wally," Edna complained to Lester, who sat at the kitchen table. "I'm going out there!"

Lester peered over his crossword puzzle. "Out where?"

"My brother's old place. I'm going out there, and don't try to stop me."

"I wasn't planning to," Lester muttered. "This time, pick up some apple cider. But, before you go, what's a six-letter word for lazy?"

"That would be Lester, L E S T E R," Edna remarked without skipping a beat.

Lester yawned, "No, it has to have a 'p' in it."

Twenty minutes later, Kitty saw a jet-black Cadillac pull into the driveway. The car had barely stopped when a woman jumped out, slammed the door, and strode determinedly up to her front door. The front door was open, so she vigorously rapped on the metal screen door leading to the porch. With the side of her fist, Edna pounded on the pitiful door.

Kitty was rattled by the unexpected visitor and the aggressive knocking. She tiptoed into the living room, but paused when she saw the hawkish stance of the glaring redhead.

"I see you," Edna called out.

Kitty shuffled closer to the door but paused again when she was still two feet away. "Yes? What is it?" All that stood between Kitty and the woman with her hair on fire on the other side of an inch-thick 25-pound aluminum door. Kitty frantically looked around the living room, as if she could defend herself with a sofa pillow or an Afghan anyway.

"I'll tell you what it is," Edna bellowed as she yanked open the locked door and stormed in. Kitty jumped back, folded her arms into her chest, and yelled, "What the—"

"Just who are you, anyway?" Edna's clipped question caught Kitty off guard.

"I'm, um, I'm Kitty," her voice floundered." I'm staying here until the son of the previous owners shows up," she replied. "And by the way, you just broke into this house, that's breaking and entering, and I just might call the police," Kitty snipped.

Edna ignored the threat. "Why?" "For how long?" "Which son?" "What's his name?" Edna peppered an alarmed Kitty, who was gradually backing away into the kitchen.

"Connor. Connor Larson." Kitty was dumbfounded by Edna's lack of decorum.

Edna needed further confirmation. "Connor, you say? Blond or brunette?"

"I wouldn't know, I've never seen him. But I know he grew up here; his parents were Karl and Roberta. I also know he works for 3M."

"Where's Connor now?" Edna snarled.

"He's in, um, Belgium, from what I understand. He's supposed to be here either at the end of the month or early October. If you'd like to stop by then," Kitty suggested in a slow and easy mellifluous tone that would have made her mother proud.

"I doubt it. I'm here on business!" Edna shook her bony finger at Kitty. "My brother and his family lived in this house for a lifetime. Connor is my nephew. He told me once that his mother kept a diary in a trunk in the basement. I'm here to get it before it's too late." Edna bombarded Kitty with her bluster, leaving her defenseless on the front line.

"But, if it's not *your* diary," Kitty patronized Edna with a righteous nose in the air. "Then what makes you think —"

"I need to see that trunk, and I need to see it now!" Edna's gritty face protruded, driving Kitty steadily backward in retreat.

Kitty's iPhone chirped, but she let it go to voicemail. She'd call Robie back later.

"And I'm here to make sure that diary doesn't end up in the wrong hands," Edna declared. "Someone like yours, maybe?"

"Well, I don't know anything about that. Like I said, I'm just staying here temporarily. But if you want to go down into the basement, feel free. I've never been down there." Kitty's demure attitude did little to check Edna's unrelenting pluck.

Other than her most recent break-in, Edna had only been in the basement a few times.

Kitty followed her down the stairs and, with a smug look on her face, watched as Edna rubbed her hand on the ledge below the basement window.

"Where's the key? It's not here." Edna, of course, knew it was too late for a key. Grabbing an abandoned tablecloth, she wiped the dust off her hand.

"I have no idea. What key?" Kitty's mouth remained open as she held her hands out and shrugged in surrender.

Edna went over to the trunk and examined the lock with her fingertips. "This lock has been jimmied. Who did that?" Edna dropped her jaw, letting her mouth hang open in a sham look of dismay.

Kitty nervously paced the floor, pausing occasionally to fidget with whatever she could find to distract her. She wished Lana were there. She glanced at the stairs.

Edna hauled the clothes out of the trunk by the armfuls and tossed them onto the floor. When she finally got to the bottom, she saw there was no dairy in the trunk. She sifted through the pile of clothes on the floor.

"It's gone. I want it!" Edna demanded.

"What's gone?" Kitty's contrived innocence only made Edna more impatient.

"The diary!" Edna yelled. "My sister-in-law's diary! Don't try to play dumb with me!" Edna moved in on Kitty as she lashed out.

Kitty needed to do something, to be strong, like her father would want her to be.

"I don't know who you really are or if what you're saying is even true, but if you don't leave right now, I'm calling the cops," Kitty threatened in a commanding voice she never knew she had.

Edna was not intimidated. "You just go right ahead and do that. Here, use my phone. Wally is the chief, and I have him listed in my favorites." She held out her phone in mockery.

While she waited to see if Kitty would accept her offer, Edna scanned the basement and soon spotted the safe. "Well, well. What have we here?" Edna walked over to the safe and pulled the latch. "Locked. I might have known," she muttered to herself.

Kitty's eyes again darted to the stairs, hoping to see Lana swooping down them to rescue her. Edna could see the strain in Kitty's sagging shoulders and downcast eyes.

Sensing Kitty's vulnerable state, Edna seized the moment. "Honey, how old are you? I'm guessing eighteen, or even seventeen. I think you're in over your head."

Kitty started to whimper. "It wasn't my idea. I'm just helping."

Edna waited for Kitty to collect herself.

"What's your name, again?"

"Kitty."

Edna's head tilted. "Kitty, why don't you just tell me what this is all about. I think you'll feel a lot better," Edna said, softening her harsh tone to that of a caring grandmother.

Kitty wrestled with Edna's suggestion as Edna stood silent.

"Oh, well, why not?" Kitty said. "What does it matter at this point, anyway?"

Edna moved closer to Kitty and put her hand on Kitty's shoulder. "Go ahead, honey," she whispered. Edna had seen the good-cop-bad-cop routine many times on her crime shows.

"Connor and his brothers want to sell the farm. When their mother died, her will made no mention of the money in the safe," Kitty explained. "Connor sent Lana here to find the diary his mother kept. The diary had clues on how to open the safe. Lana invited me along. We found the diary, figured out the clues, and opened the safe." Kitty slumped, letting out a torrent of distress in a sustained sigh of relief.

Edna gave Kitty time to catch her breath.

"So, who is this Lana you mentioned?" the good cop asked. "And where is she?"

"She rented a house in town. Connor convinced her to do this for him. She's the one who dragged me into it." Kitty's frazzled nerves were beginning to calm down, her shaky voice fading away.

"Well, well. Connor wants to steal from his brothers. But why didn't Connor just come and do what you two did himself? Edna asked.

"Apparently, Connor knows that it might take some time to go through the diary and find the clues. He planned to do it before they sold the farm, but his company sent him to Belgium at the last minute." Edna knew she could easily verify that with a mere phone call.

"What made Connor believe there was even money in the safe?" Edna asked.

"Again, I only know what Lana's told me. Apparently, he saw his mother stuffing money into socks and putting them in the safe. I don't know how he managed to see all that. His brothers only *suspect* there is money in the safe." Kitty, a cusp away from hyperventilating, closed the trunk and sat down on it, folding her hands between her legs and vacantly gazing at the basement floor.

"I guess that explains the pile of socks," Edna snickered. "But why didn't Connor just get the money when he was here for his mother's funeral?"

Kitty answered without making eye contact with Edna. "I've told you all I know. This was all Connor's idea. Lana just asked me to help her get the money out of the house and wait for Connor's arrival. So, I did." Defeated, Kitty made a simple request. "Please leave," she pleaded.

Edna wasn't quite finished. "There's more to all this than you know. Let me help you get out of this, what I call, a leaky operation. I think you're being used, and when all is said and done, those two will drop you like a used condom."

Kitty cringed at Edna's analogy. "Lana would never do that; we're cousins," Kitty glowered at Edna's accusation.

"Well, if brothers can steal money from each other, then so can cousins."

Kitty flinched at Edna's accusatory analogy.

"You know, Kitty, I'm only thinking of you. Why don't you just show me the money? And maybe we can come up with a way for you to fix all this." Edna's soothing tone swaddled Kitty into a state of reprieve.

"I can't show you the money. We put it back in the safe and locked it. Lana has the combination with her." Kitty held her breath while Edna said nothing.

"I'll be back tomorrow. Make sure Lana's here," Edna demanded as she stabbed the air with three fingers pointed at Kitty. Edna waddled as she climbed the stairs, hoisting herself with her left hand on the precarious handrail.

Once Edna had gone, Kitty, depleted of energy, poured herself an orange juice and collapsed onto the living room sofa, releasing a puff of dust into the air. She sat in complete silence, her right leg bouncing up and down. *Was Lana really using her? Would she ditch her and leave her with nothing? She had to admit, this Lana wasn't the same one she practically grew up with,* she concluded.

She was never so happy to see Virgil when he came in the door moments later, holding four trout on a string in front of an endless grin.

# CHAPTER 19

# HURRICANE EDNA

## Enough Is Enough

Even though it was Tuesday, it felt like a dreary Monday to Edna. With the sun rising later each morning, it was easy to linger in bed. A late sunrise, obfuscated by dark clouds and rain, just wasn't Edna's kind of day.

She sat at the kitchen table, on her third cup of coffee, and was still waking up. Patty and Paige, her two cats, were bewildered by her pensive mood—usually, she was banging and clanging around the kitchen, driving them as far away from the kitchen as possible. They turned their attention to Lester, who came through the back door with a carton of orange juice.

"I had to go to the Stop and Rob." That was his supposedly humorous name for the convenience store on Spring Street. "We were out of orange juice, so I got some." He plopped the carton onto the counter to accentuate his aggravation at having to leave the house so early, especially on such a nasty day. "You don't look so good. Something wrong?" he grunted.

Knowing that was about as sympathetic as Lester could be, Edna merely sighed, her classic prelude to what would follow. "Oh, nothing, just a little tired," Edna yawned. "I didn't sleep so well last night. I fell asleep on the couch and never made it up to bed."

But Edna was not on the couch all night. Instead of parking her car in the garage, she had parked it down the street and around the corner. After peeking in on Lester to make sure he was asleep, she eased out the back door and made her way to her black Cadillac, the one she called Raven.

Edna saw Kitty's car at Wanda's Wasteland but drove on by. She parked behind the abandoned warehouse next to Wanda's in case someone saw her very noticeable car and mentioned it to Lester. Edna could never remember the warehouse ever being used for anything other than a place where local teenagers had their first smoke, their first kiss, and their first whatever they call it nowadays. She smiled as she remembered her first, and it was everything but a cigarette.

A few heads turned when Edna walked in, and a couple nodded. Edna ignored them and headed for the table.

"I'll have a bourbon on the rocks. Make it a double and not the cheap stuff." Edna folded her arms and muttered to herself as she watched with contempt as the scantily dressed waitress bounced her way back to the bar, muttering to herself. Edna was scandalized by the current fashion. "Not enough fabric and too much money," was how she described it.

After what Edna felt was an eternity, the waitress set the drink on Edna's table. "You call that a double?" Edna snarled. "And what took you so long?" The waitress ignored Edna's questions.

"Double, my ass," Edna muttered as the waitress strolled away.

Out of the corner of her eye, Edna saw Kitty enter the bar and sit on a barstool next to the gas station attendant where Edna bought her gas. In no time, Edna could see they were talking about her by their sporadic glances at her.

"She's coming over here," the man said with his hand in front of his mouth as he whispered to Kitty.

"Good evening, Kitty. Out on the town tonight, are we?" Edna snickered. "And who's your young friend?

"That's none of your business. What do you want?" Kitty had had enough of Edna for one day. Maybe even a lifetime.

"Why don't the two of us use the powder room, where we can have a private chat?" Edna snidely suggested. "I think you'd find it interesting to hear what I have to say. Unless, of course, you want me to say it right here." Edna's sing-song ultimatum drew Kitty from her barstool.

"Fine." Kitty snapped as she purposefully strode toward the ladies' room, with Edna right behind.

As soon as Edna locked the door, Kitty spun around and faced her. "What on earth, Edna?" Kitty's nostrils flared as she faced Edna with a sharp gaze.

Edna ignored Kitty with a sniff induced by the recently painted room. She looked around the room to inspect the paint job. The inspection ended when she saw the handwritten 'out of order' sign on the cloth towel dispenser. The roll of paper towels that sat on top of it was nearly depleted. Edna would let Wanda know.

"Now, Miss Kitty, there's no reason to have a hissy fit. I thought we were square when I left earlier today."

Kitty answered Edna's oily, patronizing tone and its synthetic Southern accent with a cross between a snicker and a scoff.

"What?" Kitty snapped as she put her hands on her hips. "You've got to be kidding!" Kitty's eyes squinted as she drew her cheeks high and tight, letting her crooked mouth sag open. "I mean, really, do you even have any people skills?"

Nobody had ever asked Edna that question before, or so bluntly. She dipped her head and swallowed hard as the question echoed in her head. She lifted her eyes before lifting her head.

"I, I, just want to make sure you aren't sharing too much with other people, like that young man at the bar."

"You mean my cousin, Virgil? He's staying with me for a few days. But don't worry, he knows nothing about what's going on," Kitty assured Edna.

"Good. I'm glad to hear that. I guess I'd better get back to my drink." Edna unlocked the door and left, too adrift in her thoughts to tell Wanda about the paper towels.

## She Did What?

The following morning, Lana drove to the farmhouse.

When Kitty heard Lana's car pull onto the driveway, she darted to the back door, opened it, and stood in the doorway, frantically waving Lana in.

"Lana, I'm so glad to see you!" Kitty gasped. "Come in, come in!" Lana reeled back in an unfocused gaze, wondering why Kitty was in panic mode.

Once inside, Kitty held on to the back of a chair and dissolved into sobs.

Lana cupped Kitty's hand between hers. Kitty, honey, what's wrong?" Lana whispered. "Just tell me. Come on, let's sit down," Lana led Kitty to a kitchen chair and poured her a glass of water.

"Lana, I could hardly sleep a wink last night," Kitty bewailed as she sat on the edge of her chair. She reached for the ballpoint pen on the table. *Click, click. Click, click. Click*—Lana took the pen from Kitty's hand.

Kitty panted as she related the events of the day before, starting with the black Cadillac pulling into the driveway and ending with Edna's departure. Her glass of water was empty by the time she had finished.

"I did the best I could, Lana, but she's a very pushy woman. I wish you had been there," Kitty moaned.

Lana could see the toll Edna's interference had on Kitty. "Kitty, let me fix you some tea. We'll work through this." Lana's composed presence eased Kitty's anxiety. But not for long.

"And, then again, last night, when I stopped at Wandar's for a class of wine, she accosted me again."

They both heard the tires crackling on the gravel driveway. Lana, next to the microwave, threw a startled look at Kitty, who then went to the window. It was the same black Cadillac.

"It's her. She's back," Kitty hissed. "She's headed for the back door this time."

"I'll handle it, Kitty. You just relax." Lana walked over to the door to confront Edna.

Edna was about to knock when Lana pulled the door open with a whoosh.

"Oh, it's you, Edna. I remember you. I was in the church kitchen when you staged that pathetic apron scene. Is there something you want?" Lana snarled.

Lana stood in front of the formidable Edna Stern, but what Lana saw was the pushy cheerleader who made her work alone in Biology class. Except this time, she wouldn't back down. "Yes, Lana, I remember you, you and your trashy outfit." Edna flung her shoulders back and forth as she spat out the insult. You didn't even know what lefse was!" Edna tittered.

"You came all the way out here to tell me that? So, you said it, goodbye." Lana reached to slam the door in Edna's face, but the sturdy Dr. Scholls on Edna's left foot somehow got in the way.

"Not so fast, missy. We gotta talk. Now. Either at this door or inside. You choose. But I ain't going away. Except, maybe, to go to the police station, or call one of Connor's brothers. Probably Matt, he's the eldest." Edna's jaw jutted out as she pushed her face closer to Lana.

"Ha!" Lana scoffed at Edna, throwing her head back in defiance. "Go ahead and call whomever you want. But you might have better reception if you stand in the middle of the road."

Kitty, gasping at Lana's antagonistic taunt, held her breath, fearing an avalanche of hostility catapulting from Edna's mouth.

"Come in if you must," Lana snipped, "but I won't be offering you a chair."

"Edna Stern doesn't need a chair, but you might," Edna smirked.

"None of what's going on here is of any concern to you." Lana pointed her finger at Edna. "Connor asked me to come here and get some money out of the safe, money that his mother wanted him to have." Edna ignored her as she gazed around the kitchen.

"It's been a long time since I've been in this kitchen," Edna recalled. "Hasn't changed much, though. I used to come out here with food for Karl; he could barely make toast." She looked around the kitchen. "But that was before he married that hideous woman who suckered him into a forced marriage." Edna spewed out the words, going from zero to sixty in one sentence.

Lana, yet to see Edna in full throttle as Kitty had, glanced at Kitty, who in turn shrugged her shoulders and turned out her hands in a 'how should I know' pose.

"Sometimes, I would cook his meals right here, in this kitchen," Edna continued. "We were so close growing up. After they were married, I rarely saw Karl, except when he came into town for church or on business," Edna trailed off with a woe-begotten sigh.

"Aw, I'm touched, Edna, genuinely touched," Lana's mocked empathy was short-lived.

"But this has nothing to do with you, so stop meddling!" Lana barked. "So, now, why don't you take your fond memories and go home and leave it at that?"

Edna abruptly put her hands on her hips and thrust her head forward. "Very funny, Laaanaaa," she jeered. "I don't even need to know all the details of this operation you have going on here, but none of that money is getting out of this house without some of it ending up in my hands!" Edna declared.

"You have absolutely no stake in this. This is Connor's money, plain and simple." Lana's succinct characterization of the matter bounced off Edna like an errant ping-pong ball.

"You might want to rethink that," Edna suggested. "You two removing that money from this house just might be illegal. And if a call to our local police chief, Wally, who happens to be a good friend of mine, doesn't raise a red flag, then certainly a call to Connor's brothers would shake things up."

Lana's shoulders sagged in defeat while Kitty dropped her chin to her chest, picking at a loose button on the plaid shirt she had appropriated from Virgil before he left. Edna savored the moment with a subtle grin of success.

In a relaxed pose, Edna leaned her elbows on the kitchen counter. "So, anyway, how does Connor even know about the money in the safe? Or how much there is?" she asked.

"What difference does it make?" Lana snarled.

"Then here's the deal. Take it or leave it. I get a chunk of that money, or else. And you know what that *else* is by now."

"Kitty and I need to discuss this, just the two of us. Wait for us outside," Lana commanded.

"Oh, no," Edna emphatically shook her head. "You aren't about to—"

"No, Edna, we won't lock you out," Lana finished Edna's thought.

Kitty was the first to speak. "She's got us, Lana. I mean, what else can we do? Walk away?"

"I can't walk away," Lana replied. "You can bail out if you want, but I have to see this through. I told Connor I would do this for him, and I will. Besides, he guaranteed me a minimum of $20,000, of which I plan to give you half. Let's just play along with her for a while and see what happens," Lana suggested. Kitty nodded in agreement.

Lana let Edna back into the house.

"So, what is it? If I'm not in, then nobody is." Edna stood akimbo.

With sarcastic disbelief, Lana winced at Edna. "What kind of a person would steal money from her own nephew?"

"The same kind of person who would steal money from his brothers!" Edna shot back.

"We are doing nothing illegal. So, you know the chief of police? Big deal," Lana shrugged her right shoulder, playing down Edna's threats. "Call him right now and have him come out here."

"If Connor wants you to have some of his money, that's up to him, not you, or us," Kitty finally joined in the squabble. "Right, Lana?"

"Just who is Connor to you two anyway, to get you involved in this?" Edna blustered.

"Lana and Connor had an affair when she was—" Kitty blurted out, eliciting a frosty glare from Lana.

"But Connor's married, and has been for several years. They have two sons. Not only that, he doesn't need this money. He's very successful at his job and is married to a wealthy woman whose parents own several restaurants. Apparently, his wife's parents are from Greece," Edna explained.

Kitty, realizing what she had done, closed her eyes and drooped in shame.

"I want to see that money, and I'm not leaving until I do!" Edna demanded.

But Lana wasn't listening. The shock of Edna confirming what she had strongly suspected left Lana in a daze. All Lana could hear was the screeching sound of the old windmill blades outside. All she could see was Connor at her door on their first date. An awakened whiff of his woodsy Bois d'Argent Dior cologne enticed her to inhale slowly to prolong the moment.

Edna and Kitty stared at Lana, waiting for a response. But her mind was in Chicago. She could hear Connor's voice telling her she was not included in the invitation to what he called a business dinner. She remembered hearing voices in the background, foreign-speaking voices—it was Greek! She saw herself sitting at a table at Benedict's Supper Club, where she first met Connor, at that table with the stylish guests. *One of those couples was his in-laws! He played me,* she reasoned. *He made me fall in love with him while he was married.* Lana hung her head and joined Kitty in the slumped stance of a fool.

"Girls, I got an idea!" Edna proclaimed in a folksy voice that snapped them both to attention. "Why don't we work together on this? We can split the money three ways. Connor won't pursue it. What can he do? Call the cops? He has no proof that this is his money." Edna glanced back and forth between Kitty and Lana, her designs on the money swelling like a balloon about to burst.

"He claims the diary is proof. Apparently, his mother specified in the diary that the money is his," Kitty explained. "But, we stopped reading the diary once we found the money. So, we really don't know."

"Even so, that diary could, you know, easily disappear," Edna puckishly suggested as she bounced her shoulders.

Lana, now rebounding from her stupor, chimed in.

"Edna, why are you even getting involved in this? If we turn the money over to Connor, then we've done nothing illegal. But now, what you're proposing is clearly illegal," Lana pointed out.

## Edna Lays the Foundation

Edna sat down at the table and motioned for Kitty and Lana to join her.

"There's something you need to know about the Larson family," Edna began. "Karl was my brother. He was the most easy-going man I knew. He worked hard on the farm, day in and day out. But that Roberta, she did nothing," Edna declared, with a heavy emphasis on nothing. "Oh, she put up some pickles and other things, but only because some of the neighboring women helped her out. She was a lazy, spoooooky woman. She almost always wore black or grey. She only went to church with Karl a couple of times a year. She was always growing weird plants. How she managed to grow some of that stuff around here was beyond me. She grew Belladonna. Right here, in—"

"Edna, get to the point," Kitty sharply interrupted. Both Edna and Lana jolted at Kitty's brash remark.

"The point is that she gradually poisoned Karl over the years. Sure, my brother wasn't the most educated man around, but he was always social and fun to be around. That poison turned him into a spiteful, angry old man by the time he was forty. He looked terrible when he died. She poisoned him; that's what she did." Edna slapped her hand on the table, causing an empty glass to tip over and shatter when it hit the floor. But that was of no concern to Edna.

"Of course, there was no proof." Edna shook her head in frustration. "That's because she knew what she was doing. It was reported that he died quietly in his sleep. And I don't doubt that." Edna paused when Kitty's phone rang.

"It's Robie," Kitty said, letting the call go to voicemail.

"Not only that," Edna continued, "I think Connor was in on it. One time, he showed me some of those so-called herbs she was growing. He seemed to know an awful lot about them." Edna lowered her voice even though there was no one to hear the accusation other than the three women. Kitty stood and fetched a broom.

"So, what?" Lana grumbled. "What does that have to do with anything?"

"Connor and his mother were very close. Karl knew he wasn't Connor's biological father and did his best to deal with the situation by keeping his mouth shut." Edna paused to watch Kitty as she swept up the broken glass.

"Oh, Connor was good at making people feel sorry for him, pretending to be left out when he was the one who arranged it that way. Always blaming others when things went wrong." Edna used her foot to move a chair so Kitty could reach some of the glass that had flown under the table.

"He knew how to work his mother, that's for sure. He played on her guilt without even knowing what that guilt was. And now, once again, it's poor me, poor suffering Connor, the self-proclaimed victim who now deserves everything for himself." Edna embellished her closing argument with a whiny face and sneering voice.

"Edna, enough already," Lana complained as she started to get up from her chair.

Edna grabbed her by the arm and pulled her back into the chair. "Hear me out," she commanded.

"Roberta's parents had money. After they were killed in a car crash, there was a lawsuit. Roberta inherited big. She claimed she didn't, that the attorneys ended up with most of it. But *I* know otherwise." Edna's puffery mirrored that of a lowly stock trader sharing inside information with a high roller.

"Let's take that money and split it three ways. I remind you, one quick call to one of Connor's brothers would immediately kill this operation, and you'd have absolutely nothing. Do you really believe that Connor will share any of the money with either of you?" Edna's doubtful eyes shifted between Lana and Kitty as each waited for the other to answer her rhetorical question.

"You know, Lana, I think Edna might be right," Kitty blinked first. "Connor is a greedy man, greedy in love, greedy in money."

Lana cocked her head and looked at Kitty out of the corner of her eyes as the clarity of Kitty's terse assessment set in her bones.

"On second thought," Kitty continued, "What we planned was nothing illegal. But what you're now suggesting *is*." Kitty recalled what Edna had said about getting out before it was too late. With her shoulders back and her head held high, Kitty shook her head as she clarified her stance. "I mean, all I bargained for was to get the money out of the house and into Connor's hands."

Lana sat back thinking. After hearing about Connor's wife and family, she decided to cut Connor out completely. It wasn't passion-inspired revenge, she told herself; it was vengeance for the sake of justice. In Lana's mind, it was nothing more than a simple balance sheet.

"But who needs Connor's hands? We're six of them right here." Edna held up her hands. Remembering Lana's catatonic response upon hearing that Connor was married, Edna continued. "Lana, he was using you then, in Saint Paul, and he's using you again now." Edna's pithy accusation had the effect she intended—to arouse Lana's desire for revenge.

Lana said nothing as she nervously tapped her fingers on the table.

"Now, can I finally get a look at the money?" Edna asked.

The three went into the basement, and Lana opened the safe.

"Roberta." Edna bent slightly over to speak to the money. "I never thought I'd ever have anything good to say to you, but now, all I can say is 'thanks'." Edna jerked back and looked at Lana. "You did count it, right?"

But Kitty answered. "Yes, three times. It's over a million dollars."

"How do I know that you two won't just take all this money and run?" Edna raised her head, her shifty eyes squinting as a canvas of suspicion crossed her face.

"Oh, come on, Edna. You already know the answer to that. For one, I saw you writing our license plate numbers down before you barged in here," Kitty interjected.

Kitty's revelation surprised Lana, whose jaws tightened with fury.

"Is that true? You wrote our license plate numbers down?" Lana snapped.

"Of course, I did. It's just a bit of insurance on my part. Edna Stern is no fool," she gloated. "If you didn't already know that, you do now!"

Expecting Lana would stew all night over Kitty and Edna's accusations about Connor, Edna announced she needed to get home to make supper.

"But we need to finalize this. You can't just leave now," Lana firmly protested as she closed the safe, giving the dial a spin.

"OK, let's meet tonight at Wanda's, on Main Street. Eight o'clock." Edna walked away, not noticing Lana's contemptuous glare that followed her up the stairs.

Kitty and Lana watched from the kitchen window as Edna drove away. The two then sat quietly at the table, Kitty slumped in her chair with her arms crossed in a defiant teenage pose, and Lana calmly stared at the kitchen floor with her hands folded on her lap.

Lana broke the silence. "You know, Connor said his mother died in late June of this year and that she lived in this house until she died, right here, right here on this kitchen floor." Lana nodded at the floor, drawing Kitty's attention to it.

"That creeps me out now that I hear that. And to think, after all this time, we've been sitting here, right where she dropped dead," Kitty shuddered.

"It was an aneurysm in her brain," Lana explained. "Connor said she was as sharp as a tack right up to the very end."

"Could Edna be right about the poison?" Kitty conjectured. "Did Connor help his mother poison his father? Did Connor poison his mother? Did *he* poison his own *mother*? I saw a book about poisonous plants on the front porch." Kitty's eyes were opening wider and wider. "Maybe his father saw the book and was poisoning himself, thinking the authorities would learn about Roberta's special garden and arrest her. Or maybe he knew she was poisoning him but didn't care. Or maybe—"

"Whoa, slow down, Miss Kitty Hitchcock. Just because Edna has that crazy story about Roberta poisoning him doesn't mean it's true. Surely, a doctor could have run some tests and would have found any poison in his blood or tissue," Lana suggested as she slid her chair back and stood up. "At any rate, it's time for me to go home. I'll see you later at Wanda's. Somehow, we need to get rid of that woman." Kitty looked askance at Lana, not knowing what she meant by 'get rid of'.

Lana was pensive as she left that old farmhouse, a house she was glad to be leaving soon. As she approached her car, she turned back to take in the scene. She stood there in the moonlight comparing Connor's life to hers. She grew up in a stable home with loving parents. She wondered if Connor had invented a past life of hardship, strife, and alienation just to soften her. And then there was his wife. Lana nodded as she admitted to herself that Kitty and Edna were right about Connor.

"Goodbye, old house," Lana whispered." Maybe they should burn you down too."

## Roberta Signs Off

After Lana and Edna left, Kitty brought out the diary. She had nothing else to do and still wondered if they had missed an entry stating that the money was Connor's alone, not that that even mattered anymore. Paying more attention to the pages they had hastily paged through, she eventually came to the blank pages at the end. She and Lana had stopped there, believing that it was the end of the diary. Kitty yawned as she looked at the clock, but went through the empty pages before going to bed. And there it was, another entry, buried between empty pages.

*January 8, 2008*

*Finally, he's dead.*

Kitty turned to the next page.

*January 13, 2008*

*And buried.*

Kitty looked at the clock again. She missed Virgil already. She would spend her first night alone at the farmhouse, and she was dreading it already. After reading about Karl's death, Kitty closed the diary. She called Robie, but her call went to voicemail. *Should she call her father? Maybe even her mother?* Kitty put her elbow on the table, sank her heavy head into the palm of her hand, and closed her eyes.

She opened the door of a kitchen cabinet and found a can of SpaghettiOs. She opened the can, poured the mixture into a glass bowl, and heated it in the microwave. She washed it down with a Diet Coke.

She looked at the clock again, then at the diary. As the following several pages of the diary were blank, she had assumed that the clipped entries about Karl's death were the final entries. With time to kill before the meeting at Wanda's, she opened the diary and thumbed through the remaining pages. And then, on the very last page of the diary, Kitty found the final entry.

*June 17, 2021*

*I haven't been as diligent as I once was in writing in my diary. Of course, years ago, with my boys at home, I had much more to write about. People say it's more difficult to raise girls, but*

*I'm not so sure. At least my four boys stayed out of major trouble and are now married, notice I didn't write 'happily married'. Nobody understands that better than I do.*

*Now, I have some things I must admit.*

*I must admit, I wasn't the kind of wife Karl deserved. I was never a farm wife who spent her time cooking, baking, canning, and volunteering at the church.*

*My parents were both university professors, and I grew up in an urban academic setting. At least some of that rubbed off on Connor. He was rarely seen on the farm without a book in his hands.*

*And now, I sit alone in this wretched farmhouse, as much a prisoner now as I was from the start. At first, I was so in love with Karl, if, in fact, one could be in love at first. When he talked about his farm, it sounded so idyllic. I fancied myself another Willa Cather, writing books about the challenges and rewards of a bucolic rural life. But none of that ever happened, and now, in retrospect, I realize that I unfairly blamed Karl for the bitterness that thwarted my literary ambition.*

*I must admit that Connor, my baby, was the joy of my life. Not that I loved him more than I did his brothers; we just had so much more in common, like reading, watching the clouds and stars, writing poems and short stories, and working in my garden. He never connected with his brothers nor with Karl. He was a lonely boy who never had the chance to learn how to lose.*

*And the last thing I must admit is that Karl was right all along about the money. But none of that matters now. The million dollars will soon be in Connor's hands, I hope. I left him one last treasure hunt for him to find.*

*I remember how much he loved those treasure hunts as a child. I had him running all over this farm as he followed my clues. He especially liked it when I wrote the clues in silly poems. When he was little, the treasures started out as toys or candy, then moved to comic books, and later, a library card and a blank diary. But this, this final treasure hunt, will be one he'll never forget.*

*Connor, I know you know about the money and that it's in the safe. You watched me put it there at least once. You also know I've kept this diary over the years and that I hide it in an old trunk in the basement.*

*When they read my will, they'll find no mention of the money in that safe; the four boys will only inherit the farm and any other holdings I have. But I know Connor, he will put two and two together and try to get the money out before the place is sold. So, have fun, Connor, and spend the money wisely.*

*P.S. This is the final entry in my diary.*

*Roberta Larson 1945-*

Kitty didn't know if she should finish off the date with 2021. She'd ask Lana.

# CHAPTER 20

# WANDA'S

## A Wet Night

Kitty brought the diary with her to Wanda's, figuring that Lana would arrive early, as she often did. She waited in her car until she saw Lana pull in. When Lana got out of her car, Kitty stepped out of her car, reached back in, and beeped her horn. She waved Lana over.

"Kitty, what's up? I hope it's not bad news." Lana had enough bad news for one day.

"Hop in, I have to show you something."

Once they were both in the car, Kitty slid the diary from under her seat. "I didn't have anything else to do, so I spent some more time with the diary. I found three more entries." Kitty opened the diary and handed it over to Lana.

"Let me open my flashlight app so you can read it." Kitty already had her phone out.

Lana read the three entries aloud. In the meantime, the light mist from earlier had turned into a steady downpour. Kitty slid the diary back under her seat, and the two of them made a dash for the door. After they got a bottle of white wine at the bar, along with two glasses, they were lured by a lit stone fireplace with an empty table in front of it.

"This is perfect for a night like this," Kitty observed. They sat quietly watching the fire, yielding to the flames as they danced away the bluster of the afternoon.

"That Edna sure is a pain in the you-know-what," Kitty decided.

"I know. But what can we do? We either split the money three ways or end up with nothing." Lana took a sip of her beer.

"I can't believe we are doing this. And the way you took charge! My mother always called you a shrinking violet. But if she could see you now!" Kitty gushed.

"Thanks for telling me that, Kitty. But I won't tell you what my father called your mother."

"You don't have to." They both burst into a laughing jag.

## A Dry Martini

As usual, Wanda's was busy. Edna drove through the small parking lot twice but found nothing. She ended up parking on the street, more than a block away. Edna sat in her car, waiting for the rain to let up. Losing all hope, she reached for the travel umbrella she kept under the passenger's seat. It wasn't there.

"Shit."

She buttoned the top button of the red cloth coat she bought at a garage sale years ago. Lester said it looked "Christmasie" when she modeled it for him. "Maybe you can accessorize it with some silver bells or tinsel come Christmas time." Lester wasn't surprised when she did just that.

Edna was past the point in her life when running was an option. Her right hip was getting worse, and her doctor saw a hip replacement in her future. Edna waddled as fast as she could toward Wanda's, cursing the rain with every step.

"Hey, Edna," someone yelled from across the oval-shaped bar as she crashed through the door. "You need to get out of that wet coat and into a dry martini."

Edna laughed at the comment, as did others, including Wanda.

"How does that sound, Edna?" Wanda asked. "A dry martini on a wet night? This one's on me."

"Sounds good," Edna said, already feeling better. "Make it a Beefeater. And leave the damn olive out."

Edna slid a chair closer to the fireplace and hung her wet coat over it. By the time she got to the bar, the martini sat waiting for her. The glass was filled to the brim, so she took a few sips before moving to the table where Kitty and Lana were seated.

She set the glass down, stooped over with her head near the fire, and fluffed her soggy red hair with her dry fingers. "Damn, this rain is a pain in the ass. I had to park a mile away," she said, as she turned back to the table.

A few people greeted Edna as they walked by on their way to the pool table or to the noisy and flashy electronic games that lined the walls. She made it a point to introduce Lana and Kitty to most of them. Who says Edna has no friends?

## Uninvited Guests

Lana saw Kyle and Wally come into the bar together. They sat at the bar and each ordered a beer.

"That fire sure looks good on a night like this," Kyle observed. "Too bad there—" Wait a minute, I know that woman, she's renting Gracie's sister Sonia's house. And that's got to be Edna over there, who could mistake that mop of red hair." The quizzical smile on Wally's face told Kyle what was coming.

"Let's say we mosey on over there, under the guise of warming our chilled bones."

"Ever the detective you are, Wally, ever the detective."

They approached the table unnoticed.

"So, can two happily married men be seen in the company of three women? Edna, aren't you going to ask us to join you?" Wally asked.

"Of course, Wally, you two happily married men just need to pull up your own chair," Edna replied as she pointed to two empty chairs at a nearby table.

"I'm wondering what brings you three together?" Wally asked as he slid his chair in between Lana and Kitty.

"I met Lana at church. She helped out with the smorgasbord. As for Kitty, I met her at the Larson farmhouse," Edna explained. "The Larson boys asked me to keep an eye on the place, so I did."

Wally's cell phone interrupted the conversation. "Excuse me, I need to take this," he said as he stood. He walked over to a hopefully quieter area while Edna continued with her explanation.

"Since they're both new in town, I introduced Kitty to Lana and the three of us have had several games of cribbage and cards, had a few meals together, and who knows what else we'll do?" Edna kicked Lana under the table.

"Hmm. I don't see a cribbage board or a deck of cards on the table. So, what's the entertainment tonight?" Kyle joshed. "You're not planning a bank heist or something like that?" He looked at Edna when he made the joke. Kitty kicked Lana under the table.

Edna was quick on the draw. "How did you guess, Kyle? We need a driver. You in?"

"Touché, Edna, touché," Kyle interjected without answering her final question.

"We're here tonight because we are planning an outing to Reno, girls only," Edna announced, carefully watching Lana and Kitty's reaction.

Kyle leaned into the conversation. "My wife Evie and I have been to Reno many times. Tell me more about your plans. Gambling? Shows? Nightlife?"

The four talked about Reno until Wally came back to the table.

"Reno," Wally asked. "Don't tell me you and Evie are going to Reno again."

"No, we're not, but these three are," Kyle nodded toward the three women as she said it.

"Anyway, I need to go; my presence is needed elsewhere," Wally announced as he turned away. Kyle said he needed to go too, so he and Wally walked out together.

## Not Reno, Vegas!

"Thank God, they're gone," Lana breathed a sigh of relief as she collapsed back into her chair.

"I like your Reno idea. Funny how that just popped into your head. How exciting. I can't wait." Kitty was ready to get out of town, and the sooner, the better.

"We're not going to Reno, Kitty. Edna just made that up," Lana brushed the idea aside.

"I've been thinking. I think it would be best if we weren't here when Connor and his brothers get here. Sure, you two can just take off, but what can I do?" Edna shrugged.

"Too bad, Edna, you're the one who nosed your way into this," Lana replied.

"I know, I know. But what's done is done. When Connor finds out the money is gone, he's not just going to turn around and go home; he'll go to Wally. Wally will connect the three of us. Then he'll come to my house, see I'm gone, put two and two together, and contact the authorities in Reno."

"All the more reason not to go to Reno," Lana shook her head in disbelief.

"Come on, Lana," Edna replied, "Connor will tell Wally that you stole the money. He has no reason to believe that Kitty and I had anything to do with it. We can deny knowing anything about the money—the three of us are just going on a trip to Reno."

All that remained of Edna's martini was the olive. She chewed it leisurely, giving her words a chance to sink in.

"But here's the deal," Edna scanned the crowd, leaned in, and, with two fingers, motioned for Lana and Kitty to do likewise. After a glance in both directions, Edna whispered. "We're not going to Reno. We're going to—" Edna mouthed the words— "Las Vegas."

"To me, this just seems unnecessary. I just want my share and leave," Lana declared. "I've had enough of this whole affair."

"You know, you're right, Lana," Edna bobbed her head in agreement. "Let's just each of us take our share and leave it at that. Kitty and I will be free and clear; it's you they'll come after, not us."

Lana sat quietly, staring at her empty wine glass as she spun it between her thumb and index finger.

"Lana, I think it would be fun. It's been all work and no play since we've been here. Robie's working a construction job in Lexington and won't be back until next week." Kitty's lower lip extruded just enough to be noticed.

Lana looked over her glasses at Kitty, voicing an exasperated sigh. "Kitty, that only works on your father."

"I just don't know what the big deal is, Lana. I mean, come on." Kitty reasoned. "I went along with your plan and came to Gailsprings, thinking we were only getting the money for Connor. But this changes everything. I'm an unwitting criminal thanks to you."

"I wouldn't exactly say unwitting," Edna clarified.

"Kitty, you don't have to be a part of this new twist if you don't want to," Lana told Kitty.

"Now just wait a minute," Edna scowled. "Kitty's already a part of this. If she bails out now, she could tell Connor and the law everything."

"I could never do that to Lana," Kitty whimpered.

"But you could do it to me. And then *I* could do it to Lana." Edna delivered the lines like she was on the set of 'The Sopranos'. "Kitty, it's too late to bail out now."

"Edna, that sounds like blackmail to me," Lana replied.

"Maybe it does because maybe it is." Edna softened after her flip comment. "But, I'll tell you what I'll do. Since you two did all the work getting that money out of the safe, I am willing to settle for 20% and you two can split the rest."

Edna sat back with her hands clasped behind her head, allowing her offer to sweeten the pot and mollify any remaining wobbly commitments.

"Let's do it, Lana. It would be like sisters on a trip together." This time, Kitty played the sister card.

"Lana, face it. You may have come here with the intention of giving that money to Connor, but that's no longer the case. Is it?" Edna ventured. "No need to answer. Connor played you for a fool, and now it's your turn to do the same."

"C'mon, Lana. Let's end this with something fun," Kitty urged.

Lana pictured the map of Mexico from the atlas. *It's really not that far from Vegas,* she realized. Lana drew a protracted breath through her nose and let it out slowly. " Well, I suppose," Lana conceded. "What do we have to lose?" Lana threw her hands up in the air in surrender. "I just want to get this over with."

## The Leading Lady

"I'm glad I packed some nice things, especially now that we're going to Las Vegas," Kitty declared, letting her anticipation show.

"Edna, how about we take your car? It's so classy, perfect for Las Vegas." Kitty purred, knowing her flattery would land on fertile ground.

"Of course, good idea, Raven would love to grace Las Vegas with her presence," Edna agreed. "So, the way I see it, this is how this is going to play out. First we—"

"No, Edna," Lana butted in. "This is how this is going to all play out."

Edna winced, a prelude to indignation.

"We leave town this Thursday. Kitty burns the diary the day before. You got that, Kitty?"

"Yes."

"Early Thursday morning, we open the safe and divide the money. Be sure to bring a bag or a large purse. We then head to Vegas."

Lana felt good about being at the helm, where the chief of operations should be. Kitty sat and listened with deferential admiration, while Edna's anger smoldered like a vat of gurgling acid.

"We should stay in Vegas for a few days, hang out by the pool, take in a show, maybe play some Blackjack. We are supposedly on a vacation." Lana was on a roll. "Edna, can you arrange the hotel reservation?"

Edna nodded, pleased to feel she was needed after all.

Lana grabbed her phone and searched 'Gailsprings to Las Vegas.' "Make it for three nights, starting on Sunday night. I just looked it up. Vegas is a twenty-four-hour drive. We could do it in three days, but that would mean some very long days."

"I say we take our time. There's really no reason to rush," Kitty proposed.

"You know, the more I think of this, I'm glad we're taking this optional mini-vacation," Lana admitted, pumped by the power of being first chair.

"They say what happens in Vegas, stays in Vegas," Edna commented with a sly grin. "But we won't be staying, and neither will our money."

"Then," Lana continued. "After a few days in Vegas, we split. Connor's in Belgium until early October. That way—"

"—that way, we'll be loooong gone," Kitty playfully finished Lana's sentence.

Lana looked at Edna. "Once Connor finds out what happened, you'd better be prepared."

"Don't worry about that. I'll be prepared," Edna declared.

"I'll just say I know nothing about it. Yes, we went to Vegas together, you two decided to stay longer, and I came back alone. As far as I know, you both are still in Vegas. What's Connor going to do anyway? Contact the FBI? There would be an investigation, and surely his brothers would be dragged into it. But we must not forget to burn that diary."

"By the way, where is the diary?" Edna asked, almost as an afterthought.

Lana glanced at Kitty, and Edna followed suit.

"It's in a safe place," Kitty responded. "I'll burn it the day before we leave. Gladly."

"And be sure to burn the diary completely, leaving no unburned pages," Edna cautioned. "I watch those CSI shows, and I've seen what they can do. Especially that weird Abby." Edna was on top of the latest developments in the field of crime investigation. Neither Lana nor Kitty asked who weird Abby was; that conversation would last for hours.

Edna left Wanda's with a spirited gait, the pain in her hip soothed by the prospects of a trip to Las Vegas and a chunk of money.

*No, Kitty, it didn't just pop into my head,* she said to herself as she looked up at the sky and saw that the clouds were gone. Edna had it all planned. She envisioned something out of a crime novel or a movie. It would be Thelma and Louise plus one, without the cliff, of course. But with the gun.

## No Vegas for Raven

Edna was frantic. It was late Wednesday afternoon when she returned home from the body shop.

"They said that they would have my car ready by today. Now they say they need it for at least three more days. Something about the supply chain. We have reservations for Vegas!" she exclaimed.

"You know, Edna, the damage to the car was more extensive than they thought. You've got to be more careful on some of those country roads. You hit that object hard. Why you always have to drive so fast, I'll never know. What was it again?"

"I've told you a dozen times, Lester, it was part of an old muffler. Probably fell off an old truck or something."

"But, Edna, it was broad daylight, for heaven's sake," Lester reminded her.

"Kitty's car is out. Too small. And Lana sold her car to Evie Tyson."

"Why don't you just take my car? I'll be fine for a few days. You've already packed the refrigerator with more than I'll ever eat. I can always call Wanda-Woo if I need anything."

Edna rolled her eyes at Lester's frisky implication. "Very funny, Lester. You wouldn't stand a chance with her. Why don't you be a sweetheart and gas up your car for me?" Edna cooed.

# CHAPTER 21

# AND THEY'RE OFF

**Thursday, September 24**

Edna and Lester had just finished a light breakfast. Edna's lone suitcase sat open on a kitchen chair. Edna went to the closet, took out a large empty purse, and put it in her suitcase. Lester lowered his newspaper to see what the commotion was.

"Why would you need another purse, especially such a large one?" Lester asked in his usual stony way.

"It's for my winnings," Edna smartly replied.

"Just don't gamble away my car," Lester warned from behind the newspaper.

The night before, with Edna at the steering wheel, Lester gave Edna a quick rundown on the knobs, buttons, and dashboard displays.

Lester closed Edna's suitcase and put it in the trunk of his car. He then backed the car out of the garage and left it running. He waited for Edna outside, chatting with a neighbor who was walking her dog.

Edna was in the driver's seat and ready to close the door when Lester grabbed the door. "Okay, Edna, now listen. You've only driven this car a few times. True, it's just as new as your Raven, but every car has its own idiosyncrasies." Lester bent over and gave Edna a slight peck on the cheek so he wouldn't smear her rouge.

Lester watched Edna drive away at a speed the car had rarely seen. "My God. What did I do?" he lamented to his neighbor.

"She's not running away, is she?" his neighbor asked with an undercurrent of hope in her voice.

When Edna arrived at Lana's, she pulled into the driveway and blew the horn. She waited. She blew the horn again. Finally, Lana came out, lugging a defiant suitcase.

"Finally, it's about time," Edna sneered.

"You could have come in, you know, and helped me with my luggage," Lana challenged.

"You seem to be doing just fine on your own."

"This isn't all of it. There are two more cases in the house," Lana panted as she approached the car. "Could you at least open the trunk?" Lana cuttingly asked.

Edna got out of the car and reached for the key fob in her pocket to open the trunk. Lana went back into the house and came out with the two remaining bags. She tossed one in the trunk and the other on the back seat on the driver's side of the car.

"But this isn't your car, Edna," Lana commented.

"That's right, it's Lester's, Edna confirmed. "Mine's still in the shop. So, you sold your car to Evie Tyson, I hear."

"Yes. I can buy another car in Vegas," Lana replied. Lana relished the thought of Connor noticing her car around town, only to find out it was Evie driving it.

## Ashes to Ashes

When Kitty saw a strange car pull up to the farmhouse, a frisson of panic froze her to the chair by the kitchen window. She sat back in the chair and carefully moved the curtain with the back of her two fingers. *Could this be Connor?* Certainly, if it were Connor, he would just come in. The driver's door inched open, a foot touched the ground, and then a body appeared.

"Come on, Kitty, let's get a move on!" Edna yelled.

Lana and Edna passed Kitty's large suitcase as they entered the kitchen.

"What have you got in there? The Queen Mary?" Edna sniped. But no one waited for an answer.

After clamoring down the wooden stairs, they assembled in front of the safe, each with a large bag in their hand, like three overgrown children trick-or-treating. Lana opened the safe and took out the money, including the slip of paper at the bottom of the safe with an amount written on it. She showed the amount to Edna, used her phone to calculate 20%, and paid Edna. She then split the rest between her and Kitty, dropping Kitty's share into her Gucci bag.

Back up the stairs, Edna gave Kitty a hand in getting her suitcase over the threshold of the back door until they had it down the steps and onto the ground.

"Wait, I'll bring the car up closer," Edna said.

Lana stood alone in the kitchen. She grabbed a clean napkin and an ink pen. She wrote something on it and left it on the table. Then, she exited the house for the last time.

Edna drove slowly at first, Lana riding shotgun and Kitty in the back. About to leave the gravel driveway and onto the paved county road, Edna stepped hard on the accelerator, kicking up gravel and dust while leaving some rubber on the pavement.

"Did you burn the diary?" Lana asked Kitty, who was fussing around in the back seat, rearranging haphazardly tossed bags for more legroom.

"Yes. I even buried the ashes behind the old outhouse. I can't imagine having to use one of those. This one had two seats in it," Kitty said.

## Omaha

Soon after joining the interstate at Lake Delton, Edna told Lana to reach under the passenger's seat for the atlas. "Lester always keeps a current atlas in his car, even though he rarely crosses the county line."

Lana reached under her seat and pulled out the atlas. "Yes, I can see it's brand new." Lana flattened it out on her lap.

"You any good at maps?" Edna asked Lana.

"I am very good at maps. You keep driving, and I'll work out a route," Lana assured her.

Lana suggested they continue on I-94 until they get to Madison, then take US 151. "From there, we'll get on—"

"Lana, how about just one stretch at a time?" Edna suggested.

"Fine." Lana closed the atlas and was about to place it under her seat when she stopped, distracted by the dashboard.

"Something wrong, Lana?"

"No. I'm just wondering if there is a GPS in this car," she said.

"Yes, it does have GPS. Lester talks about it all the time. But that's about it; he just talks about it. He's too daft to figure the damn thing out," Edna laughed. *Apparently, you are too,* Lana held her tongue.

Edna started looking at the display screen, and Edna joined in.

"Edna, you keep your eyes on the road. I'll deal with the GPS." Soon Lana had their destination in the system.

"I muted the voice for now, but when we go through a congested area, we can turn it back on."

"Lana, you're kind of like a co-pilot," Kitty observed. "Or maybe more like the navigator, like Chekov on Star Trek. I'm not a Trekkie, but I have seen a lot of the shows. William Shatner was totally hot on that show, unlike now."

"What the hell is a Trekkie? As if I need to know."

Kitty wasn't sure how to answer Edna's trick question since she apparently didn't want to know.

"They're die-hard fans of the TV series Star Trek," Lana answered for Kitty. "They have conventions, dress like characters from the series, and try to act and talk like the characters from the show. And I agree with Kitty about William Shatner."

Edna saw the sign first but said nothing. Kitty did.

"Did you see that sign? Welcome to Iowa, it said. Home of John Wayne. My father loves those old westerns," Kitty wistfully recalled.

"Lester likes those too, especially when they're in black and white," Edna said.

"My dad likes the History Channel," Lana chimed in. "Especially all those war documentaries."

They rode in silence; each lost in their own thoughts.

With the open atlas once again on her lap, Lana made a suggestion, "It looks to me like Des Moines might be a good stop for lunch."

Two hours later, and on the other side of Des Moines, Edna exited the highway. Kitty spotted an Arby's and declared that as their destination. After lunch, Lana took over the driving and Kitty sat up front. Barely on the highway, Edna was snoring lightly, and Kitty was nodding off and on. Lana turned on the radio and found a station that played country music. She was glad she had bought a coffee to go when they left the restaurant.

When they got to Omaha, Lana put on the blinker, and they exited the highway.

"I figure we can stay here tonight," Lana announced. Neither Kitty nor Edna protested. They had a nice dinner at a local bar and grill, where Edna ordered a double bourbon, Kitty a white wine, and Lana a Tanqueray martini. When their meal was done, they were ready to call it a day.

"Hoooooooah," Edna let out a hearty yawn as she unlocked the door to her room. "I'm bushed. See you tomorrow." The door clicked shut.

Lana and Kitty's room was three doors down the hall. Lana had barely opened the door when Kitty darted in and plopped face down on her bed. With her elbows propping her up, she held her phone in her hands as she reread an earlier message from Robie—for the tenth time. "I miss you. I love you. I have a question for you."

She grabbed a pillow and stuffed it under her dreamy head. She saw her father walking her down the aisle of a packed church. Robie stood at the altar in a classic black wedding tuxedo. Her mother's sniffles were just audible enough for Kitty to hear.

The running water of someone showering on the floor above lulled Kitty into a slumber. When Lana came out of the bathroom, she retrieved the extra blanket from the closet and carefully draped it over Kitty. Lana turned off the light and slid into bed with a muffled yawn.

---- CHAPTER 22 ----

# EDNA SHOWS INTEREST

**Friday, September 25**

The day dawned cloudy with a light mist in the air. After eating the complimentary breakfast at the hotel, they returned to their rooms and then regrouped in the lobby to check out. Edna insisted she start off driving. Kitty was fine in the back seat, and Lana was again up front with the atlas on her lap. Having noticed a large dumpster at the back of the parking lot, Lana instructed Edna to pull up next to it.

"What's this all about?" Edna asked.

"You'll see," Lana replied.

Once they were parked next to the dumpster, Lana explained.

"Here's where we get rid of our phones. They're too easy to trace. We can pick up some prepaid phones down the road; they're much more difficult to trace. So, turn off your phones and hand them to me."

"What?" Kitty grumbled. "But, but what—"

"Kitty, listen to me. I know what I'm doing." Lana was firm.

"But what about my leopard print case? Can I keep that?" Kitty whined.

"Yes, of course," Lana tenderly replied in an effort to soften Kitty's exaggerated distress about being without her phone.

Around noon, Edna exited the highway at Ogallala, Nebraska, where they had a quick lunch at Taco Bell.

When they made a brief pit stop in Fort Morgan, Kitty picked up a brochure about Colorado.

"I'll take over from here." Lana was heading to the driver's side of the car. Edna said nothing as she slipped into the back seat. Kitty sat in front, looking over the brochure.

"So, those are the Rocky Mountains up ahead," Kitty said.

Edna quelled any snide remarks about Kitty's extraordinary grasp of geography.

"It says here that they go all the way into Canada," Kitty announced in her best tour guide voice.

"I wonder how tall they are." Edna's sudden interest in the matter sparked grins and glances between Kitty and Lana.

"The highest point is some 14,440 feet," Kitty read. "That's a lot of feet. What would be that in miles, Lana?"

Kitty was confident that Lana would surely know.

"Just under three miles," Lana answered.

Edna had seen some of the bluffs along the Mississippi River between Wisconsin and Minnesota, but these mountains captivated her.

"I remember reading about how people in covered wagons crossed these mountains to get to the west," Edna said as she stared out the window. "Sometimes, they got caught in snowstorms, were attacked by Indians, or bitten by rattlesnakes. The hardships they endured!"

A mile later, Edna continued. "Women would give birth in the covered wagons, but they would just keep heading west. And here we are, driving along like it was nothing."

Both Kitty and Lana's eyes opened wide as they looked at each other with disbelief, both wondering if the cantankerous Edna they had left Wisconsin with was mellowing as they crossed state lines. Edna slid over to the center of the back seat.

"Edna, your head's blocking my rearview mirror," said Lana. "Move to one side or the other."

"I suppose I could move to the left. That is if I wanted to sit on top of one of your *many* pieces of luggage," Edna teased. "I've been thinking, Lana, you have no intention of returning to Galesprings, do you? That's why you brought so much luggage along and sold your car."

"It's only three pieces. A girl's got to have some accouterments on a trip like this," Lana sportively replied.

"Lana's right," Kitty agreed. "I wish I had brought more along myself."

"It's a good thing I left most of my clothes at my apartment in Louisville," Lana added. "Now, Edna, please stop blocking my rearview mirror."

Edna slid back to her right, declaring that she would move to the front seat at the next stop. "It seems like we've been driving and driving, and yet those mountains don't seem any closer," Edna whined.

"They'll still be there when we get there," Kitty reassured Edna.

Edna's lighthearted laughter at Kitty's flip remark further revealed a veiled side of Edna's personality that she seldom shared. Lana and Kitty once again shared a glance, thinking, *who is this woman in the backseat?*

## Girls' Night Out

They spent the night in Sterling, Colorado. After checking into their hotel, Kitty suggested they drive around to find a place to eat.

"Let's be adventurous tonight," Kitty suggested. "We can find a local bar, have a drink there, and then move on." Lana tilted her head and nodded as she considered the idea. The roguish look that soon appeared on Lana's face belied her usual impassive mien. Kitty could see that Lana was on board.

"We're not doing one of those bar-hopping things. I'm just not up for that," Edna grumbled. "I like to stay in one place."

Neither Lana nor Kitty responded, giving Edna time to savor the weight of her disapproval. "Well, OK, I suppose. If we must. But Lana has to drive." Edna reluctantly lifted herself out of the armchair in the corner of Kitty and Lana's room. Overstating the imposition, she blustered, "So, let's get this over with." They agreed to meet in the lobby in half an hour.

It didn't surprise Edna when Kitty arrived in the hotel lobby wearing a red cocktail dress and metallic gold sandals. The black clutch purse accented the ensemble. Edna's white, wrinkle-free slacks from Target, along with the pale blue corduroy shirt she found at a thrift sale, were a sharp contrast to Kitty's haute couture. Edna would let that bother her more than usual. She was never one for fancy clothes and often reasoned by saying, "Lester never takes me anywhere decent anyway." But seeing Kitty brought back memories of a time when she did enjoy dressing up, going out in style, dancing the night away.

Moments later, Lana walked into the lobby in a tight-fitting lavender dress and stylish silver flats. The silver drop earrings inset with amethyst stones were a perfect match.

"Lana, is that you? You look stunning!" Edna gushed.

Taking offence, Kitty baited Edna. "Heavens to Betsy, Edna, what am I, chopped liver? I'm gussied up too."

Without faltering, Edna responded. "This is different, Kitty. You always look, as you put it, gussied up."

Kitty magnanimously absolved Edna of her oversight.

They drove around until they found a bar that was respectable, at least from the outside. As they opened the door to the bar, they were met by a raucous cacophony of music, chatter, and the slamming of dice boxes on the bar. Edna covered her ears with her hands, artistically framing the painful grimace on her face.

"This reminds me of Sally's," Kitty observed as Lana and Edna scouted out a table as far away from the jukebox as possible.

Not wasting time by sitting down at the table, Edna asked what Lana and Kitty wanted and elbowed her way up to the busy bar. After waiting an excruciating minute for service, Edna sent a piercing whistle down the bar. Some laughter, if not admiration, ensued as people turned to see that a 65-year-old woman was the source of the summons.

She was served promptly: a bourbon for Edna, a martini for Lana, and a gin and tonic for Kitty. A middle-aged man sitting next to Edna watched as she tried to fit three glasses between her two hands. She accepted his offer to help, sliding two glasses over to him as she took the other. After he set the drinks on their table, Edna thanked him, "It's nice to see there are still gentlemen in this country."

With only a few sips of her gin and tonic, Kitty announced she needed to use the ladies' room. She spritely waltzed through the crowd, leaving interested eyes in her wake.

She took a more measured pace in returning to the table. A man in tight blue jeans and a white T-shirt caught Kitty's attention as he caught hers. He moved in as she paused—he looked just like Robie.

Lana noticed it too. "Edna, see that man making his way towards Kitty, he looks an awful lot like Robie. She's been away from him for too long. We'd better get her out of here fast."

Edna took a large gulp of her bourbon and wiped her lips with the back of her hand.

Lana knew better than to slam a martini. They surrounded Kitty and escorted her out of the bar.

"But wait! My Cult Gaia beaded purse!" Kitty shrieked,

"I got it," Lana reassured her.

"I don't know what's going on, but this is not my idea of fun," Kitty mewed.

They drove around and ended up at Santiago's Mexican Restaurant. Edna settled for a Corona, Lana stuck with a martini, and Kitty ordered a margarita. Their server, Javier, was a classic handsome, virile, and flirtatious Latino, and they did their best to try to embarrass him. They failed but had a lot of fun doing so. Kitty suggested they leave Javier a big *propina.*

"A big *what?*" Edna asked in a mortified whisper.

"A big *propina,* you know, a tip," Kitty explained.

"I don't know about you two, but that sounds like a dirty word to me." Edna dropped five on the table as she slid her chair back.

# CHAPTER 23

# CONNOR'S DILEMMA

## Good Mother, Lousy Wife

Connor had no sooner turned into the driveway of his childhood home when the realtor pulled in.

"The deal's off, at least for now," the realtor said. "Something with the financing."

"I was afraid something like this might happen," Connor said as he shook his head in disappointment.

The two chatted a bit about possible scenarios regarding the property, and the realtor drove away. Connor quickly called his brother Matt and told him the story.

Connor then went into the house and directly down to the basement. He easily found the trunk, opened it, and tossed the clothing onto the floor. Good, the diary was gone, and things were going as planned. He then walked over to the safe, pleased to see nothing in it, but puzzled that it was unlocked. Lana was supposed to lock the safe after removing the money. Connor was about to lock it, but stopped short. He needed to think things through.

Connor looked at the pile of clothes on the floor. One item of clothing drew Connor's attention. It was his mother's floral dress. He picked it up from the floor and held it out in front of him. He glared at the dress until the soft floral colors blurred into a blotchy mélange.

Growing up in that house, Connor never thought much about his mother's clothing, but seeing some of her clothes now gave him pause. *Why did she always wear such drab clothes? Was it so that people would think Karl prevented her from buying nice things? Was she trying to make Karl look cheap?* Connor dropped the dress on the floor. He looked at it again. He concluded his thoughts with a pronounced sigh. "You were a good mother, but a lousy wife."

Connor slowly climbed the stairs, which he had climbed countless times before. He sat at the kitchen table. Among the clutter dominating the table, he found a slip of paper with an address on it. He recognized the street name as one in a residual area of Gailsprings. *This must be where I'll find Lana.* He went to his car, entered the address into his GPS, and headed for town.

He parked in the driveway of the address, noticing that the garage door was shut. He rang the doorbell, but no one came to the door. Even though he heard the doorbell ring, he pounded on the front door with his fist. Again, no answer. He walked around to the back of the property and found nothing but some clothes hanging on the clothesline.

When he returned to the front of the property, an elderly woman approached him.

"Can I help you? If you're interested in renting the house, it's already rented," the woman informed him.

Connor hesitated. "Someone told me to look up the person who lives here."

"You're one of the Larson boys, aren't you? Yes, the youngest one, Conrad, I believe," the woman guessed.

"Yes, I am one of the Larson boys. But my name is Connor, not Conrad," he graciously corrected her.

"So, you were supposed to look up Lana, you say?" Gracie Sanderson asked. "But she left two days ago. Left in kind of a hurry, too. She sold her car to Evie down the street," Gracie said, pointing to the Tysons' house. "Nice woman. Helped out at the church, she did."

Connor said nothing as his nostrils flared, and his breathing intensified.

"She took off so fast I didn't have time to return her deposit and some of the rent money. She left some stuff here, if that helps."

Gracie froze when she saw Connor's eyes bulge as his fists clenched. Feeling increasingly in danger, she looked around, hoping someone would happen by. She started to back away as his face got redder. "Do you need some water? Do you want to sit down?"

"No, I'm fine." Connor curtly snapped out of his rage. He jumped into his car and sped away. Gracie walked back to her house, shaking her head as she processed the peculiar encounter.

Having skipped breakfast, Connor stopped for lunch at the Gailsprings Family Diner before returning to the farm.

## Tres Bandidas

Back at the farmhouse, Connor paced around the kitchen floor. It had never captured his attention before, but any evidence of his father was gone: the microwave stand his father had built years ago, his favorite kitchen chair with the worn leather cushion, and the framed serenity prayer he received after teaching Sunday school. He bowed and shook his head in both sadness and dismay: his mother had erased any trace of Karl from the house.

Connor dialed Edna and Lester's landline. Lester answered on the fourth ring.

"Hi, Uncle Lester, it's Connor. I'm at the old farmhouse, and things just don't look right. You know anything about that?"

Lester shook his head as he answered. "Sure don't."

"How about Edna? Is she there?"

"No, she went to Reno." Lester paused, causing wrinkles of suspicion on Connor's forehead.

"Come to think of it, that woman who was living at your old house went with her," Lester continued. "I think her name was Caitlin, no wait, Kitty, yes, that's it, Kitty." Lester was distracted by the hurricane forecasts on the Weather Channel.

"Just the two of them?" Connor asked.

"No, another woman by the name of Lana. They were supposed to take Edna's car, but it's in the shop. Again!" Lester commented with breezy sarcasm. "She ran over a muffler in the light of day. So, I let them take my car."

"Did they say why they were going to Reno?" Connor casually asked.

"Yep. They wanted to see some shows, do a few slots, and hang out at the pool," Lester replied.

At that point, Connor knew that Lana had double-crossed him. He felt rage surging through his body and clenched his teeth. He knew the real reason they left town, but would not tell Lester.

"So, that must mean they're coming back," Connor assumed, suppressing his anger with a spurious neutral tone.

"Edna is, she has my car. I don't care if she stays in Reno, though, just so I get my car back. As for the other two, I don't know."

"How did Edna hook up with the other two women?" Connor asked.

"How should I know? You know Edna. She barges in when and where she wants to. You in town for long?" Lester asked.

"I'm not sure. That depends on a few things. When did they leave for Reno? You still got that personalized license plate?"

"I think it was Wednesday, no, wait, I got that wrong, it was Thursday, yesterday in fact, and yes, I still have that same plate. B4U-D1E. Edna hates it. She thinks it has something to do with her. All it means is that we need to live our lives before we die, like I'm even doing that," he bemoaned, his voice fading into nowhere.

Connor fell silent as he processed the situation.

"Connor, you still there? Is something wrong?" Lester asked.

"Nah, I just have to make some more calls, Uncle Lester. I'll talk to you later." Connor hurried the conversation to a close.

But for now, he needed to think clearly. He sat at the kitchen table, trying to contain his rage. "Damn it!" he yelled as he backhanded a box of graham crackers off the table, scattering them around the kitchen floor. He would call Wally.

Wally's phone number was still at the top of a list glued to the wall by the telephone in the kitchen. The list hadn't been updated for years and still included telephone numbers of people who had passed away years ago. Connor dialed Wally's number. It was a landline phone, and Ruth took the call.

"Hello."

"Hi, Mrs. Simonson. It's Connor, Connor Larson." Connor's abrupt and starchy voice drew a frown to Ruth's face.

"Oh, Connor! How nice to hear from you. But is everything alright?" she cautiously asked.

"I'm out at the house. Something's been going on around here, and I wonder if Wally knows anything about it."

Connor's voice was stiff and urgent, a signal to Ruth to restrain her curiosity instead of asking what was wrong. "I'll get him," Ruth said mechanically.

Many calls had come in on their landline over the years, and Ruth knew that sometimes time was of the essence. She covered the mouthpiece of the receiver and whispered, "It's Connor Larson."

"Hey, Connor. Ruth has an alarmed look on her face, so what's up?" Wally asked.

"Do you think you…could drive out here…so we can talk about this face-to-face? It's, um, sort of confidential," Connor sputtered, both embarrassed and enraged by the situation now facing him.

"Whatever you say, son. But unless it's an emergency, I'd like to have my lunch first and then make a couple of other stops."

"No, Wally, it's not an emergency." *Oh, but it is!* "But it is something big," Connor stressed.

"I'll be there when I can," Wally assured him.

"Sure, Wally. See you later."

Connor sat on the living room sofa, jumbled speculation swirling in his head. There were questions: *Was he naïve in trusting Lana? Why would she double-cross him? How could she be so deceptive?* There were promises: *She'll pay for this. Kitty and Edna will too.* An acidic cocktail of raw emotions bubbled through his veins: anger, revenge, hatred, malice.

Connor needed a distraction. Stepping out the kitchen door at the back of the house, he drew in several deep breaths. The late September sun was already working its way south after the autumn equinox. Beyond the cornfield, he could almost picture his father on the tractor, picking corn. The maples had lost their vibrant hues; the few leaves that clung to the branches had turned brittle and brown. Memories surfaced—his brothers raking leaves into a towering pile, then leaping into them from the roof of the granary. Nearby, the charred foundation of a once-sturdy barn stirred another memory, one he had never been able to forget. Turning back toward the house, he tried to summon an image of it alive with love, laughter, and warmth. No matter how hard he pushed, the fantasy dissolved before it could take shape.

He walked around the place while he was waiting for Wally to come. The old tire swing was still hanging from the oak tree out front. He couldn't remember which brother it was, but one of them pushed Connor so high that he fell off the swing. *Did his brother do that on purpose?* He remembered his bloody knees and palms and how his mother's panic escalated the gravity of the incident.

He entered the front porch, where he and his mother spent many summer hours reading. Looking in the small cabinet, he found a book about poisonous plants. He took it out and thumbed through it, pleased with himself that he could still identify most of the plants.

Suddenly, he tossed the book onto the floor. He hadn't thought of it until now—what if Wally asked him how Lana got in the house? He went into the kitchen and dug out the heavy meat pounder. *Perfect.* He was about to swing it against the kitchen window from the inside, but hesitated. *I have to do it from the outside.*

He went out the back door, rounded the lilac bushes that he used to hide in, and, with the stance of a designated hitter at home plate, swung the meat pounder against the brittle glass. Fueled by his anger, what might have only required a gentle tap sent shards of glass raining onto the kitchen floor. He wiped his fingerprints off the handle of the meat pounder and, for added effect, tossed it through the broken window. The crash, as it hit the kitchen floor, was cathartic.

Back in the kitchen, and considering the scene of the crime, he felt something nagging at him; something was off. *Who brings a meat pounder to break into a house?* He returned the meat pounder to the cupboard and went outside to find a rock. Choosing one about the size of his fist, he returned to the kitchen to reset the stage, placing the rock among the chips of glass that glistened like diamonds in the sunlight. With the broken window, the shattered glass, and the rock on the floor, he had achieved the cinematographic representation he needed.

## Whose Money?

Connor sat at the kitchen table, organizing documents, deeds, tax records, and other important papers until he finally heard the sound of a car on the gravel driveway. When he saw it was Wally, he darted out the back door. And with bounding long strides. He met Wally as he was opening the door of his squad car.

Wally could see the agitation in Connor's grimace as he initiated a handshake that Connor quickly dispensed with.

"Wally, let's go into the house." Connor's crisp suggestion further advanced Wally's perception that Connor was clearly anxious about something. They sat at the kitchen table. Wally looked around the room, noticing Graham crackers and shattered glass scattered on the floor.

"A lot of memories in this room. Not to mention this house and farm. We found your mother right over there," Wally said, pointing to a spot on the floor. "Hannah Severson called it in. She was supposed to take your mother into town for groceries. I always thought it was odd that Roberta never learned to drive."

Connor crossed and uncrossed his legs as his impatience grew.

Wally continued, "She was kind of a recluse, people thought. She was a looker, though, in her day. Ruth offered to take her shopping in Eau Claire more than once, so she could buy some nicer clothes. Was all that Karl's doing? Did he not want her to look nice?"

Connor flipped his arms into the air. "Pfft. How should I know?"

"So, what's going on out here?" Wally asked as he pointed to the broken window. "Obviously, something's up."

"You can say that again. As you see, someone broke into the house," Connor nodded toward the window. "And, apparently, she used a rock to do it."

"*She*?" Wally abruptly turned his eyes from the scene of the crime to Connor.

"Yes, she. I hooked up with a woman in Saint Paul. We had a fling. She seemed unusually interested in my past. More than once, I talked about this place, my parents, the way my brothers treated me, and how my dad burned down the barn."

"I was here that night. I saw you looking out a window. Your Aunt Edna was in the car with me. She had reason to believe Karl was out of his wits about something. And she was right."

"Anyway, I told her about my mother's treasure hunts. I told her about a few other things, too. I knew my mother kept a diary, and she kept it locked in a basement trunk."

Wally put his elbows on the table and leaned in.

"I also knew she had stashed a lot of money away in the safe. So, when I told her I thought my mother had left clues in the diary on how to get the safe open, she was very curious."

"People speculated about the settlement your mother got from her parents' deaths, believing it must not have been much, by the way you lived. But, apparently, it was. Any idea how much?" Wally asked.

"Over a million." Connor pulled his lips together as he stared at Wally.

"So, when I came here to meet my brothers since we're selling the house, I went into the basement and found the safe unlocked and no money in it. She suckered me in with her seductive wiles, like she had me pegged as an easy mark. She played me," he hissed.

Connor's disingenuous sneer and appraising stare at Wally was a look Wally had seen many times; he had heard many fabricated stories behind those theatrics.

"That's some story, Connor. And you didn't find the diary anywhere?"

"No. And then, when I called Lester, he told me that Lana, the woman I met in college, someone named Kitty, and my Aunt Edna had skipped town—with our money. They went to Reno, with our money!" Connor howled.

"Why didn't you boys get that money right after your mother's death?" Wally noticed a slight twitch in Connor's left eye.

"I had to get back to school. We've tried many times to meet here, but we never seem to be able to pull it off. We finally agreed to meet here the last weekend in September, but that changed when 3M sent me to Brussels. But we finished our project early, which explains why I'm here now."

"But it doesn't explain how she knew you were in Brussels, or that you were selling the house."

"I think I know the answer to that. During one of her calls to me while I was in Belgium, my wife told me that a woman had called, saying that she knew me from high school and that they were planning a class reunion. I didn't think anything of it at the time, but now I'm convinced it was Lana."

Do you have any proof that your mother left a specific amount of money in that safe?" Wally asked.

"One time, I saw her put money into a sock and toss it into the safe. It looked like a lot of money to me. The safe was almost full of socks. Plus, one time she told me I would be a millionaire when she died."

"I see," Wally remarked, as he carefully watched for the telltale signs those in his profession look for: eye movements, body language, nervous tics.

"I thought she was just predicting my future. My mother could be a spooky woman at times. She claimed she could communicate with the dead and see the future."

"Why didn't she just include the combination in the diary?" Wally asked.

"Who knows? Like I said, she often set up treasure hunts for me around the house and farm. Maybe she wanted to send me on one last treasure hunt," Connor speculated. "She could be a bit prankish with me sometimes. She also might have thought that my father would find the diary and eventually open the safe, I don't know, I just don't know," he admitted. "Nobody could ever figure out my mother."

"There must have been a will of some kind?" Wally reasoned.

"Yes, but there was no mention of the safe," Connor replied.

"Is the safe open now?"

"Yes."

"Can I see it?" Wally stood as he asked.

They went into the basement, where Wally looked around, careful not to touch anything. When he saw the empty safe, he turned to Connor and said, "So, what now?"

As they ascended the stairs, Connor's rage intensified with each step. Once in the kitchen, he exploded. "Those three stole my—our money! And to think my Aunt Edna is in on it?" Connor yelled as he paced the floor.

"Don't ever put anything past your Aunt Edna, Connor," Wally said as he stood and walked over to the window to watch a flock of Canada geese cutting through the sky in a V-formation.

"We'll be seeing and hearing a lot of that over the next few weeks," Wally observed, still looking out the window, hoping the interruption would calm down Connor.

"You say they have Lester's car?" Wally asked before he turned around.

"Yes."

"I could put a BOLO on it. I know his license plate by heart. Been seeing it around town for years. I hope you didn't compromise anything in the basement. There's bound to be some evidence of their presence down there: fingerprints, fibers, who knows? Wally said.

"I did touch the trunk and the safe," Connor replied.

"We can deal with that if and when the time comes. In the meantime, I'll call Reno. Did Lester tell you when they left town?"

"Yes, it was Thursday, yesterday. I missed them by a day."

"And that's probably a good thing. Who knows what might have happened?" Wally's eyes fixed on Connor, who stood with a distant gaze in his eyes as he looked out the broken window.

"Connor, why don't you follow me back to our house. It would do you no good to spend the night out here." Wally walked out the door, knowing Connor would follow.

## Connor's Queries

Wally called Ruth on his drive back into town.

"Connor Larson is behind me. I told him he could spend the night with us. I hope that's OK."

"Of course it is. But why is he here? Is everything all right?" Ruth's question deserved a detailed answer.

"I'll tell you about it later."

Wally parked in the garage and Connor on the street. Ruth met them at the door leading from the garage to the kitchen.

"Connor, come on over here. Give me a big hug."

"It's good to see you, Mrs. Simonson."

"Mrs. Simonson? Oh, Connor, just call me Ruth. I'm not your high school English teacher anymore. Your room is up these stairs and to the right. There's a bathroom right next door. Make yourself comfortable. I'll call you when supper is on the table. I'm making stuffed cabbage rolls and an apple crisp for supper."

Connor unpacked his Louis Vuitton suitcase and took a shower. While he waited for Ruth to call him down for supper, he phoned Lana. The call went to voicemail. His message was brief:"Where the hell are you? And where is my money?" Of course, since Lana's phone was now in a dumpster in Omaha, his message would go unanswered.

Around the supper table, they traded updates—news from Galesprings and stories from Connor's life.

"So, Connor, Edna tells me you're married. We would like to hear about it, wouldn't we, Wally?" Ruth looked at Wally as he nodded in agreement. The conversation went on until Ruth stood to clear the table.

Wally grabbed two beers and led Connor out to the front porch.

There were a few lingering clouds in the sky, and a light, gentle breeze played at the wind chimes on the porch. They sat in silence. That's what Wally thought Connor needed. The shadows around them were getting longer as the sky turned a pinkish yellow.

"Wally, aren't you close to retirement by now?" Connor eventually asked.

"I could have retired years ago. But what would I do? True, this town has changed over the years, but I still know a lot of people. In some cases, three generations worth."

"Wally, I don't think I ever saw you trying to chase down a runner."

"I've done a few. You boys weren't in town as often as some of the other country boys. I'd see your older brothers in town once in a while, but not so much you."

"Yes, they were always more gregarious than I was," Connor admitted.

"As for retirement, I will do it at the end of next year. How Ruth is going to put up with me puttering around the place, I don't know."

They sat in silence again until Ruth came out to say goodnight.

"I'm going to call it a night. I'll do some reading upstairs. Connor, you were a voracious reader in high school. I hope you still are."

"When I have the time, two boys, a wife, and a full-time job keep me on the go."

"Wally, should I turn on the porch light?" Ruth asked.

"Naw, it just attracts bugs."

"Well, goodnight then," Ruth said.

The two men quietly watched the stars emerge in the inky sky.

"Connor, you got something on your mind?" Wally asked.

"Yes, I guess I do. It has to do with my parents, the relationship they had with each other, and how my father was always so distant with me," Conner explained.

"Ok, I'm listening," Wally encouraged Connor to continue.

"My dad was a kind, gentle, and compassionate man. He was always helping other people. I think his working all the time was also an escape mechanism, to get out of the house, away from my mother." Connor set his empty beer can on the porch floor. "They were so different. I never considered it much as a small boy, but as I got older, it was clear they both held a grudge against each other."

"Well, Connor, there was a lot going on out there. And I'm no therapist, so I'll leave it to you to draw your own conclusions."

"It's odd. Now that I am a father, I see my father differently," Connor said.

"There's nothing odd about it. That's how it works."

"Growing up, I often heard comments about how different I was from my brothers. I also overheard my father accusing my mother of doing something in the past, something he called a carnal sin."

"It's too bad you had to hear all that," Wally replied. "But every family has its drama, dysfunction, and blemishes. We may not get over the hurt they caused, but we do need to get through it."

"You know, I think my father wanted to die. He put off going to the doctor until it was too late. It was his way out of that marriage."

"Things like that happen sometimes. Putting an end to one's life takes many forms and with many reasons." Wally professed. "Being in the profession I'm in, I've heard so many hurtful things people say to each other that I could write a book."

"At the time, I gave little thought to what she had done. But after my father's death, something happened; memories started popping up in my head. When they had those heated discussions, my father often said, 'Your son Connor. ' I must have suppressed that." Connor hesitated before he asked Wally the question that had eaten at him for years.

"Was Karl implying that he wasn't my biological father?" Connor was fishing, and he wanted Wally to bite.

Wally's posture stiffened.

"Be careful, Connor. Sometimes skeletons are best left in the closet," Wally counselled.

"Let me ask you point-blank. Was Karl my biological father?" Connor looked straight at Wally.

"Did either of them tell you that, *point blank?*"

"No. But you could," Connor proffered.

"I don't know what to say, Connor. What would you do if you found out he wasn't? What would it change?"

"It would give me peace of mind, Wally. It would lift this weight off my mind."

"It might give you peace of mind, but what if it turns out to be true that Karl wasn't your biological father? Something like can tear apart families, yours and any others involved."

Connor fixed his eyes on the floor of the wooden porch and let Wally's comments percolate in his head.

"You know what they say about playing with fire," Wally wisely advised, looking Connor squarely in the eye. Connor's intuition coaxed him to ask one more question.

"So, who was he?

"Connor, even if I knew, I wouldn't tell you."

Wally rose out of the rocking chair, leaving it to continue rocking as he stood.

"Good night, Connor."

"Good night, Wally. And thanks." The screen slammed shut with a springy twang.

# CHAPTER 24

# KITTY COCKTAIL

**Saturday, September 26**

After a light breakfast, the three fugitives left Sterling with the wind at their backs. As they walked to the car, Kitty surprised them with a question. "How about if I drive this time?"

Lana's skeptical glance at Edna was met with the guarded look of someone worried about her husband's car.

"Don't worry, I'm a good driver." Kitty approached the driver's door.

"Well, I suppose," Edna begrudgingly conceded. "But once we get close to Denver, I'm taking over."

"No," Lana corrected Edna. "Then, I'm taking over. Edna, the way you drove around Des Moines left me with white knuckles. Denver isn't Galesprings. I'll do the driving, and you do the gawking."

"Well, I'll think about it," Edna huffed.

"Lana's right, Edna," Kitty concurred.

"I said I'll think about it. Now let's get going." Edna would ride shotgun to keep an eye on Kitty's driving. Lana grabbed the atlas and sat in the back, concentrating on the map of Mexico.

Soon, the traffic was picking up, and Edna ordered Kitty to pull off the highway.

"Lana, the steering wheel's all yours," Edna declared. "Kitty, how about you join Lana up front?"

Back on the highway, Edna opened the atlas to find where they were.

"What state are we in anyway?" Edna wondered aloud.

"Colorado," Kitty answered. "We're just approaching Denver," Lana clarified. As they got closer to Denver, Lana unmuted the GPS.

"We're going to hit some heavy traffic now, so don't distract me," Lana said while adjusting the rear-view mirror.

Edna struggled to buckle her seatbelt for the first time since they left Galesprings. Lana spirited them through the relentless Denver traffic, weaving in and out of lanes like a local. Kitty and Edna held their breath a couple of times as Lana crisscrossed multiple lanes. But they admitted they found the ride exhilarating.

That night, they stayed in Grand Junction, Colorado. Edna said that either Lana or Kitty could have a private room, but they both declined. After they freshened up, they met in the lobby to go out for dinner.

"I hope we can go where I can get a cocktail," Kitty surprised both Lana and Edna with her suggestion. "This has been a long day, and after that petrifying drive through Denver, I need something strong." They agreed to meet in Lana and Kitty's room at six.

Lana pulled out a pair of black dress slacks and a leopard skin print top from her suitcase. She added gold slingback shoes and gold earrings. Kitty opted for black Givenchy boot cut jeans, red sandals, and a crimson red Versace draped neckline blouse. She chose a silver theme for her jewelry. Edna entered their room wearing the same white slacks from the night before, but this time with a floral blouse.

"Edna, I have the perfect necklace to go with that blouse." Kitty took her jewelry box out of her suitcase and produced a rose gold necklace with a trio of brilliant sapphires. Kitty put the necklace around Edna's neck and clasped it from behind.

After they were seated at the restaurant, Kitty ordered a martini, Edna a white wine, and Lana a gin and tonic.

All three ordered the ribeye steak special. The effect of Kitty's first-ever martini became obvious even before it was half finished. All three laughed boisterously at the alliteration Lana coined: Giddy Kitty. Lana slid Kitty's martini glass off to the side and moved her water glass in its place. They lingered at the table, talking about misadventures in the past.

Edna talked about last year when she backed into the mayor's car that was parked in front of a fire hydrant. "It was worth it. He got a parking ticket, and there was a picture of the scene all over social media."

Kitty told about the time she jumped her horse over a police car at the county fair. "My father thought it was a beautiful jump, but the two officers inside weren't amused."

Lana recalled her introduction to Jello shots at a frat party in Saint Paul. "I now stay away from Jello in any form."

During their walk back to the hotel, they tried to sing "Viva Las Vegas," but those were the only three words they knew from the movie. Kitty, with one shoe in hand, suggested that Lana sing *viva*, Edna sing *las* and Kitty sing *Vegas*. Edna and Lana went along with it, and they might have passed as schoolgirls on a sugar high.

## Forget About Justice

When Wally and Ruth returned from visiting Ruth's aged mother in an assisted living facility in Sparta, Ruth went directly to the kitchen where a pot roast was simmering in the crockpot.

Wally poured himself and Connor a small glass of Mogen David wine, and they sat on the front porch.

"I heard from Reno. They'll watch for the plates and keep an eye on them."

"So, they split the money three ways. Is that what you think?" Connor asked.

"They might," Wally speculated. "Then again, who knows how this might all play out."

"Do you think Edna will come back to Galesprings?" Connor wondered as he stood and paced the creaky porch floor.

"Yes, I do. And when I approach her, she'll say she didn't know anything about Lana's plan to steal your money." Wally looked Connor straight in the eye. "That is what happened, right? I'd hate to find out later that there is an alternate version of the story."

"Yes, of course. I told Lana about the money, never thinking she'd cheat me out of it. Why would she?"

"Well, Connor, when you've been in law enforcement as long as I have, there are many answers to your question, way more answers than we have time for."

Connor heightened his pace, the coiled tension on his face casting a menacing aura.

"If the other two fly out of Reno, then that's easy to track. But they might each buy a car, most likely a used one, so they don't attract attention. But I doubt whether they will leave together," Wally reasoned.

Connor stopped pacing and looked squarely at Wally.

"I want them caught, and I want the book thrown at them!" Connor's taut voice was uncharacteristic of the Connor Wally knew as a boy. The bulging veins in Connor's neck, along with his red face, made it apparent to Wally that he needed to do something to diffuse Connor.

"Let's take it down a notch, son," Wally suggested with both hands pushing downward in front of him. "You want justice, and so do I."

"I don't care about justice," Connor icily snapped as he looked down at Wally, who was still seated. With flared nostrils and raised eyebrows, Connor bitterly whispered, "I want revenge."

Wally stiffened as he winced at Connor's confession but said nothing. Connor glanced away and stared at the floor.

"Wally, Connor, lunch is ready," Ruth called out from the kitchen, not knowing that her timing was the interruption they both needed.

With their lunch of pot roast, mashed potatoes, and glazed carrots on the table, the three sat down to eat.

Wally took a nap after the meal, and Connor and Ruth played cribbage in the kitchen. After two rounds, Connor announced that he'd like to drop in on some friends from high school.

"Of course, sure. Might I ask who?" Ruth wondered.

"Willie Madison, for one. We were on the debate team together. He was vicious when he debated, sometimes a bit too much." Connor opined. "And then, if there's time, I'll pop in at the bowling alley. I'm sure to find someone there I know."

"Are you coming back this evening? We'll probably have leftovers," Ruth said as she put away the cribbage board.

"If you're not getting sick of me, yes, that sounds good," Connor said.

Wally, refreshed from his nap, walked into the kitchen and heard the exchange. "Let's have a brandy Manhattan before dinner tonight. It's been a while," he suggested. "And it being a Saturday night, maybe even two."

# CHAPTER 25

# A WHITE POWDER

**Sunday, September 27**

The next morning, after a hearty breakfast of buttermilk pancakes and sausage, Connor declined an invitation to join Wally and Ruth at church, opting instead to drive out to the farm and then back to Minneapolis.

It was a sunny day, so he strolled around the buildings for what should have been the last time. When he approached the old outhouse, he remembered he had carved his name into the back of it. *Was it still there?*

It was late in the season, and the hollyhocks around the outhouse were losing their color. He saw that some plants had been trampled on. Was it a deer? Or a bear?

He slowly moved closer, keenly listening for sounds other than the wind. It was clear that someone had recently dug there. He doubted it was an animal because the topsoil had been replaced. A person had recently buried something there, he surmised. He went back to his father's old tool shed for a shovel and approached the area, wielding the shovel as a weapon. You never know, he thought. He stomped on the ground, but nothing happened. He jammed the shovel into the ground and started to dig.

He stopped when he first saw something white and powdery mixed in with the dark soil. He bent over and, with his hand, scooped up a small amount of the mixture. Standing next to the withering hollyhocks, he moistened his index finger with his tongue and dipped it into the white powder. "Ashes," he said aloud.

The wind was turning the long-abandoned windmill blades that once supplied water for the livestock. The screeching sound from the rusted gears distracted Connor, who stared vacantly at the revolving windmill blades. It was the sound that lulled him to sleep on many a fitful night while growing up.

Taking the shovel once again, Connor continued digging. He discovered a small piece of something. Was it a small rock? Maybe a bone? He picked it up and blew the dirt and ashes away.

He held the small corner of the cover of his mother's diary and squeezed it tightly. Seething with vengeance, he looked at the horizon and bellowed, "Lana, you're going to pay for this!"

Moments later, he heard a car pulling onto the gravel driveway. He put the potential evidence in his pocket and went to meet him. He was sure Wally would want to see what he found. He walked to the front of the house where the realtor was getting out of his car.

"Well, Connor, as it turns out, the financing came through. You can close next weekend." Connor quickly called Matt and told him the good news. They would need to come to Galesprings on the first Saturday in October.

## Enroute to Vegas

The novelty of the trip was waning with Las Vegas their next stop. Edna had just finished paging through the atlas, and Kitty had just put her nail polish away after unsuccessfully trying to paint her nails in a moving vehicle.

Suddenly, Kitty blurted out a revelation. "Hey, I got it. We can call ourselves ELK."

"What?" Edna scowled from the rear seat.

"ELK, as in Edna, Lana, and Kitty. I don't mind being the last. And Edna, surely, you'd want to go first."

"Why do we need to call ourselves anything? It's not like we're starting a sorority, Kitty. You understand that we're not a team, an association, or an order." Lana kept her eyes on the road while she said it.

"Maybe we could use it as a password or a code word," Kitty persisted.

"A password for what? We're not spies, Kitty," Edna snickered. "And why would we need a code word?"

"How about we stick to Edna, Lana, and Kitty?" Lana suggested. "In any order."

"You two are no fun. I'm just trying to lighten things up, you know, make the trip go faster." Kitty felt deflated. She wasn't nearly as thick-skinned as Edna and Lana. Not many were.

Kitty saw the sign for a rest area and suggested they stop. "I need to go."

Lana gladly took the exit for the rest area, craving some time for herself more than anything else.

With the necessities out of the way, Lana strolled around the rest area, relishing her momentary solitude. Edna cornered a couple whose car had a Wisconsin license plate. "Oh, I see you're from Wisconsin. What part?"

The elderly couple stretched as they stood next to the open doors of their car. "We're from the Beaver Dam area. Just off US ten to the north."

"Heading for Vegas, I suppose," Edna speculated.

"Oh, no, the woman seemed scandalized by the suggestion." Our grandson and his wife just had a baby." With the photo of the infant now on the screen of her phone, she approached Edna to show her. "Isn't she precious?" the woman gurgled.

"Oh, yes, now *that's* a baby," Edna agreed, giving her the pat answer she used every time someone showed her a picture of a baby.

Lana continued driving, and soon they turned south on I-15. "This is the last stretch that will take us all the way to Vegas."

Kitty and Edna both cheered.

"We'll be in Nevada soon," Lana added.

"Nevada," Kitty repeated the state name. "Now, let me think. There must be a song about Nevada. Back in Alabama, we have 'The Stars Fell on Alabama' and in Kentucky, there's 'Kentucky Moon Keep on Shining'. It was in Sally's jukebox. What about Tennessee, Lana?"

"For one, we have 'The Tennessee Waltz'. I'm sure there's more, it's Tennessee, after all. Then there's 'Rocky Top', by the Osborne Brothers."

"And you, Edna, anything with Wisconsin in it?" Kitty turned around to face Edna.

"Honestly, Kitty. How should I know? But I suppose we have something. Now that I think of it, we have 'On Wisconsin', which is somehow connected to sports. Other than that, the only other song I would suggest as our state song would be "Ninety-Nine Bottles of Beer on the Wall."

Kitty started to sing the song.

"Oh, God. What have I done?" Edna looked to the heavens for divine intervention.

Lana turned the radio on full blast.

A mile later, the challenge was over and peace regained, if only for a moment.

"Thank God!" Edna didn't address the heavens this time.

Kitty continued trying to come up with songs with either state or city names in them.

"Of course, there's also 'Sweet Home Alabama.' I loved that movie. Josh Lucas was totally hot," Kitty crossed her hands over her heart.

"Never heard of him." Of course, Edna had never heard of him, but she did think Robert Conrad was hot in her day.

"'All My Exes Live in Texas' That's another one. But I think Alan Jackson is much hotter than George Strait," Kitty volunteered.

"Tennessee is also mentioned in that song—That's why I hang my hat in Tennessee." Lana sang the line.

"Then there's 'Shenandoah.' That's not a state, of course. That was such a sad movie, except at the end when one of the sons returns home and walks into that church. I cry every time I see that scene," Kitty confessed. "Edna, have you ever cried during a movie?"

Kitty doubted Edna would admit something like that.

"Well, for one, Love Story. I thought that line about 'love means never having to say you're sorry' was a bunch of bunk. But it was a sad movie," Edna admitted wistfully.

"And you, Lana?" Kitty asked.

"I'd have to say Steel Magnolias. True, there's a lot of humor in the movie, but when Shelby dies at the end, I can't imagine anyone not crying."

Lana, hoping to change the mood in the car, came up with 'I Left My Heart in San Francisco'. Again, she sang it.

"I got one," Edna jumped in. "California Dreamin'. All the leaves are brown, and the sky is gray," she belted out the words as if she were Mama Cass herself.

With their song-a-thon exhausted and still unable to find one for Nevada, the three turned their attention to the scenery.

## Cacti

With only hours before their arrival in Las Vegas, Edna made an observation. "I don't know when I have seen so many cactuses."

Kitty jumped at the chance for payback. "Cactuses, Edna, did you just say cactuses? I suppose being from Galesprings, Wisconsin, you wouldn't know that the plural of cactus is cacti. As in 'I don't know when I have seen so many cacti'."

"I don't care what the plural form is. There's just a lot of them, that's all."

"I remember that from high school Latin," Kitty proudly professed.

"Don't tell us they let *you* take Latin," Edna added.

Now somewhat inured to Edna's insults, Kitty wasn't fazed.

"Does that mean that you went to a Catholic high school?" Lana asked.

"No, I went to a private school, but it wasn't just Catholic. I took Latin as an elective. I was good at it too, I'll have you know." Kitty declared as she looked back at Edna.

The mood turned subdued as the three marveled at the unusual scenery. How different this was from the places the three had spent all, if not most, of their lives; Kitty in the flat terrain of Alabama, Lana in the foothills of the Smoky Mountains, and Edna in the driftless area of Wisconsin.

"I'm not sure if those are buttes or mesas," Lana wondered aloud. "I took a geology course at Macalester, but it really wasn't my thing."

"This scenery is kind of spooky in a way. Like we're on another planet. A planet from Star Wars, maybe. I wonder if they shot some of those scenes right here?" Kitty figured Lana would know what she was talking about, but as for Edna, probably not.

Edna knew enough not to ask Chatty Kitty to elaborate. That was Edna's new moniker for Kitty, even though she had yet to disclose it.

Since it was fall, many of the flowers native to Utah were past their prime. They saw some purple thistles and white buckwheat, several types of grasses and shrubs, and some pinyon goosefoot stems sticking up. As they got closer to southern Utah, the flowers became more abundant and more colorful. Some yellow columbines were still in bloom, though not for long. Lana had rarely paid attention to flowers and wished she was in the back seat instead of driving.

"Kitty, look at those pale blue flowers to your left." Edna meant the chicory blossoms.

Later, Lana spotted some chokecherry trees, now turning a reddish purple in tune with the season. Edna recognized some purple coneflowers on their right and called Lana's attention to them.

"Lana, don't you love those purple flowers on your left?" Kitty asked in an effort to get Lana to enjoy at least some of the scenery.

"They look like thistles to me." Lana was right, they were Purple Bull Thistles.

Her dismissive comment belied her increasing interest in the flora and fauna of their journey. Her mother had flower gardens all around their property, but Lana took little interest in them.

When they got to Mezquite, Lana pulled off the highway for gas. Before she got out of the car, Kitty asked her to open the trunk. Edna got out to stretch her legs as Kitty fumbled around in her open suitcase while it was still in the trunk. When she found what she was after, she slipped off her Christian Louboutin flats and put on her black Prada heels.

"Las Vegas, here I come," Kitty announced to the world as she sashayed around the gas pumps, pirouetting at the end of each bank of pumps before launching into a variety of affectations.

Edna stood aghast. With her right hand over her mouth, she hastily scanned the area for onlookers. Lana squealed with delight, clapping her hands until Kitty's maneuvers ended and the bearded cowboy at a nearby gas pump started to whistle. "I'd go to Vegas with you anytime, pussycat," he pledged.

"Well, her name *is* Kitty," Edna told the cowboy out of the side of her mouth.

Lana continued driving. They would be in Vegas traffic soon, and Kitty would be arriving in heels.

"It will be nice to be in Las Vegas, where I can finally dress up. Wait until you two see the fabulous black Versace dress I bought the last time my mother and I went to Atlanta to go shopping. We had so much fun. She is a different person when she gets away from home. I miss her for that." Kitty turned to look out the side window as soft tears gradually streamed down her cheeks.

Having composed herself over the next few miles, Kitty began thinking about things to do in Vegas. "I doubt I'll gamble. We'll have to go to some fine restaurants. I wonder what shows are on in Vegas? I'd like to go to one of those shows where those hunky men strip down to barely anything. The Chip..., chip something."

"Chippendales, Kitty. Chippendales." Edna's off-the-cuff response amused Kitty and Lana, who looked sideways at each other with endearing grins.

"Kitty, it appears there's more to Edna than we know."

Edna picked up on Lana's playful cadence with a boastful confession. "I've been around. I've had my fun," Edna foxishly gloated. "Don't think I haven't."

Neither Kitty nor Lana spoke right away, which gave Edna room to reminisce and left them with an unwanted moment to imagine.

"I had one of their calendars in my bedroom back home. My mother pretended to be mortified by it. Funny thing, though, I caught her staring at it more than once." Kitty's words trailed off as the memory precipitated another pang of homesickness.

"If we're going to eat at fancy restaurants, I'll need to do some shopping first."

The uncharacteristic excitement in Edna's voice fed Kitty's inclination to offer her expertise in the world of fashion. "I'll go with you, Edna. This will be fun," Kitty gushed.

Lana, who still had a few surprises in her luggage from her shopping sprees in Louisville, said she'd bow out of a shopping trip.

## Blue Lights

They were approaching Las Vegas, and the traffic was picking up but not slowing down. Lana had entered the address of their hotel into the GPS and unmuted the system once again. Surrounded by cars, trucks, and construction equipment, Edna once again put on her seatbelt. As she fought with it, she revealed her frustration with a pithy comment. "I hate these damn things!" Once it clicked, she settled down. "There!"

"Now, Lana," Edna advised. "Try not to make those scary maneuvers you made back in Denver. We want to live to spend this money."

And that's when Lana saw the flashing red and blue lights coming up from behind.

"Shit. It's the cops," she announced. Both Kitty and Edna turned around, repeating the expletive.

Lana could see the vehicles behind them pulling off to the side of the road. She did the same. The squad car parked at an angle in front of them. An officer got out of the car and walked toward the driver's door. Lana rolled down her window.

"Good afternoon, ma'am. Can I see your license and registration?" The officer asked.

"Officer, Waldman, I see. Why did you stop us?" Lana asked.

"First things first, license and registration, please."

The officer took both documents to her squad car. Kitty blathered nervously while Edna and Lana remained silent.

"You two, let me do the talking when she returns!" It wasn't a suggestion; Lana was emphatic. After what seemed like an eternity, the officer returned.

"The license checks out, but this car is registered in the name of someone else." The officer handed Lana her license but kept the registration. "You mind explaining that?" she asked.

The officer stiffened when she saw someone in the back seat suddenly lean forward.

"It's my husband's car. Lester Stern is his name." Edna blurted.

The officer responded. "Can I see some identification from you, ma'am?"

Edna sat back in her seat and anxiously rifled through her purse. Once she found her driver's license, she handed it to Lana, who gave it to the officer. Satisfied that nothing was amiss, she returned both documents to Lana. "You ladies have a safe trip now."

"Excuse me, officer, but why did you stop us?" Lana asked.

"I stopped you because someone reported a car like this one speeding and weaving in and out of traffic. But I can see it's not you. Have a safe trip, and sorry for the interruption."

Lana rolled up the window, put on her left blinker, and eased onto the highway.

Kitty stopped biting her nails. "That was close. My heart is still racing," she said with an audible exhale.

"I saw myself in handcuffs," Edna admitted. "Then I realized they would need a warrant to search the trunk."

Lana spoke next. "This is Lester's car. We could have said we had no idea the money was there."

"That is chillingly ruthless, Lana," Edna said from the back seat. "And to think that it was Lester's idea to let us use his car."

Wally received a call an hour later. "We stopped them just north of Las Vegas. We then tailed them to the Hampton Inn Tropicana," Office Pérez said."

"So, Reno was a subterfuge. Probably Edna's idea. I got a guy in Vegas. I'll call him to keep an eye on the three. Thanks, Officer Pérez."

## Modista Mode

Before checking in at the Hampton Inn Tropicana, Lana suggested they splurge and all get separate rooms.

"I don't know, Lana," Kitty said. "I might miss your snoring."

"Very funny, Kitty. And I might miss you talking about Robie in your sleep. I've learned a lot over the past few days. Some of it is titillating."

Edna raised a supercilious eyebrow in Kitty's direction.

"That's not true, and you know it!" Kitty coyly denounced.

Edna and Kitty agreed to meet at 4:30 in the main lobby to go shopping.

Kitty tried to steer Edna into some of the more high-end boutiques, but Edna wouldn't have it.

"I'm taking a taxi to Target. No use spending all that money on a dress I'll probably never wear outside of Vegas. Are you coming along?" Edna asked.

When they got to the store, Kitty trailed Edna, who somehow knew the layout of the place. Kitty, shifting into modista mode, eagerly pulled dresses off the racks and shoved them at Edna, who looked at the price tag before she looked at the dress. Weary of the ordeal, Edna caved in and grabbed a dress out of Kitty's hand, relieved not to have to hear another, "this one's perfect for you."

As planned, the three met for drinks in the hotel lounge. Lana walked in first, wearing a violet chiffon sleeveless halter top dress with mauve two-inch pumps. Her diamond earrings sparkled in the ambient light of the bar. She sat at the bar and ordered a Gibson martini, aware of the glances she was getting.

Moments later, Kitty arrived, gliding in like a Hollywood star over the red carpet on Oscar night. Her Donna Karan black sheath with gold brush strokes was perfect with the Prada heels she had modeled at the gas station. The string of pearls around her neck swayed gracefully over her breasts as she bobbed her way to the bar. But it was her peacock flapper headband that stole the show. She gently set her gold Gucci clutch on the bar and ordered Champagne.

"Kitty," Lana said. "Imagine if Robie could see you now. He would be down on one knee, and there wouldn't be a dry eye in the house." Kitty was so touched by Lana's words that she had to suppress the tears lest her mascara run.

It wasn't until some twenty minutes later that Edna slipped unnoticed into the lounge.

"Edna, you look lovely," Lana gushed. "And that gold necklace is stunning over the emerald green dress."

Edna fondled the necklace. "Kitty loaned it to me." Edna held her open hand to block Kitty from seeing her lips. "Let's hope she forgets about it before the night is over," Edna replied with a wink.

Kitty faked a startled look and then joined in the laughter. Edna ordered a double bourbon on the rocks.

When the bartender returned with Edna's drink, he leaned back to size up the three women. "Something tells me I'm serving three generations of the same family. And all lovely women at that."

Lana was quick to dispel his observation. "Actually, we barely know each other. We're here on business." She saw no reason to lie.

They finished their drinks and took a taxi to the Flamingo Casino, where Lana, following Kyle's advice, had earlier reserved a table at Bugsy and Meyers. Since they weren't driving, and this was Vegas, they had another round of drinks. Then they splurged on a pricey meal that Kitty found routine, Lana was becoming increasingly comfortable with, and Edna couldn't wait to describe to Lester so he could be flabbergasted.

# CHAPTER 26

# THE RUNNING OF THE ELK

## Wednesday, September 30

It was Wednesday morning, and as they had agreed the night before, it was time to leave Las Vegas. At Lana's suggestion, the three spent their casino time converting their smaller bills into larger ones at the cashier's stand. "Why bother with anything under a hundred?" Lana shrugged. "And besides, this way we reduce the bulk and not the value."

Edna gave Lana an approving nod. *Maybe she's not so bad after all.*

"So, where should I drop you off?" Edna asked Kitty and Lana. Edna's role would end soon. She played it well, she thought. Sitting around the pool, she pretended to be on guard, imagining FBI agents crashing through the gate. While at the casino, she scouted out the exits, in case she needed to make a run for it. Even at the cashiers' windows, she pretended to be passing off freshly minted bills. Granted, she was no Barbara Stanwyck or Sharon Stone. But starring in her own movie, one she also directed, was all she needed.

Kitty answered first. "I talked to my mother last night. She wants me to come home. She bought me a plane ticket from here to Birmingham. You could drop me at the airport."

"And you, Lana?"

"I'm going to stay here until I make up my mind where I want to settle down. I hear Oregon's nice, but maybe too cold, now that I think of it. Maybe somewhere in California. You can drop me off at the Bellagio. I plan to check the classifieds and buy a car. I'm sure I can find a seller who wants to deal in cash."

Edna dropped Lana off first. She was just going to say goodbye from the driver's seat until she saw Kitty get out of the car. She joined Kitty and Lana as they stood at the entrance to the casino and hotel.

"You know, Lana, you're alright. I wish you the best. It's not too late to settle down as you say. Get married. You and Connor would've made a good match." Edna paused to scrutinize Lana, tilting her head and scrunching her eyes. "But then again, maybe not; you're both so," Edna searched for a kinder word, "so driven." Edna gave Lana a back-slapping hug and returned to the driver's seat, leaving Kitty and Lana to themselves.

"You know, I'll miss you, Lana. We were so close growing up, and then we reconnected, and now we have to say goodbye. Maybe even for—forever." Kitty broke into tears with the word forever.

Lana pulled her in and held her tight." We'll see what happens, Kitty, once things settle down."

Kitty pulled away, wiping her tears with the tissue Lana handed her.

"Bye, Kitty. I'm so glad you're going home. Call Robie. He told me he wants to marry you. He's just a little shy. He'll make a good husband and father."

Kitty's sobs halted Lana's next words.

"If you're smart, Kitty, you'd somehow get rid of that money before you leave here. It will haunt you for the rest of your life. And it's not worth the risk."

"Are you suggesting that I give it to you?"

"No, Kitty, I'm not. But Edna is a volatile and reckless person; if she gets caught, then so do we. Just leave it somewhere at the airport, somewhere away from cameras, maybe the restroom."

"Maybe I should do that," Kitty whimpered.

"And one last thing, Kitty. I want you to have this." Lana handed Kitty a large envelope. "In there are the two key fobs for a Volvo I bought. It's in storage in Louisville. You'll find the address inside, along with the title, which I have signed over to you. Consider it an early wedding present."

"That's too much," Kitty said, shaking her head no.

"Not for what I got you into. The key to my apartment is also in there. As is the address. Take anything you want. I have an extensive wardrobe, much of which should fit you. The combination to the safe is also in there. Everything in there is yours; the money, the jewelry, everything."

Kitty made no effort to stanch the flow of tears as Lana hugged her.

"I love you, Kitty. As of now, I am likely to end up in Mexico. Somehow, I will contact you and let you know for sure." Lana walked away before Kitty could ask any questions.

Instead of dropping Kitty off at the airport, Edna parked and went in with her. They saw that Kitty's flight wasn't until three hours later.

"Do you want me to wait with you, Kitty?"

Edna's warm-hearted question was a sharp contrast to the surly Edna that Kitty had seen in the basement and kitchen of the farmhouse. Kitty thought back to the conversation she and Lana had had the night before.

"I still can't believe she settled for only 20%. But, then again, I wonder if it was really less about the money and more about revenge of some kind. From what I heard in the kitchen of that Lutheran church, Edna doesn't lack for money," Lana had said.

"Maybe so," Kitty replied. "But what I wonder is if she was in more for the adventure than anything. She was the one who orchestrated the trip to Las Vegas. I think instead of vicariously living those crime shows she's always talking about, she simply wanted some action in her otherwise mundane life."

"How perspicacious of you, Kitty. I think you're right," Lana pursed her lips as she nodded in agreement.

A thunderous jet taking off distracted Edna and Kitty. "No, Edna, no need for you to wait. You know, deep down, I see you as a caring person. Maybe you should let others see that too." For the second time, Kitty's observations rang true, and Edna knew it.

"You're doing the right thing, you know, going home to your mother. I think you will both understand each other better now. And besides, you have to find yourself a husband."

"You sound like my mother," Kitty joked.

"I'm sure she's very proud of you and will be delighted to have you home again," Edna tenderly replied. "And what about Robie?"

"He's still in Louisville. I talked to him last night. He says he has a surprise for me when I get back to Louisville. But I can't go back there. Connor knows Lana was in Louisville. Once they connect me to Lana, I'm doomed."

"Call him as soon as you get home. If he loves you and wants to marry you, he will come to Alabama. You will be a wonderful wife and mother." Edna held Kitty's hands in hers.

"Edna, I don't want this—this money. I just want to be with Robie," Kitty stammered as her words filled the gaps between her sobs.

Edna drew Kitty in close, letting her tears fall freely. Once Kitty composed herself, Edna handed her a tissue.

"I got into this as a favor to Lana," Kitty quivered as she went on. "I was dragged into this by Lana, convinced that we were doing nothing wrong. But, this, this has turned out all wrong."

Edna waited as Kitty blew her nose. "This is not what I do; I do not steal for other people," Kitty steadfastly declared, jutting out her chin.

"Kitty, Kitty, Kitty," Edna sputtered. "You remember, I told you that you were in over your head before. But it's not too late," Edna consoled. "If you think what you're doing is wrong, then it is," Edna reasoned.

"Edna, let's go into the ladies' room, where it's private. I will give you my share of this dirty money," Kitty calmly offered. "Either you take it, or I'll get rid of it some other way," she firmly added.

Stunned by the recent turn of events. Edna followed Kitty with a blank stare of befuddlement as they weaved through a throng of passengers hastily arriving at a nearby gate. *Is this really happening?* Edna asked herself. *Is she just giving me that money?*

There were several empty stalls in the restroom, so they easily found two next to each other. Kitty took her luggage into the stall with her, which made for tight quarters. After struggling to get the suitcase open just enough to retrieve the two bags of money, the restroom door opened. Kitty froze as the woman entered the stall next to her. Kitty and Edna waited. Once the woman left the stall, she washed her hands and left the restroom.

"Edna, slide your bag over to me," Kitty said. "That expandable tote you bought from a street vendor yesterday should hold it all."

With Edna's tote now at Kitty's feet, Kitty looked above the door to make sure the coast was clear. She wrestled the two bags of money out of the suitcase, stuffed them into Edna's tote, and zipped her suitcase shut. Using her foot, Kitty slid the tote over to Edna.

"Wait a few minutes before you come out," Kitty suggested.

When Edna came out of the restroom, Kitty was gone.

When Kitty checked in at the counter, she told the agent her name was Kitty Barr, but the agent couldn't find a reservation under that name. After a slight panic, Kitty realized that her mother must have booked the flight with her given name.

"Try Katherine Barrington," she suggested.

"Yes, I do have a Katherine Barrington." The confusion over the name on the reservation raised a red flag with the agent, who, rather than dutifully asking for a valid form of identification, scrutinized Kitty with an air of suspicion. "I need to see your ID before we continue," the agent curtly demanded.

Kitty panicked. Her downcast eyes were fixed on the counter. She already had her fake ID in her hand. The agent stared at her, waiting for her to hand over the ID.

"Please, Miss, your ID. Others are waiting." Kitty had to think fast.

"I just realized I grabbed my sister's ID by mistake. She's waiting for me so we can say goodbye. I'll come back after."

"Next in line," the undaunted agent announced.

Kitty found a secluded spot and rifled through her purse. After frantically digging around with her fingers, she began taking items out and setting them on the empty chair next to her. The woman sitting on the other side of the empty chair was watching with an uneasy look on her face.

"Don't worry. Nothing's wrong. I just can't find my ID," Kitty assured her.

"I know the feeling. I couldn't help but notice that lovely wallet you have. Is that a Christian Dior?"

Kitty picked it up off the chair, thinking how easy it would be for the woman to grab the wallet and run.

"Yes, it is. A gift from my mother." Kitty put the wallet between her purse and her stomach and continued her search.

"Here it is!" Kitty waved her original ID in the air.

The elderly couple sitting across from her applauded. She crammed everything back into her purse as fast as she could and returned to the check-in counter, hoping she wouldn't get the same agent. She did.

Kitty minced her way to the counter with the proper ID in hand.

"So, you found your ID. If you hand it to me, I'll check you in. Just one bag to check?" Kitty watched the agent as she multitasked through the process.

"Yes, just one." Kitty lifted her bag onto the scale, using her knee as she did.

The agent gave Kitty her boarding pass and returned her ID.

"Everything you need to know is on your boarding pass. TSA is to your left. You're fortunate, the line is short. Have a safe trip. Next."

With her boarding pass and Alabama ID in hand, Kitty approached the TSA checkpoint line. Once in line, she realized something—she needed to get rid of her fake ID. She stepped out of the line. She had no scissors or access to a shredder, so that was out. And she didn't think she should flush it down the toilet. She settled on the only option left; she would toss it in the trash. So what if someone finds it and tries to use it? she concluded.

## As We Make Our Approach

Kitty didn't know that her mother had booked her into first class until she boarded the plane. Once on board, she was offered a drink, and she chose a ginger ale. She realized she had drunk more alcohol on the trip with Lana and Edna than she had in a year.

Kitty looked out the window and allowed her thoughts to meander. She thought about her childhood and how she never realized how charming it was until now. She could smell her father's Cuban cigars and her mother's cigarettes. The sound of horses running free echoed in her head and made her wonder if Maple, her first horse, would still recognize her. She thought of the Dr. Seuss book her parents read to her on her birthday, even when she was in high school. "Oh, the places you'll go," they would say in unison and with the profoundness of a guru.

Her gap year was over in just four months, but Lana and Edna were both right; the place she needed to go was home.

She thought of Robie. Did she get caught up in something the way he predicted? Kitty started to sob.

A passing flight attendant squatted to meet her eyes. "I hope you don't mind me asking, but is everything alright?" he asked in a gentle southern drawl that made Kitty feel like she was already home.

She so wanted him to take her into his arms and tell her everything would be alright. *That's what Robie would do*, she imagined.

"Can I get you anything? Another ginger ale?" he asked.

Kitty dried her eyes with her cocktail napkin and managed a weak, "Yes, please."

He returned with the ginger ale, water, and a small package of tissues.

"Let me know if you need anything else. We'll be landing in Birmingham soon," he reassured her.

"Thanks. I'm better now," Kitty responded with her head down.

By the time they made the usual announcements regarding their landing, Kitty was at peace; she would just walk away and become Katherine Barrington again—make that Katherine Campbell.

It was drizzling when they landed, and the raindrops on the window of the aircraft mimicked the tears she had recently shed. As they stopped at the gate, a few harried passengers left their seats and gathered their belongings. A flight attendant reminded everyone to remain seated with their seatbelts on. Soon, the doors were open, but the passengers were still seated.

The captain came out of the cockpit, and he and a flight attendant stepped off the plane and into the jetway. Kitty could hear hushed voices and was sure she heard the word money. She slid deeper into her seat, spinning the birthstone ring on her right hand.

As she was in first class, Kitty was one of the first to deplane. She tensed when she walked past the security officer who stood near the door of the airplane. As she went up the jetway, she glanced over her shoulder more than once, but the rush of other passengers bustling forward blocked her view.

## Unclaimed Baggage

Kitty's mother waited for her daughter at the baggage claim carousel. She watched until a baggage agent removed the last two unclaimed bags from the belt. She approached the agent.

"Excuse me, sir. I wonder if I might be at the wrong carousel. I was supposed to meet my daughter here. She was supposed to fly in from Las Vegas. And I don't see her anywhere."

"What's your daughter's name, ma'am?"

"Katherine Barrington."

The agent checked the name tags on the two unclaimed bags.

"Don't see that name on either of these two bags. Sorry."

"But I could swear that's my daughter's bag."

"Ma'am. I can't tell you how many bags look alike," the agent declared.

By then, two uniformed security officers had approached the scene.

"Is there something wrong?" one of the officers asked.

With a shaky voice, Eunice replied, "I am here to meet my daughter. She was supposed to fly in from Las Vegas today. She has not shown up. I hope she's okay."

"Would you mind showing us some identification?"

Eunice opened her Gucci bag, extracted her beige Bottega Veneta wallet, and showed it to the officers.

"Please remove your license from your wallet and hand it to us."

As she fumbled to remove the license from the transparent window in her wallet, Eunice asked, "What is this all about? Is my daughter okay?"

Neither officer replied; she would find out soon enough.

"Maybe you need to talk to an agent from the airline she was supposed to come in on. Maybe your daughter didn't even check a bag," the baggage agent suggested.

The baggage agent told Eunice where to find someone who could help her, but her worried look remained.

Eunice was returning her ID to her wallet when the announcement came on. "Eunice Barrington, please meet your party at the courtesy counter on the main level." The announcement repeated.

Eunice felt a sigh of relief. Katherine was alright. Maybe the baggage agent was right; she didn't check a bag.

The two police officers watched as Eunice walked away. Then they asked the baggage agent to scan the information on the airline tag attached to the bag. It was checked in under the name of Katherine Barrington.

Kitty stood near the courtesy counter, standing on her toes as she scanned the busy area for her mother.

"Mom. Eunice. Over here," she called out when she saw her mother walking aimlessly in the terminal.

Vacillating between a fast walk and a slow run, Eunice's heart raced as her two-inch Valentino Garavani pumps clicked their way across the shiny epoxy floor. Kitty met her halfway, where they fell into each other's arms.

"Mom, I am so glad to be home."

Eunice held her daughter tight as Kitty shook with sobs of relief.

The officers from the baggage claim area had followed Eunice. Seeing them approach, Eunice joyfully declared, "I found her. I found her. She's safe!"

"Yes, Mrs. Barrington, we have found her, too. Miss, is this your bag?"

"Yes, it is. Why?" Kitty was surprised that the officer had her bag.

"Why didn't you claim it?" the officer asked.

"I was going to. After I met my mother." Kitty motioned toward her mother.

"Why does the tag say Kitty Barr when it was checked in as belonging to Katherine Barrington?" the second officer asked.

"I don't understand what this is all about. I sometimes call myself Kitty Barr; it's nothing but a shortened version of my given name. It's not like it's an alias, or an AKA." Wary of all the questions, Kitty's tone sharpened.

"Why are you harassing my daughter like this? I mean, really!" Eunice spouted. "So, she wasn't the first one to retrieve her luggage. And if she wants to call herself Kitty Barr, what's it to you?" Eunice glared at the officer with brazen defiance as she pressed her face closer to his.

"Please, ma'am, just take it easy. We're just doing our job," one of the officers calmly explained.

"Well, I'm not so sure. What is the meaning of this? This is my daughter, Katherine Barrington. I am Eunice Barrington, and Charles Barrington is her father," she huffed with deep-rooted indignation.

A female officer who had approached the group interrupted the conversation. "Could we see some identification, miss?" she asked Kitty, who set her purse on a nearby chair and carefully pulled out her one and only ID.

"Now," the woman continued as she returned Katherine's ID. "You need to come with us so we can open your bag in private. Please bring your bag and follow us." "Wait a minute!" Eunice intervened. "You need a search warrant for that."

"No, ma'am, we do not. This is an airport. We have every right, every duty, to ask people to open their luggage. Now, if you don't step aside and let us do our job, you may be at risk of being arrested yourself." The female officer was firm as she fixed her unblinking eyes on Eunice.

"Well, I never…!" Eunice muttered as she stalked over to a nearby empty wheelchair and sat down. With a pugnacious glare, she announced, "We will see about this. I am calling our attorney." Eunice pulled out her Paloma Picasso leather-bound address book in haste, catching it on the strap of her purse, and sending it onto the floor. She bent over to pick it up, and when she raised her head, she saw a small group of onlookers.

Eunice narrowed her brows and glared at the group, who stood gawking with their mouths agape.

Noticing Eunice's menacing glare and hoping to de-escalate a potential confrontation, one officer called out to the group, "Folks, please move along."

With a female agent now present, the officers brought Kitty to a private room. Eunice followed, now talking to their attorney. "Kitty!" Eunice yelled out. "Harlan says to just say 'no answer' to their questions."

Once they were in the security room, one of the officers closed the door. "You need to stay out here, ma'am," he declared. Eunice answered him with an exasperated sigh. Kitty opened her suitcase and watched as the officers rifled through her designer clothes. They then searched her purse. Kitty said nothing, inwardly thanking Lana for her advice.

## The Last of Lana

The next day, Lana checked out of her hotel and found a small car dealership a few blocks off the strip. After haggling over the price, Lana bought a used Mustang. Paying in cash sealed the deal. The salesman told Lana how to get out of Las Vegas and onto I-15 to San Diego. As for going into Mexico, he admitted he knew little about it.

The five-hour drive from Las Vegas to the border gave Lana plenty of time to consider where she had been and where she was going.

Within slightly over a year, she had cheated Sally out of several hundred thousand dollars. Then, she orchestrated Connor's scheme to cheat his brothers out of over a million dollars, but with a different finale. She envisioned herself living in an expat community in Mexico, where she could operate an unofficial accounting firm out of her home.

She imagined Kitty and Robie, holding hands at the altar. From Kitty, her mind jumped to Sally's. She remembered the scene, Sally unloading unmarked boxes of liquor in the back alley.

And finally, Connor, an unruly curl of black hair touched with silver, hung over his right eye. "Lana, I need your help."

*Too bad, Connor,* she thought. *You duped me, and now I duped you.*

In Nogales, Arizona, Lana pulled into a busy truck stop and parked as close as she could to the truck parking area. She sat in her car, watching the truck drivers come and go. The safest thing to do, she told herself, would be to find a female driver, but she wouldn't rule out a man if he seemed harmless. Lana still had the handgun her father had taught her how to shoot with. He called her a natural at handling the gun.

After being turned down by two women and one man, Lana finally closed a deal.

"Excuse me," Lana said through the open window of her car

"Yes, what is it?" the woman asked. "You need help?"

"In a way, yes. Are you, by chance, heading into Mexico?" Lana asked.

"Yes, I am. But I will not deliver a package for you," the woman said as she turned to walk away.

"No, please wait," Lana called out.

The driver turned back to Lana.

"It's not a package, it's me. I need to sneak into Mexico," Lana explained.

The woman laughed. "Now that's a first. Someone trying to sneak into Mexico. Are you running from something?

"No, I'm running from *someone.*" Lana had practiced for this moment; her eyes darted from left to right, her lips trembled, and her voice was shaky.

"What's in it for me?"

"I'll pay you," Lana whispered, her eyes still searching the area.

"Is this someone here right now? Will he see you leave with me? I don't want to be in the middle of something dangerous," the driver stepped back away from the window of Lana's car.

"If I hang around here much longer, he will find me. I'll give you a thousand bucks up front and another thousand when I'm safely across the border." Lana's offer brought the woman in closer.

"What about your car? You can't just leave here," the driver pointed out.

"I'll pull it around back; make it look like it belongs to an employee." I'll remove the plates and take the title with me." Lana had worked out everything on her drive down to Nogales.

The driver accepted Lana's offer.

"OK, so park your car, and I'll swing around the back. There'll be cameras back there. I'll park my truck between you and the cameras. I'll get out and pretend to be checking something on the trailer. You then slip into my truck through the passenger door and hide in the sleeping compartment."

OK, but why all the rigamarole?" Lana asked.

"This way, when they find your car, or if someone comes looking for you, I can say you snuck into my truck while I was double-checking the trailer and didn't discover you until we were in Mexico," the driver explained.

"Sounds like you've done this before."

"I ain't saying I did, and I ain't saying I didn't."

Lana stayed in the sleeping compartment as they pulled out of the truck stop.

"Can I sit in the passenger seat?" she asked the driver.

"Best not to. They have cameras all over the place down here."

As they approached the border crossing, the driver made an observation.

"OK, the truck lane is fairly long, but they seem to be moving them through at a good pace. I've done this run dozens of times. Just be quiet and be patient."

The driver had all the necessary paperwork to get into Mexico. The trailer she was hauling was an empty car carrier, but the agents had their dog sniff around the tires anyway.

A short time later, the driver looked in the rearview mirror. "You can move up front now if you want. We're now in Mexico. I'll take you as far as Hermosillo, then you're on your own," the driver said.

"Thanks—oh, I don't even know your name," Lana said.

"No names. Better that way." The driver pulled out a joint and shared it with Lana.

"Just what I need right now," Lana smiled.

Lana knew she had entered Mexico without entry documents. But she would deal with that later, now that she was Gloria Rivera of San Bernardino, CA, thanks to her uncle Calvin.

# CHAPTER 27

# GOODBYES

## Edna Plays Aunt Bea

Edna would make the drive back to Galesprings alone and stay at the same hotels. She called Lester at the end of the first day. "Not much happenin' around here," he said the first two nights.

But when he repeated it on the third night, something jarred his memory. "Oh, ya, I forgot to tell you about this business with Connor. I guess they finally sold the place, and him and his brothers are cleanin' and moving things out this weekend."

Edna jolted as her knuckle slipped in between her teeth. "Oh, I see. I thought he was supposed to be in Belgium until early October."

"Well, I don't know anything about that."

*Of course, you don't, Lester. If it's not on TV, you know nothing about it,* she thought.

"But, he called again last night. They will close on the place this Saturday. He'll be here again with his brothers."

Just as Lana had planned her exit scene, Edna had plenty of time to strategize her return to Gailsprings.

She would be like Aunt Bea, returning to Mayberry, anxious to be back in her own kitchen again. True, Lester was no Andy, but Edna would make it work. People would wave and smile at her while she drove down Main Street. Lester would come out to the car, welcome her home with a hug, and carry her suitcase into the house and up the stairs to their bedroom. Patty and Paige would be at the kitchen door, welcoming her home with gentle purrs.

## A Key

It was the first Saturday in October. Connor intentionally arrived at the farmhouse early; he needed to lock the safe. When his brothers arrived with their wives, they all began sorting through the house and property that had been the home to three generations. Knowing that they would eventually get to the safe and find it empty, Connor played the scene with the serenity of a Tibetan monk.

As the day went on, the brothers walked around the grounds while the wives continued in the house.

"The new owners are fine with our leaving the property the way it is," Connor told his brothers. "I didn't think any of us would want any of this old equipment, anyway."

"I would imagine there wouldn't be much of a market for any of it. Let them have it, as far as I'm concerned." Matt's comment drew nods of agreement.

They continued their saunter around the property, the three older brothers sharing memories, while Connor merely listened. Soon they found themselves in front of the tool shed.

Matt, the oldest of the four, changed the subject. "Hey, let's grab some tools and get at that safe," he suggested with gusto.

"Ya, I suppose we should get that out of the way," Connor responded casually while easing his way into the tool shed ahead of his brothers. They grabbed a variety of tools, not knowing what would work.

Unwittingly following in order from the oldest to the youngest, the four Larson boys thudded down the stairs in a syncopated cacophony heard throughout the house.

"I knew there was a safe down here, but I never saw it before now," Ernest, who was the third-born son, said curiously. "Maybe that table next to it was in front of it, or something."

"Something looks different down here." Ruben scratched the back of his neck as his eyes panned the basement. "What's that speaker doing on the floor like that?"

Connor had to think fast. "Oh, that's right, Mom sold a few things shortly before she died. I think it was a couple of tables and some mason jars. She sure had a collection of empty mason jars," Connor chortled, hoping his levity would redirect the conversation from the obviously disheveled basement. "Maybe someone knocked over that speaker."

"Well, apparently she didn't sell any socks," Ernest jokingly said as he pointed to the pile next to the safe.

With the selection of tools on the basement floor, on both sides of the safe, the four men pondered the situation.

"I remember hearing once that this safe's been in this basement since they built the house," Matt recalled.

"You'd think that door would just fall off with a swift kick; it looks so fragile. And with all that rust," Connor reckoned as he picked up the decades-old sledgehammer.

"Connor," Matt reached for the hammer and eased it from Connor's hands. " You'd better let me do that. I don't think I've ever seen you wielding a hammer."

All four laughed at the comment.

Matt put on the gloves and goggles he had brought with him.

"Of course, Matt thinks of everything," one of them said seconds before the clang of a hammer on steel echoed through the basement. It took the four men several tries, several minutes, several different tools, and several curses before the door finally popped halfway open. With his flashlight app, Ernest illuminated the inside of the safe, pulling out a small key.

"What the hell!" Ruben blurted out as they all looked at the key, shaking their heads in disbelief.

"A key?" Connor's voice sank in disappointment. "Nothing but a key," he added as he threw his hands in the air. But this isn't over! he gritted between his teeth.

It was late afternoon when Connor and his brothers stood on the gravel driveway bidding their final goodbyes to their homestead. The two large dumpsters were piled high with nearly everything from the house. They all vowed to keep in touch, and Connor's three brothers drove off.

With his brothers gone, Connor was somehow drawn toward the house one last time. As the wind wrapped around the house, it seemed to carry his mother's voice: "Connor, it's time to come in, supper's almost ready." But he would not answer her call. He waited for the wind to call out again. But it was Karl's voice he longed to hear, calling Connor to join him in the fields, or to play catch, or just to be by his side. He closed his eyes and hung his head, a gesture he had mastered years earlier. Disappointed in the wind, he left the farm forever.

## C'mon Wally, for Old Times' Sake?

Edna finally approached her house as dusk was setting in. There were no waves or smiles as she slowly drove down Main Street. And it wasn't only Lester there to welcome her home. Wally and Connor were waiting too. The blank looks on their faces were far from the fanfare she had scripted. The garage door was open, and she saw that her car had been returned. All three men stood akimbo at the top of the recently repaved concrete driveway, preventing Edna from driving Lester's car into the garage.

In an attempt to disguise the angst Edna felt at the sight of Wally and Connor, she joked as she got out of the car, "Well, isn't this a fine welcoming party?"

It turned out otherwise.

"I'm telling you, all three of you, I only went along with this scheme so I could get some of that money back to Connor. You all know I don't need money. My divorce left me set for life," Edna initiated a nod of agreement, hoping it would spread. "Connor, honey, I did it for you," she cooed.

With Lester's permission, Wally had searched his car and found the cash. The large purse sat next to Wally's feet.

"Those two were going to split it two ways. That's when I stepped in. I knew those two were up to something. More than once, I saw both of their cars parked out there." Edna's words gushed from her mouth—a torrent of desperation.

They knew each other before they came here. Lana said Connor wanted her to get the money out of the safe so he could have it all for himself—never mind his brothers." Edna edged closer to Lester as Wally gave Connor a suspicious we'll-talk-about-this-later glance. "Lana managed the scheme. And Kitty, that poor thing, Lana sucked her into this. When I caught them with the money a few days before they left town, I told them I wanted in. I only agreed to help them so I could at least save some of the money for Connor and his brothers." Edna's self-attributed altruism might have garnered a moan or a scoff on another stage.

"Why didn't you just call me?" Wally wasn't buying any of it. "Or the FBI?"

"Aunt Edna, you stole from me! From me and my family." The hurt look on Connor's face didn't play on Edna.

"Ha, don't give me that, Connor! You were stealing it from your brothers, from your family," Edna boorishly replied, leaving Connor speechless as he felt his face flush with chagrin.

"Wally, just give that bag of money back to Connor, and we can all just forget this ever happened," Edna instructed. "I was able to talk Kitty out of her share, so I managed to save two-thirds of the money for Connor and his brothers. Don't you see?" Edna uselessly pleaded.

Edna wasn't ready to give up yet and directed her next remark to Connor. "You can still find Lana, after all, you had an affair with her, you two-timing fink!" Edna roared.

Wally shot a glance at Connor, who quickly focused on the driveway.

Edna again turned to Wally. "Wally, we go way back; let's just let this play out without the expense of trials, lawyers, and who knows what other costs?"

"I'm afraid I can't do that." Wally shook his head and lightened his lips. "This is bigger than me, bigger than Galesprings. The FBI has taken over the case. You'd better get yourself an attorney."

"Edna, how could you? Of all the harebrained things you have done, and now this?" Lester walked around his car to check on its condition.

He sat behind the steering wheel and started the engine. He opened the window and, with a raised voice directed at Edna, he barked. "And you couldn't even spring for a tank of gas before you returned my car?"

Lester's comment launched Edna into a consuming rage.

"Connor doesn't deserve that money! Roberta poisoned Karl over the years, and Connor was in on it! My brother had to die a slow and agonizing death just so Connor could have all the money!" Edna's strident voice intensified.

Edna turned to face Connor and, with unfettered fury, continued her bluster.

"That's blood money!" Edna snarled at Connor, her face getting redder and redder. "My brother's blood, blood pumped full of poisons by you and your wretched mother! I hope you're happy. Karl wasn't even your biological father. Did you know that? Huh? Did you know that? Edna moved in closer as Connor stepped back. "Of course, Roberta wouldn't admit it. I had a feeling, though, a feeling that it was one of Karl's brothers," Edna conjectured.

Edna turned to Wally. "Connor's nefarious scheme to get that money was the impetus for all of this. And it has ruined lives."

"May it ruin yours, too." Edna turned her cold stare into Connor's eyes, sharpening her curse.

Edna rambled on, muttering unrelated grievances as Wally cuffed her and escorted her to his police car.

As they drove away, she stared back at Connor and Lester through the back window with her head held high and a defiant look on her face, playing her best Scarlett O'Hara, determined to save Tara.

## A Single Shoe Holds Another Clue

Earlier that same day, long before his brothers arrived at the farmhouse to open the safe, Connor had decided to look for his old diary. He remembered how he had kept it upside down under his mattress until the day he discovered it right side up. Suspecting one of his brothers, he'd moved it to a different place. But he couldn't remember where he had hidden it.

Standing in his former bedroom, he looked around, hoping something would jar his memory. He opened all the drawers in the dresser, starting with the bottom drawer and working his way up. He got on his knees and looked under the bed, finding nothing but dust and a single sock. The open door to his closet summoned him over.

After tossing what was left of his belongings onto the floor of the bedroom and not finding his diary, Connor slammed the closet door and sat at the foot of the bed, rubbing his forehead.

But then he saw the shoe. One of his mother's shoes.

He walked over to the shoe, picked it up, and found a note inside. He removed the note and saw it was another clue. With a sigh of despair laced with irritation, he looked up and yelled at his mother, "I've had it with your God-damned clues!"

Connor paced the floor in circles, muttering to himself about the mess he was in. He stood in front of the mirror on the dresser, looked at himself and said, "Connor, get a grip on yourself. Solve the clue and get the hell out!"

He muttered the clue aloud. "It won't be found lying down. Once it was there, so now you know where." Connor had learned to zero in on key words in this mother's clues. "Lying down, lying down." He looked at the bed. "Once it was there, where," he whispered. "Got it!" Connor dropped the note to the floor and flipped the mattress off his bed. There was his diary. He concluded that his mother must have found his diary wherever he had hid it. *Was she the one who had discovered it under the mattress to begin with?* he wondered.

But there was something sticking out of it. He saw it was an envelope, a sealed envelope. *Money?* he hoped. He broke the seal and took out a sheet of lined paper, torn from a spiral notebook.

It was a list of numbers and letters, the likes of which he'd seen before. He opened his wallet and took out several bills. His hunch was right; they were serial numbers from bank notes, dozens of them. He knew the FBI would be happy to see the list of serial numbers, but not nearly as happy as Connor was to show it to them.

With a smile, he grabbed the diary and the list and walked out of his former bedroom. "I got you now, Lana!" his voice echoed down the hallway.

With the adrenaline of revenge coursing through his veins, he flew down the stairs, jumping over the final three steps. *Thud.* He hit the floor hard, his clenched fists rising above him in triumph.

Connor stuffed the list in the pocket of his favorite jacket, where it would stay until he pulled it out after his family left the farm for the last time.

## Ramifications

It didn't take long for Connor's brothers to learn the truth since their Aunt Edna's arrest spread like wild fire. Initially, they bought Connor's story about Lana stealing the money without his knowledge. But as they questioned Connor further, they wondered how he knew about the money to begin with, how he knew about the diary, and why their mother had hoarded all that money.

Connor simply told the truth; he saw it all. Several serial numbers on Roberta's list matched the bills found in Edna's purse.

Kitty claimed to know nothing about the money; she had just gone along to see Las Vegas. Her attorney advised her to admit only that she and Virgil had visited Lana at the farmhouse. She also told the attorneys at the deposition that Lana and Edna had spent a lot of time in the basement, saying they were refurbishing an old trunk. The charge of accessory to a crime was dropped.

In an effort to protect Kitty, Edna agreed with Connor's story, putting all the blame on Lana. Throughout the legal proceedings, she maintained she was only trying to protect Connor's interests. While the prosecution thought otherwise, the jury did not. "She did return with the money in plain sight," were her attorney's final words to the jury. The judge ordered that the recovered money be split equally among the four brothers. With his share of the money and the sale of the farm, he was, as Karl would have put it, sitting pretty.

Edna's and Kitty's prints were everywhere. As were those of a person yet to be apprehended.

As for Lana, Edna told the authorities as much as she could while casting Kitty as an innocent bystander. The FBI traced Lana back to Sally's, but there the trail went cold.

## Six Months Later

Lana, known by locals as Gloria Rivera, settled in San Miguel de Allende amid the many expats. She moved in with the owner of a popular bed and breakfast hotel that catered to customers who wanted a colonial ambience with modern amenities. Operating out of her home, she gained a reputation as a skilled tax consultant.

Kitty's father walked her down the aisle and into Robie's arms. Eunice's sobs only faded when her husband sat next to her and put his arms around her. Following a lavish reception at the country club,

Robie and Kitty drove off in their new Volvo, their destination undisclosed. Upon their return, Robie was hired by Barrington Enterprises and Kitty returned to college.

Edna's scrape with the law briefly fazed her. After keeping a low profile for a month, she was soon driving a new silver Cadillac she called Silvia, terrorizing the church kitchen, and ignoring Lester much to his delight.

Connor's affair with Lana in Minneapolis came to light, and his marriage ended in a divorce. Following the success of his project in Belgium, along with other feats, Connor finally got his corner office on a high floor. Sitting there alone on many evenings, he watched the sun set in the Minnesota sky, delaying the drive to his lifeless condo near Loring Park.

Yes, he had that corner office, that trendy condo, that money in the bank. But it had cost him too: brothers now forever alienated, limited time with his two sons, and the betrayal of someone he trusted. And it was to Lana Paulson that he directed his greatest grievance. He didn't want justice, as he had told Wally; he wanted revenge. And none of that had changed. But that revenge was out of reach, at least for now. And that's what kept him going; the obsession to some day orchestrate the last reprisal.

# ABOUT THE AUTHOR

Richard E. Olson was born in Eau Claire, Wisconsin, in 1952 and raised among the rolling green hills and small-town traditions of nearby Elk Mound. His childhood was filled with country adventures—duck ponds, a trout stream, and endless trees just begging to be climbed. Sundays meant church, potlucks, and the kind of Lutheran smorgasbords that would later find their way into his writing.

A lifelong reader, Richard still has the grade-school certificates that listed the books he devoured. They're proof that he was destined for a life surrounded by words, or at least that he was really good at avoiding chores.

After high school, Richard earned degrees in Journalism and Spanish from the University of Wisconsin–Eau Claire, with plans to become a foreign correspondent. Instead, he spent three decades teaching Spanish at Stevens Point Area Senior High and another four years at Northcentral Technical College. He insists the best part of retirement is not the free time, but the newfound freedom to "go to the bathroom whenever I want."

Richard's travels have taken him to Spain, Ecuador, Guatemala, Costa Rica, Mexico, and beyond. He even earned a master's degree in Hispanic Literature in Guadalajara, Mexico. More recently, he's taken up Brazilian Portuguese, though he admits he now speaks Spanish with a Portuguese accent and Portuguese with a Spanish accent. His luggage, he jokes, has logged even more miles than he has—his parents must have known what they were doing when they gave it to him as a college graduation gift.

He's also explored England, Italy, and Germany, landing in Berlin just after the Wall came down. To this day, he keeps a piece of the Wall handy and is never shy about showing it off.

An unapologetic bookworm, Richard often says, "No two people read the same book." After rereading *Zen and the Art of Motorcycle Maintenance* nearly 50 years apart, he added a new twist: "And no one ever reads the same book twice."

When he's not reading, Richard spends his retirement tackling crossword puzzles, gardening, and cooking. He is active at The Landing senior center in Wausau, Wisconsin, where he has taught Spanish and led lively presentations on topics ranging from Frida Kahlo and Diego Rivera to Georgia O'Keeffe and the history of the United States through art. His students once accused him of being a closeted art teacher, and he didn't entirely deny it.

Richard and his partner of 36 years, Ray, have made countless road trips together—mostly heading south to visit family. His motto remains: *"You've got to leave the party when you're still having fun,"* which is exactly what he did when he retired from teaching.